C

Lightning ... that it lit up the courtyard almost as bright as day. Alexander stopped for a moment and glanced up. The lightning bolt was still tracing its path across the sky, a spreading stream of molten light, with many small tributaries branching off from yet other tributaries. For an instant the boiling clouds glowed like tarnished silver in the night sky, sculpted into fantastic, fleeting shapes, constantly forming, constantly changing.

Just as the light faded into blackness, in that last glimmering, Alexander thought that he could see a castle sailing by on the clouds. It seemed almost real, solid, a thing of stone walls, battlements, and high towers. As darkness swallowed it up again, however, Alexander began to doubt what he had seen. Surely it had been a trick of the light, of the clouds, or of his imagination. Castles do not fly . . .

King's Quest is the #1 bestselling computer game series of all time, with over two million copies sold. Now, Boulevard Books presents a new series of fantasy novels based on the characters from the King's Quest games.

KING'S QUEST

—THE—
FLOATING CASTLE

CRAIG MILLS

BOULEVARD BOOKS, NEW YORK

For Elizabeth Danforth,
with thanks

And for Dorrie Nelson,
as always

KING'S QUEST: THE FLOATING CASTLE

A Boulevard Book / published by arrangement with
Sierra On-Line, Inc.

PRINTING HISTORY
Boulevard edition / July 1995

ISBN: 1-57297-009-X

BOULEVARD
Boulevard Books are published by The Berkley Publishing Group,
200 Madison Avenue, New York, New York 10016.
BOULEVARD and its logo
are trademarks belonging to Berkley Publishing Corporation.

PRINTED IN THE UNITED STATES OF AMERICA

10 9 8 7 6 5 4 3 2 1

·1·

The oak tree had grown across the moat from Castle Daventry for as long as anyone could remember. It was a fine tree, its gnarled trunk sturdy and thick, branches both low enough and strong enough to climb on. Now it was burning, split down the middle and burning. The tree's two halves were splayed wide apart, and flames crackled from the splintered fork between. Red sparks rose with the flames, but they could not long survive the slashing rain. Even the fire burning at the tree's heart had begun to diminish under the onslaught; soon, it seemed, there would be nothing left but smoke and glowing embers.

Cold, his garments sodden and heavy, Prince Alexander paused to watch the tree burn, feeling a slight but real sense of grief. He had often watched the children of Daventry playing in its branches, and now it was no more. The storm had ended it.

Lightning flashed suddenly, cutting a livid scar across the eastern sky. Then came the thunder: a low, ominous rumble that continued, and even gained strength, long after it seemed the last of it should have been wrung out. Alexander was reminded that he should not linger out in the open any longer than necessary. The storm could end his life as easily as it had the tree's. Putting his head down, the prince hastened on his way, toward the warmth and safety of Castle Daventry.

Driven by fierce gusts of wind, the rain came down in blinding sheets, but Alexander could make out the castle's welcoming lights through the blur of streaming water and he knew the way as well as he knew anything. He quickly found the narrow bridge that spanned the moat and crossed it, careful not to slip on the wet stonework and wind up as food for the moat monsters.

He was relieved to see that the main gate was open, the portcullis drawn up, its iron teeth barely visible. Entering the sheltering recess beyond the portcullis, he met the lone guard, Henry by name, who stood there clutching his halberd, rain beaded in his beard.

"Good evening, Prince Alexander," the man said. "You chose a poor day to go out walking, as it turns out."

"Yes, as it turns out," Alexander said. "It was sunny when I started out this morning. Who'd have guessed the day would end like this?"

"Not I, certainly. I've never seen a storm come on so quickly. Not a storm this bad, anyway."

A sharp, cold gust of wind blew in through the gate, and Alexander did his best to suppress the shiver that it brought him. "Well, I'd better go in, before I catch my death," he said, moving past the other man. "Take care, Henry. Try not to get too wet."

"I'll certainly try, Prince Alexander."

Upon reaching the other side of the passage, Alexander entered the courtyard. Ahead was the keep, a tall, strong structure of grey stone, with many small windows, square sides, and a crenelated top. Hunching his shoulders against the rain, which seemed to be getting worse by the moment, he hurried across the courtyard, splashing his way through the deep puddles that had gathered on the flagstones. He heard fierce winds roaring through the towers and battlements of Castle Daventry: a mournful sound.

Lightning flared overhead again, so close this time that it lit up the courtyard almost as bright as day. Alexander stopped for a moment and glanced up. The lightning bolt was still tracing its path across the sky, a spreading stream of molten light, with many small tributaries branching off from yet other tributaries. For an instant the boiling clouds glowed like tarnished silver in the night sky, sculpted into fantastic, fleeting shapes, constantly forming, constantly changing.

Just as the light faded into blackness, in that last glimmering, Alexander thought that he could see a castle sailing by on the clouds. It seemed almost real, solid, a thing of stone walls, battlements, and high towers. As darkness swallowed it up again, however, Alexander began to doubt what he had seen. Surely it had been a trick of the light, of the clouds, or of his imagination. Castles do not fly.

Still, as Alexander continued across the court, he kept glancing over his shoulder, to where he had spied the phantom castle. He did not see it again, however, and by the time he reached the Great Hall he was largely convinced that he never had.

Supported by brass sconces, partially sheltered by an overhanging stone lintel, the torches set beside the massive door flared and roared in the gusting wind. With a strong sense of relief, Alexander placed his hands on the door and pushed it open. The unsettled air rushed into the antechamber beyond the door, carrying with it slanting rain turned gold by the yellow torchlight.

There were two guards inside the antechamber. One of them rushed forward to help Alexander seal the door behind him. Having gained access to the chamber, the wind seemed reluctant to surrender it; it resisted Alexander's efforts with stubborn force.

When they finally managed to close and latch the door, the guard turned to Alexander, and said, "Good evening, Prince Alexander. Your parents will be happy to see you home. They've been worried about you."

Alexander nodded. "Are they within?" he asked, indicating the door leading into the throne room.

"They are."

"I'll just go in and put their minds at rest, then." The second guard opened the door for Alexander, and he passed through into the throne room.

Alexander knew of no room more beautiful than the throne room of Castle Daventry. Though built to a grand scale, with high ceilings and vast expanses of polished marble flooring, it was harmonious in design, and conveyed an impression that was almost intimate. Along one side of the room ran the great gallery, built of dark wood oiled to a soft luster and containing three long ranks of benches, padded and upholstered with dark purple velvet. It was here where the knights and their ladies would sit during important assemblages.

At the head of the room was a raised dais, upon which were set the thrones of Daventry's king and queen, flanked by banners embroidered with the kingdom's venerable crest. To the right of the dais, set into a shallow niche, hung the mirror that was one of the irreplaceable treasures of Daventry, for it was a magic mirror, with the power to foresee the future and show events occurring in faraway places.

The mirror had served the kings and queens of Daventry for more than two centuries, Alexander knew—until that day, now many years past, when a wicked sorcerer had used his cunning to cheat old King Edward of it, with dire consequences for the realm. It had been Alexander's father who had finally recovered the mirror from the sorcerer's dark lair and returned it to Castle Daventry, where it had remained ever since, there on the wall beside the throne.

It was in this place, standing before the mirror, that Alexander found his parents. His mother, Queen Valanice, was the first to see him. She was a tall woman, with dark hair smoothed back and clasped behind her head. She carried with her an aura of serene dignity, even now, when the relief was plain on her face.

"Alexander!" she said, coming forward to embrace

him. "I'm so glad that you're home. I was beginning to fear that you'd been hurt. This storm—"

Almost as soon as Valanice touched Alexander, however, she drew away slightly. "Why, you're soaked to the skin! You'd better go up and get into some dry clothes, before you become ill."

Alexander smiled at this rebuke. "I'm on my way. I just wanted to let you know that I'd made it home. But . . . is something wrong? Father looks troubled."

Frowning, thoughtful, King Graham had barely glanced at Alexander. The whole of his attention seemed bound up in the mirror. Alexander could not see what it was that the mirror was showing his father, but he knew that it had to be something worrisome.

Valanice said, "Your father was concerned that the mirror didn't warn him of the storm's approach. And now . . . it seems that the mirror has gone blank."

"Blank? What do you mean? How can the mirror go blank?"

Graham, a powerfully built man dressed in plain garments, turned abruptly from the mirror. "See for yourself, Alexander," he said. "It is as though a dark veil has been drawn over the it."

Alexander caught his father's gaze for a moment, and what he saw there frightened him a little. He could not remember ever seeing his father appear so openly concerned.

Alexander moved past Graham and confronted the mirror. It was true, he saw. The mirror was blank. It showed him nothing, not even his own reflection.

Nothing. An impenetrable darkness obscured its entire face.

"How is this possible?" Alexander said, puzzled. "What could be causing it?"

"Keep looking," Graham said.

"But there's nothing here."

"There is, if you look hard enough."

Trusting to his father's judgment, Alexander continued to stare into the mirror. For a long time he saw nothing but the same featureless blackness. Gradually, however, he began to detect vague stirrings, furtive movements, deeply concealed. He realized that this was not something that he saw with his eyes alone. Rather, it seemed to impress itself directly on his mind. A potent presence lurked there beneath the darkness that masked the mirror. He could *feel* it. It was—

Giving out a gasp, Alexander stepped back from the mirror and looked away. Evil. For one instant he had brushed up against a presence of pure evil. Even that glancing touch chilled his heart.

"It's no accident that the mirror went blank," Alexander said at length. "Someone—or something— is blocking its power. There's an intelligence at work. I felt it there, somehow."

Graham nodded. "I felt it, also."

"But why—how—would anyone blank out our mirror?"

"I'm . . . not yet sure. I'd be willing to bet that it has something to do with this storm, though." Graham paused a moment, eyes narrowed with thought, then said, "Did you see anything unusual when you were out, Alexander?''

"Apart from the storm itself? No, not that I can think of.''

"Are you sure?''

". . . Well, there was one thing, perhaps. I'm sure it's nothing, but for a moment I thought that I glimpsed a great castle floating by on the clouds. It must have been my imagination. It *must* have been. I couldn't have seen what I thought I did.''

Graham did not answer.

"Could I?''

"I wonder,'' the king said pensively.

The storm continued to rage throughout the evening. After changing into dry clothes, Alexander came down to dinner with his father and mother. The meal was excellent, but the ceaseless roaring of the wind and the crashing of the thunder cast a pall over their table. They did not speak of the mirror or the storm, for there was nothing useful to be said about either. Instead, they spoke of the harvest, of the local marriages and births, and of a recent letter from Alexander's sister, Princess Rosella, who was currently visiting the nearby kingdom of Lycathia.

Alexander retired to his bedchamber shortly after dinner, but for a long time he was unable to sleep. Whenever he closed his eyes, he saw in that usually peaceful darkness the more troubled darkness that he had encountered in the mirror, and he found himself jolted fully awake, heart beating fast, flesh chilled.

He must have fallen asleep at last, for the next thing

he knew it was morning. Sunlight was streaming in through his narrow window, to fall upon the small chest at the foot of his bed. After the dismal weather of the night before, he was surprised to see that the day had dawned so bright.

Yawning, Alexander sat up in bed, supporting himself with stiffened arms. One after the other, he freed his legs from the imprisoning blankets and jerked them over the side of the bed. He sat there for a moment, thoughts still fuzzy from sleep, while he glanced slowly about the room.

The room was not opulent, but it was comfortable, and it suited him well enough. A faded old tapestry sewn with hunting scenes hung upon one wall; a walnut wardrobe occupied most of the opposing wall. To the right side of the windows was his desk, its surface supporting a silver pen tray, a bottle of ink, a thick white candle, three leather-bound books, and a rolled parchment map.

As soon as he felt sufficiently awake, Alexander slipped from the bed and went to the window. Standing there, he saw that, indeed, it was a clear, beautiful morning. The air seemed to have been scrubbed clean by the passing storm. Everything looked new, fresh.

After a moment Alexander turned from the window and got dressed, choosing simple and comfortable clothes: a full shirt of white linen, dark trousers, a sleeveless jerkin of buff leather, and soft shoes. Then, curious to see how Daventry had fared in the storm, he left his room and climbed the four steep flights of stairs that led to the top of the keep.

He was starting to breathe hard by the time he reached the top, and a slight sheen of perspiration had come to his forehead. He pushed open the door leading to the keep's battlements and stepped out into the morning sun.

The sun had just risen above the castle's east tower. The splendid purple-and-gold banners at the keep's four corners flapped noisily in the wind. Hands on the chill stone of the battlement, Alexander gazed out over all of Daventry.

The damage was not as great as he had feared. The river was swollen from the rains, but it appeared to be in no danger of overflowing its banks. There were branches down everywhere, and a few trees had been uprooted. Aside from that oak on the other side of the moat, though, he could see only one tree that had been struck by lightning: a tall pine standing atop a stony ridge, now blackened and bare.

Daventry seemed to have borne the storm well, all in all. He was pleased.

Just when Alexander was beginning think that the storm had been a thing of no lasting consequence, however, a faint flicker of light caught his eye. His gaze was drawn to a place far downriver, beyond a low bluff, where a vast marsh enveloped the riverbank. A single dark cloud hovered over that spot, and from it lightning flashed sporadically.

Below the cloud was an immense structure, where none had been the day before. The structure was partially obscured by the bluff, but Alexander could see a high wall crowned by battlements and colossal turrets, encircling several great towers, all of inky black.

Alexander was nearly overwhelmed by cold awe. He knew that structure, knew it. Without a doubt, it was the same castle that he had seen sailing by in the night sky.

·2·

Alexander stood in the far shadows of the throne room and watched while his father questioned all those who came before him. Expression attentive and grave, the king accorded all who spoke the same weighty respect, knights and common folk alike. For most of the afternoon he sat patiently listening, straight and still upon his throne. Nothing in his voice or manner betrayed the slightest trace of alarm, although there proved to be reason enough for alarm.

Four days had passed since the black castle had come to rest beside the river, time enough for the first reports to reach Castle Daventry. Those reports were making it increasingly clear that the black castle's incursion into Daventry represented a deadly threat to the realm and its people.

From the outland castle had come riders clad in all-concealing black armor—many of them. The riders had immediately set to work despoiling the surrounding countryside without mercy, seizing upon anything of value, but most especially the newly harvested crops. These they loaded onto great wagons and transported to the black castle, leaving their victims to face the coming winter with naught but empty larders.

Almost as disturbing, some said that other wicked creatures had begun to gather in the shadow of the black castle, creatures long banished from Daventry by Graham's steadfast rule: fierce ogres and murderous trolls, dark elves and malevolent spirits of the night. Any one of these dangerous entities could easily kill an unarmed man—or even an armed man lacking sufficient luck or skill.

So far, they had avoided human settlements, seeming to prefer deserted byways and the lonely margins of the woods. In time, however, they were likely to grow bolder. And if these normally solitary creatures were to start to work together, no one would be safe.

For it did seem to Alexander that the black castle was acting as a focus for all manner of lesser evils. This being so, it was not unreasonable to believe that whoever commanded the black castle might eventually marshall all those evils together in a single purpose. Should that happen, there was no way to calculate how much damage might be done to Daventry and her people. This was a frightening possibility.

As speaker after speaker enlarged upon the dark activities of the riders from the black castle, and upon all of the other ills that had come to visit Daventry, Alexander kept studying his father, increasingly impressed by the calm manner in which he accepted the onslaught of bad news. Although it was plain to see that the king was moved by the plight of his subjects, he showed no sign of dismay. His face was thoughtful as he considered what was said, his voice quiet and measured when he spoke. The evenness of his response seemed to have a calming effect on all who witnessed it. Even those who at first had appeared near panic eventually left the throne room with an attitude of renewed confidence.

It was only when the last person had spoken and all had filed out of the chamber, leaving Alexander alone with Graham, that the prince was finally able to see something of his father's true feelings.

Graham slumped back in his throne, his hands tightly gripping its carved arms. "Terrible. Terrible. Did you hear, Alexander?" His voice was hoarse.

"I heard," Alexander said, as he came forward from the shadows, to stand at the edge of the dais. "It *is* terrible."

"It was not easy to sit here and listen to what suffering this black castle has brought my people. Not easy."

Alexander nodded. He wanted to say something to comfort his father, but he could think of nothing. What *could* he say? He felt useless.

"Whoever brought this outland castle here will have much to answer for," Graham said, a deadly edge coming to his voice.

"What are we going to do, Father?"

"Do?"

"About the castle. How are we to deal with it?"

Graham suddenly sat up straight in his throne and seemed to throw off his fatigue. His eyes narrowed, as he appeared to consider the question. After a moment he said, "Before I do anything else, I must call for an assembly of all the knights of Daventry. They will help me decide on a course of action.''

Surprised by this answer, Alexander hesitated before he spoke. ''But . . . it will take *days* to gather all the knights of Daventry in one place, and during this time the dark riders will continue to oppress our people.''

Graham sighed. ''I know. If I were acting for myself, I might ride forth to confront the knights of the black castle this very day. But I am King, and must put the good of the realm before my own wants and desires. The black castle represents a great danger to all of Daventry. I must unite all Daventry behind me before I take any action against it.''

Although he was reluctant to admit it, Alexander saw that his father was right. ''I understand. Of course you must marshall support behind you before you move against the black castle and its riders.'' He pause a moment. ''But—no such restraint binds *me*. Give me a dozen men-at-arms, half a dozen, and I will ride out and attempt to hold back the riders in black.''

Graham rose from his throne, stepped down from the dais, and placed his hand on Alexander's shoulder. ''No,'' he said flatly. ''Your offer does you credit, but I can't allow it. We are simply not ready yet. I would not be willing to sacrifice a single man in such a blind gamble, let alone my own son. No. Put it from your mind.''

Frustrated and disappointed, Alexander felt his jaw muscles tighten. It was a moment before he could give a curt nod, and say, heavily, "I understand."

"You must have patience, Alexander. Soon enough we will do what must be done. It's been many years since Daventry last had to prepare for war. It will take time."

Graham let his hand drop from Alexander's shoulder. "I had hoped that this day would never come, that Daventry would never again need to take up arms against an invader. I had hoped. But it seems that fate has decreed otherwise."

Messengers went out to all corners of the realm, and over the next five days they returned. With them came all the knights of Daventry, some on foot, some on horseback, some clad in silk or velvet, some in leather or wool. All bore weapons. All looked worried.

In the days that it took for all the knights to arrive, King Graham began to make preparations for the defense of the castle, should it prove necessary. He sent scouts out in the direction of the black castle, so that there would be an advance warning if there were any large movement of troops from there. He decreed that new guards be hired and trained, to man the castle walls in case of attack. He ordered that fresh supplies be found and brought in.

These were tense days. Alexander could sense the growing apprehension wherever he went. He could hear it in the voices of everyone he spoke to, could see it on their faces and in their movements. He felt it inside himself. In a vain attempt to put aside his anxiety, he tried to make himself as useful as he could. He helped to train and arm the new guards, and carried orders from place to place for his father. A small but growing number of refugees created by the raids of the black knights began to arrive at the castle, and Alexander helped his mother see to it that they were fed and sheltered.

Finally, on the afternoon of the fifth day, the knights of Daventry gathered in the throne room of Castle Daventry at the appointed hour and took their places behind the carved balustrade of the great gallery. Hushed and expectant, their voices filled the chamber.

Alexander stationed himself beside the dais. His father and mother were upon their thrones, their features composed and solemn. He tried to follow their example and let none of his apprehension show on his face or in his posture. This was more difficult than he would have thought. He kept wanting to frown, to clench his fists at his side, to pace the room—anything to vent the tension he felt. What would be the result of this assembly? He did not know.

At last Graham raised his hand, and the room fell silent. He said, "By now, you must all be aware of why I have called you here today. The situation appears grim. A strange castle has intruded upon the peace of Daventry. I think it fair to assume that only a powerful magic could have transported it here. As yet, however, we do not know who controls this magic. Nor do we know what its limits may be."

Graham paused a moment, and a faint murmuring

arose from the gallery. He said, "It is certain that whoever commands the black castle means our land no good. You have all heard of the dark knights that have ridden forth from the castle. You have heard how sorely they have oppressed the people of Daventry. Only a power of evil would command such actions."

Graham paused again, as the assembly muttered its agreement. Alexander looked upon his father with a certain pride. Physically, the king was not the most impressive person present. He was dressed, as was his custom, in the manner of a squire or a rustic knight, and he spoke in a quiet voice. Such was the aura of vitality and inner strength he projected, however, that he overshadowed all others in that company. The authority he commanded over his knights was absolute, but it was not the authority of force and coercion. Rather, it was an authority derived from the absolute belief and trust he inspired in his people. While Graham occupied the throne, what misfortune could long hold sway over Daventry? What evil could prevail?

Graham said, "We know that we will have to oppose this black castle and its denizens. But how, when, and where? I have called you here to consult with you on these important questions."

There was a stirring within the gallery, and Sir Brian rose from his bench, a big man, with a red beard and a wide, florid face. "*How?*" he said truculently. "By force of arms. *When?* As soon as we may. *Where?* At the very gates of the black castle."

At this, Sir Kenneth arose. He was tall, slightly

stooped at the shoulders, his dark hair turning silver at the temples. "Without even attempting to talk with the leaders of the castle? That would be foolish. I say that we send a delegation to parlay first. Perhaps the matter may be resolved without violence."

"Talk? Parlay? *Hah!* The black castle has invaded Daventry. Its knights have conducted war against our people. I very much doubt that talk will achieve anything with them. Let us take a great army to them! If they wish to talk then, we will listen."

"An army may only make them feel besieged, and therefore less likely to compromise," Sir Kenneth said.

"Compromise? What sort of compromise is possible? Do we want to share Daventry with these invaders? What other sort of compromise can there be?"

Now Sir Aubrey stood, a spare, elegant, sandy-haired man. Glancing about him, he said, "I agree that a peaceful accord with the black castle is unlikely at this point. However, I also think that it would be unwise to move against the castle with our full strength now, before we can assess the capabilities of the enemy. Perhaps if we can draw them out, somehow . . ."

And so it went, with knight after knight standing to dispute the plan proposed by the previous knight. Soon enough King Graham would gently close off the debate, and start guiding the assembly toward a consensus, Alexander knew. In the end, each knight would feel that he had made an important contribution toward that consensus. All would be united in a single purpose.

As Alexander stood listening to the debate, he gradually became aware of what sounded like a disturbance outside in the courtyard. He moved to the window and looked out.

The window, narrow and composed of numerous small diamond-shaped panes, gave him only a restricted view of the courtyard. He could see that something unusual was taking place, but not what. The servants and artisans who normally bustled about the courtyard on their individual business had gathered into an inquisitive throng, which was converging slowly and cautiously on the keep. Everyone seemed to be looking at the same place, but whatever it was that so fascinated them was too near the keep for Alexander to see from this vantage.

Alexander tried without success to sort out what was happening. He quickly decided that, whatever it was, his father should know of it. It was without question unusual, and at this moment anything unusual had to be considered potentially dangerous. Just as Alexander turned to interrupt the proceedings, however, there came a shout and a violent crashing noise from the antechamber. The discussion ceased, and all heads turned to the door.

There was another shout, more muffled this time, and suddenly the door flew open, as if of its own accord. Into the room strode an ominous stranger.

The stranger was attired in voluminous dark robes. He was tall, thin, and walked with a peculiar gliding gait. In his right hand was a long staff crowned by a shining crystal sphere, which he swung in time with his step. His head was hairless, his face clean-shaven, his skin deathly pale—all of which conspired to make his black brows and deeply set eyes appear even more prominent than they were.

Flanking the stranger were two knights in black armor. Looking neither right nor left, they followed at the stranger's heels, walking with jerky, abrupt movements. Their armor rustled and clattered with every step; their long spurs chimed softly on the marble floor. The knights' faces were entirely hidden by the featureless helms they wore. Alexander could not even see their eyes through the small eye slits.

Once the three cleared the open doorway, Alexander was able to see that the two men who had stood guard in the antechamber now lay motionless on the floor, arms and legs oddly splayed. Dead? He could not tell.

The three men, if men they were, walked boldly down the center of the room, and stopped just short of the dais. The one in the dark robes slowly appraised the assembly, seemingly pleased by the dumbfounded reaction his sudden appearance had caused.

Alexander gave an uncertain glance to his father. King Graham had gripped the arms of his throne with both hands and seemed poised between rising and sitting. His gaze was locked upon the stranger with an intensity that Alexander had seldom seen before. It was an intensity that spoke of a potent fury, contained but not diminished by a tremendous act of will.

At last Graham spoke, in a deliberate and tightly controlled voice: "Who are you, that you come un-invited into this place? Who are you, that you attack men under my protection? *Answer me.*"

The stranger threw back his head and laughed. The sound was harsh and grating. "Who am I? Why, I am your new neighbor! Have you not seen my castle there in the distance?"

The man paused. He seemed to expect Graham to say something then, but the king simply stared at him. This seemed to unnerve the stranger somewhat, caus-ing his display of levity to become gradually muted.

"Who am I?" the man said at length. "I am Tel-grin, sorcerer, scholar, master of the floating castle. I am a king among kings. From this day forward, I am *your* king."

This declaration brought a clamor of outrage from the gallery. "Must we endure this affrontery!" Sir Brian said loudly. "They are but three, while we are many. I say we seize hold of them now. We will see who is whose king." Brian stepped from the gallery and started toward Telgrin, his hands spread wide be-fore him.

Telgrin gave the big knight a contemptuous glance. A dim light flickered momentarily from within the crystal sphere atop his staff, and he made a small gesture—really only a fluttering of two fingers.

Something happened then, but Alexander was not sure what it was. It appeared that the air itself rippled about Telgrin in some obscure and indefinable way, then gathered itself into a peaked vee of distortion, which flew across the room and struck Brian full in the chest. The knight gave a choked cry of alarm, as he was thrown high into the air and hard into the wall behind him. For an instant he appeared to be pinned there, several feet off the ground. Then the force that held him relented, and he fell heavily to the floor. He groaned, curled himself into a ball, and did not move again.

Stunned silence gripped the room. Telgrin let a long moment go by before saying, "Would anyone else care to try to lay hands upon me? No? Are you sure? You may never have a better chance."

Graham said, "What do you want, Telgrin? Why have you come here?"

The man shrugged. "I have come to announce my presence, that's all. The news reached me that you were gathering all your knights here today, Graham, so it seemed a convenient time."

"You've come to announce your presence? That's all?"

"That, and to make the current situation clear to you and your men. I am now King of Daventry. Those who accept this fact will be allowed to prosper. Those who do not— Well, matters will not go so well for them."

"Do you seriously believe that simply declaring yourself king will make you king in truth?"

"*Believe?* I know it. It is a fact. Who can dispute it?"

Graham rose slowly from his throne, straightened

to his full height. Unblinking, his gaze was fixed upon
Telgrin. "*I* can."

"You dare defy me?"

"I do."

A twisted smile tugged briefly at the corners of
Telgrin's mouth. "Good. I was rather hoping you
would."

The man raised his staff above his head. A sickly
amber radiance showed from the crystal sphere, giving the throne room a distorted and ugly cast.

Seized by a terrible apprehension, Alexander said,
"Father—" At the same time, almost without thinking, he took one step toward Telgrin. The air was
suddenly cold on his skin.

Staff still raised high, Telgrin held his left hand out
before him and made an abrupt grasping gesture. Graham gave out a soft gasp, and his eyes rolled up
within his head. He wavered there for a moment, but
then the strength seemed to go out of his legs and he
collapsed face forward onto the dais. Telgrin held his
closed fist before him. His face was rapt with a dreadful joy.

"*Father!*" Alexander said again, his voice shrill
with dismay. Graham did not answer, did not move
from where he had fallen. He appeared to be unconscious, or worse. What had Telgrin done to him?

Telgrin. Alexander hesitated for a moment, turning a furious look to the intruder. The magician was
still looking down on Graham, his face showing a ma-
licious satisfaction. It was almost unbearable for Alexander to be forced to see the pleasure that the man

was taking from Graham's fall.

The prince wanted to leap wildly upon Telgrin, to tear the staff from his hands and break it over his knee—anything to erase Telgrin's smug delight and make him pay for what he had done. He could do it, he thought—now, while the magician was still distracted. Perhaps he could do it. But . . .

But there was his father, a crumpled shape on the apron of the dais, motionless and fragile. Was he alive or dead? Alexander had to know.

In that one instant, a battle of indecision was fought and won. His father came first, even over the chance to be revenged upon the man who had injured him. Alexander rushed quickly to his father's side, as Telgrin turned and started serenely toward the door, his escort following behind.

Alexander's mother was already kneeling over the fallen king by the time that he reached him. Her hand was on his cheek, which was as white as chalk.

"Mother, Mother," Alexander said breathlessly, heart beating so fast that he thought it might burst. "Is he—?"

"He is alive." She paused momentarily, as she held two fingers of her right hand against the inside of her husband's wrist. "He is alive," she repeated at last, with more certainty. "His heart is strong. Yes. He's merely unconscious."

"Thank the heavens," Alexander said softly. He was not entirely reassured, however. His father did not look well. His face was almost entirely without color, and his normally strong features were strangely lifeless.

Alexander helped Valanice turn Graham over on his back, then knelt there beside him while Valanice called out for the court physician to be summoned. He felt completely useless. There was nothing that he could do for his father now. Whatever had befallen him was beyond the prince's understanding.

Alexander suddenly stood and turned toward the interior of the chamber, filled with the overwhelming need to do *something*. Telgrin and his two knights were gone. He had heard them leave, he remembered, but he had been too concerned with his father's condition to pay them any heed.

The knights of Daventry had begun, almost reluctantly, to venture down from the gallery. They appeared confused and frightened by what had happened. Their wide eyes kept glancing uneasily to the main entrance, where Telgrin had gone.

Almost overwhelmed by emotion, not even able to sort out how much of what he felt was anger, how much fear, how much grief, Alexander numbly moved to pursue the magician-king. The knights of Daventry, perhaps seeing what was in his heart, stepped out of his path one by one. He was scarcely aware of them.

When he reached the antechamber, he saw that the guards who had been felled by Telgrin were starting to awaken. One of the two men had propped himself up on one elbow, but seemed unable rise further. A short sword lay near him. Alexander paused to scoop up the sword, then continued on through the open door.

A steep stair descended into the courtyard. Gripping the sword with a trembling hand, he hurried down the stair. The courtyard now appeared deserted. Apparently everyone had fled indoors.

Alexander did not see Telgrin and his escort, so he made his way to the main gate as soon as he came off the stair, passing through the dark passage piercing the imposing thickness of the wall. As he neared the other side, he saw a man leaning heavily against the side of the passage, there under the portcullis. He had his hand on his forehead, covering both eyes. At his feet was a halberd, its shaft broken in two.

It was the guard Henry.

"Henry," Alexander said. "Are you all right?"

At the first sound of his voice, the guard gave a slight jump and flattened himself against the wall, as if to protect himself. When he lowered his hand from his face, Alexander saw that he had an angry purple bruise forming over his left eyebrow, a streak of dried blood at the corner of his mouth. His gaze darted about wildly, but finally settled on Alexander. He gave a sigh and seemed to relax slightly. "Your Highness!" he said. "I . . . I'm fine, just a bit . . . shaken."

"Where did they go, Henry?"

"I tried to stop them, Alexander. I tried."

"I know that you did, Henry."

"What . . . did they want here?"

Alexander grimaced. "My father. They attacked my father."

"No. Oh, *no.* Is he all right?"

"I don't know. He's still unconscious."

The man scowled. "It's my fault. I should have never let them through. I should have stopped them, somehow."

"You did everything that you could. There was no way to stop them. Did you see them leave, Henry?"

"Yes."

"Where did they go?"

"They got on their horses and rode off. That way."

Alexander tightened his left hand into a fist. "A horse," he said. "I need a horse."

"You're not thinking of going after them, are you, Alexander?"

"I am. I must."

"But—" the man said, frowning. "Even if you should catch them, what would you do then?"

"What?" Alexander said dully. His thoughts had been centered on where he might get a horse most quickly.

"What would you do with them, should you catch them?"

Alexander hesitated. He contemplated the sword clenched in his right hand. Now that the first surge of emotion had left him, he realized that it would be quite useless against the likes of Telgrin. What *would* he do?

He did not know.

"You must not, Your Highness," the guard said. "Daventry needs you, especially now. You must not endanger yourself in this ill-considered plan. No good can come of it.''

Alexander stared at Henry for a moment. He drew a breath to speak, but could think of nothing he could say that would justify what he was doing. At last he let out his breath with a sigh and glanced away. "You're right, Henry," he said softly. "You're right. I wasn't thinking."

Lowering the sword slowly to his side, the prince turned and started back toward the keep, his thoughts troubled and his steps heavy.

·3·

A soft coverlet drawn up to the center of his chest, Alexander's father lay motionless on his bed. His eyes were shut, his face slack and without intelligence.

The room was but dimly lit. A thick drape covered the only window, and a single fluttering lamp burned on the small table set beside the bed. Those who came into the room spoke in hushed tones, when they spoke at all, and moved with a soft, hesitant tread. Everything seemed muted, vague, unreal.

The court physician, an old man with a forked beard and grey eyes, hovered over Graham for a long time, feeling the king's pulse, putting his ear against his chest, laying the back of his hand against his cheek, muttering to himself all the while.

At last the physician drew Alexander and his mother aside. He said, "I'm sorry. I'm afraid that this is beyond my powers. There's nothing that I can do."

"Nothing?" Queen Valanice said.

The physician shook his head unhappily. "The truth is, I can't find anything wrong with him, physically. Whatever was done to him, whatever the source of his ailment, is a matter of the spirit, of the soul, and that is beyond my province.''

"Is he in any danger of dying?"

The man gave a helpless shrug. "King Graham is fortunate to possess extraordinary physical vitality. A lesser man might have succumbed before now. Still . . ."

"What is it? *Tell me.*"

"It's just that I do not know how long his health can survive such a massive spiritual disruption. I do not think that he is in any danger of dying today, or even tomorrow. But over time there is bound to be a negative effect. It may weaken him to the point of death. Eventually it must."

"I see." Valanice looked away, her eyes fixing upon empty air. Alexander could see her cheek muscles tighten. After a long moment, the queen drew a deep breath, and said, "Well, do what you can. Anything you can do to maintain his physical well-being will be very much appreciated."

"Of course, Majesty. I, ah, will look back in on him in a short while." The man bowed, turned, and left the room.

Neither Alexander nor Valanice spoke for a long time. Alexander could see that his mother had been deeply affected by what the physician had said. If she had been alone, she might have cried, he thought. His heart full of helpless sorrow, Alexander reached out and took her hand in his. She looked up at him. Her eyes were moist, but the brave trace of a smile came to her lips.

"Don't worry. Everything will be all right, Mother," Alexander said.

"Will it? I wish I could believe that."

"It will."

"Oh, Alexander! What shall we do?"

Alexander considered the question, but there was no easy answer. He said pensively, "Somehow we must find help. Father was brought to this state by magic, and therefore it seems sensible that we should seek the help of a magician."

Valanice squeezed his hand, hard. "*Yes.* But what magician?"

Alexander frowned. This was the difficult part. He knew that many magicians roamed the world. Some were good and helpful, some malevolent beyond any understanding. Some were mighty enough to do almost anything they wished—alter their shapes, fly through the air, command the elements of nature, conjure up cunning demons to do their bidding. Others could wield only a few weak and imperfect spells.

Telgrin was the worst sort of magician: wicked and powerful. Alexander knew that it would require someone of equal power to negate the spell that Telgrin had placed on Graham. He was not sure that there was anyone of this description within reach of Daventry at the moment.

While Alexander was still thinking about this, Valanice suddenly said, "The wizard Morowyn still lives nearby, doesn't he?"

The prince took a moment to respond. "Yes," he said, cocking his head thoughtfully to one side. "I don't know how much use he can be to us. He was a great wizard in his day, but he's a very old man now—and he's still suffering from the effects of that unfortunate spell I once told you about.''

"Is it possible that he might still be able to help?"

"It's *possible*," Alexander conceded.

"Go to him, Alexander. Even if there's only a small chance that he will be able to do something for your father, it is a chance worth taking."

Unable to think of a better plan, the prince nodded. "All right, I'll go see him. Don't worry, Mother. Even if Morowyn can't help, we'll find a way to defeat this evil spell. Somehow we'll find a way."

The next day, Alexander left Castle Daventry before the sun could reach its highest point. He went on foot, because his path would lead him through a dense and tangled wood, where a horse would be worse than useless. At his side he wore a short sword, its edge keen, its pommel a disk of polished metal, its grip wound tightly with gold wire. A leather bag hung from his shoulder, containing a flask of water, a little bread and cheese, and a small pear.

As soon as he crossed the moat, he followed the road west for a time. On either side of him spread lush green meadows dotted with tall trees. Brightly colored birds rustled in the branches, and swooped across his path.

It was a beautiful day. The sun was warm, but a soft breeze stirred the leaves and cooled his brow. Given such a day as this, it was hard for Alexander to believe that evil had come to dwell in Daventry, that it was now so near. It was chilling to know that only a few wooded ridges separated him from Telgrin's dark castle.

The thought of Telgrin caused the prince to lengthen his stride, as he focused his mind more fully on the purpose of his journey. The road rose gradually before him, winding its way up a low summit. When Alexander reached the top, he paused beside a cairn of green stone, while he tried to catch his breath.

The cairn was very old, he knew. He could remember his father telling him that it had been erected by a people now long vanished from Daventry. Legend said that those who slept beside it were visited by prophetic dreams. Perhaps one day Alexander would try the legend, but not today.

After taking a drink from his water flask and mopping his forehead with his sleeve, he started off again. When at last he reached the far side of the summit, he looked down upon the deep green vale below.

Cupped between two ranges of sharp-edged hills, an ancient forest spread far into the west, where it faded into the faint blue mist that lay upon the horizon. The wizard Morowyn lived deep within that forest, far from any other habitation, so Alexander knew that he still had a long way to go. He hoped to reach the wizard's house before nightfall, but that was by no means assured.

Alexander started down the slope, which was steeper here than on the other side, and his legs soon began to ache from the strain of holding him back.

The road narrowed as it neared the bottom, and just before it flattened out it was framed by two gnarled outcroppings of lichen-mottled stone.

As Alexander passed between the standing stones, a white cloud passed over the face of the sun, casting a sudden shadow across the land. For a moment he could feel the air grow cool on his skin. Then the sun came out from behind the cloud, and the day's warmth returned.

Perhaps a quarter of a mile beyond the stone outcroppings, the forest began. At first it stood far back from the road, leaving a wide grassy belt of separation on both sides. Soon, however, it crowded ever closer, until great clawing branches hung above Alexander's head and the sky above was reduced to a jagged band of blue.

Alexander walked on for the better part of an hour. The forest became ever more dense, wild, and tangled. The air was rich with the earthy smells of moist fern, of leaf, of mould. At last he came to a place where a faint track left the main road and cut into the dark heart of the forest. Alexander followed this rude track, as it twisted along the base of a sloping bank overgrown with delicate vines and thorny brambles.

It was difficult going here. Covered with fallen leaves, the trail was frequently broken by roots and crossed by branches. It wound around stout tree trunks, rose and fell, followed a crumbling ledge above a narrow ravine. When it came to a fast-flowing brook, Alexander decided that he needed to rest for a while. He found a smooth grey rock veined with white partially buried in the bank above the brook, and sat there.

That part of the sky that could be seen through the leafy canopy was brightly tinged with yellow. Alexander guessed that it was late in the afternoon now. He knew that he could not afford to tarry here long. He did not want to be caught out on this trail after dark. It was difficult enough when he could see where he was going.

Alexander ate a small portion of the bread and cheese he had brought and washed it down with a sip from his flask, while he sat and wondered if his journey would be in vain. Did Morowyn still have the ability to combat a spell worked by someone as powerful as Telgrin? And if he did not, what would Alexander do next? The prince had no answers, and he badly needed some. After a short time, he got up, dusted himself off, and hastened on his way.

The trail followed the course of the brook for a time. Finally, however, it led Alexander to a crude bridge. The bridge was little more than two straight pine poles spanning the brook, to which roughly dressed crosspieces had been lashed with cord.

Alexander contemplated the bridge mistrustfully for a moment, as he had each time he had passed this way. Gingerly, he put first one foot then the other on the fragile construction. Holding his breath, he crossed the span, one slow step after another, alarmed by every creak and movement that it made. When he reached the other side and stepped down onto firm earth, he let out his breath in a soft sigh of relief.

Once again he had braved the bridge, and once again he had made it across.

The trail left the brook and from there led Alexander across an increasingly craggy landscape. As he scrabbled his way up and down the steep ridges, the forest became slightly less dense and tangled. Looking through the branches, he could see that the sun was hanging low in the sky now.

Over time, the trail rose more than it fell, and by the time the sun started to sink below the horizon he had attained the top of an isolated promontory. From here he could look back across the way he had come. A strong evening breeze had arisen; he could see it pushing its way relentlessly across the treetops. Alexander allowed himself a moment to catch his breath and savor the view. He knew that he had nearly reached Morowyn's dwelling. He would almost certainly be there before dark.

When the sun was but a red ember burning atop the farthest hill, Alexander turned and followed the trail around the crown of the promontory. Eventually he came to a high hedge, which encircled the entire center of the hill. The hedge was dense and woven through with flowering vines and inch-long thorns. Alexander circled it for a few yards, until he came to two pillars of roughly quarried stone.

He faced the hedge at this place. "Open, for a friend," he said.

The hedge rustled and began to move. Suddenly a gap in the hedge opened between the two pillars. Alexander stepped through this gap. He heard the hedge seal again behind him.

Inside the hedge wall was a small grove of trees, at the center of which was a simple house built of rough timbers. Alexander could see the light of a fire escaping its door and shutters, could smell the smoke escaping the stone chimney.

At this time of the evening, the trees and the house appeared as black shapes against a purple sky still illuminated with the last fleeting light of day. Alexander walked up the stone path leading to the house. When he entered the grove, he felt a slight uneasiness. He felt that he was being watched.

As Alexander approached the door, he heard a faint rustling to his right. He gave a quick glance in that direction, but saw only the surrounding trees. He took one more step toward the house, when suddenly a voice close beside him said: "Aren't you going to say hello, Alexander?"

Alexander gave a slight jump, and then turned to scan the grove, more attentively this time. He saw to his surprise that what he had at first taken to be a gnarled old oak was in fact the wizard Morowyn.

To be sure, there was no longer much to differentiate Morowyn from an oak tree. The wizard had taken on a brownish hue, his body had thickened and become twisted, and his arms had begun to sprout foliage. All this was the result of a spell that Morowyn had worked upon himself. The spell had been intended to extend his life, and so it had—but at an unintended cost. Morowyn was gradually becoming a tree.

Alexander was shocked at how far the spell had progressed since he had last seen Morowyn, some nine months before. Then he had looked like a man with some of the attributes of a tree. Now, he looked like a tree with some of the attributes of a man.

Alexander said, "Morowyn! I didn't see you there."

"No, I imagine not." The wizard's voice was soft, uninflected, and strangely hollow. "It has been some time since you last came here. Or has it? I lose track of time these days."

"It's been not quite a year. I've been away from Daventry for a few months."

"Ah."

"There's a reason why I came."

"I expect so. People usually have reasons for the things they do. I remember. I still remember, yes."

"I need your help, Morowyn."

"Indeed? Does this have anything to do with the black castle that has recently taken up residence nearby?"

Alexander was surprised. "You know about that?"

The wizard seemed to be trying to nod. This was difficult for him, since his shoulders had grown up to near his ears and he no longer had anything that Alexander would describe as a neck. "I have seen it, seen it in my dreams. I often dream now. Is this a dream? Who can say?"

"The black castle, Morowyn—it is ruled by a man named Telgrin."

"A terrible man. A dangerous man. Do not cross him, if you can help it. He has great power."

"Do you know him?"

"I have heard of him. He has an evil reputation."

"Telgrin has worked some manner of evil spell on my father."

"Ah, that would explain it, then."

"Explain what?"

"A dream I had. I saw your father trapped in a glass vessel."

"No, that's not what happened. My father lies in Castle Daventry. Telgrin came before him, made some sort of gesture, and my father fell unconscious. He has not moved since."

Morowyn considered this for a moment. "No. Your father is trapped in a vessel, or his essence is. His body may well rest in Castle Daventry, but not his soul. That is elsewhere."

"How is that possible?"

"Telgrin is a stealer of souls. I know of him, yes."

"A stealer of souls? What's that?"

Morowyn shifted uneasily. "Oh, you do not want to know. It is an old and unpleasant perversion."

Alexander frowned. He had come here believing that his father was under the influence of a spell. Any spell, no matter how powerful, could always be removed by another magician of sufficient skill, he knew. If Telgrin had taken Graham's soul, however, matters would be a great deal more complicated than he had thought.

After an uneasy pause, Alexander said, "I'd like you to come back with me to Castle Daventry. I want you to examine my father and see if you can do anything for him."

The wizard attempted to shake his head. He was only slightly more successful at this than he was at nodding. His entire upper body twisted back and forth slightly. "No," he said. "I'm sorry. That is impossible."

"Please, Morowyn. I don't know who else to turn to."

"No, you don't understand. I am not refusing your request. I'm merely telling you that it is impossible. Even a year ago, I might have managed it, but now . . . well, you see how it is." Morowyn inclined his head stiffly toward his feet. Alexander saw that the wizard was not wearing shoes, and that his brown toes had lengthened and curved into the ground.

"I am truly rooted to this place," Morowyn said.

"I am sorry, Morowyn. I hadn't realized. I didn't know."

"There is nothing to be sorry about. I am . . . resigned. I am trying to think if there is anything that I can do to help you. A moment." Morowyn fell silent for a long time. When the wizard was not speaking, Alexander could easily believe that he was facing nothing more than a peculiar tree.

Eventually Morowyn stirred. He said, "I cannot go

with you, but perhaps I can offer you someone to go in my place.''

''Who?''

''My apprentice, Cyril.''

Surprised, Alexander said, ''Since when do you have an apprentice?''

''It is a relatively recent thing. A month? Six? I'm afraid that time means little to me these days. It all . . . blends together. Cyril does those things that I can no longer do for myself. And he is very good at keeping the woodpeckers away.''

This did not sound like the sort of help that Alexander was looking for. He said, ''Your offer is very kind, but—''

''Before you make up your mind,'' Morowyn interrupted, ''you should know that Cyril is a very talented young man. I believe that he has it in him to be a great wizard some day. He came to me after years of studying with the magician Olkiphon, and he is well-grounded in the fundamentals of magic.''

''Well,'' Alexander said, not entirely convinced. ''Are you sure that you can spare him?''

''I could get by, I think.''

The prince took a moment to consider the offer. ''All right,'' he said at last. ''I'd be happy to have his help, then. Where can I find him?''

''Inside the house. Knock on the door and ask him to come out. I will introduce you.''

Alexander nodded to Morowyn, then went to the door of the small house and gave a quiet knock. At first there was no answer, but after a moment a muffled voice from within the house said: "Eh? Who's there?"

"Prince Alexander of Daventry. Morowyn asked me to summon you outside."

There was a slight hesitation, then: "A moment, Prince Alexander."

Alexander heard footsteps approaching the door. After a moment, the door opened. Yellow light flooded into the night, making Alexander blink. He saw a dark silhouette centered in the open doorway. As his eyes adjusted to the light, he was able to see in detail the person who stood before him, and he found himself dismayed.

Cyril was a pale youth of perhaps sixteen. Short and slightly plump, he was clad in brown homespun trousers and a dingy shirt that was frayed about the cuffs and collar. A faint, downy beard framed his pink cheeks. His straight blond hair appeared hopelessly disordered. He looked for all the world like a stable boy freshly awakened from a nap.

It seemed quite impossible that such a one could do anything against the likes of Telgrin. Still, Alexander tried not to let his face drop at the sight of the apprentice wizard, tried not to let his disappointment show.

Cyril gazed up at Alexander with an open and curious expression. "What can I do for you, Prince Alexander?" he said.

·4·

Sunlight filtered through closed shutters and fell upon Alexander's face. He felt its faint warmth on his cheek, encouraging him to full awareness. He blinked at his surroundings, for a moment not quite certain of where he was. Then it came to him: Morowyn's house. He had spent the night on a straw mattress before the fire, his cloak for a blanket. He had dreamed a dream, vivid, frightening, but now he found himself unable to remember a single detail of it. He brought only a vague and fleeting sense of dread to the waking world.

After a moment Alexander collected his thoughts enough to pull his cloak from him and sit up. He saw that the front door stood open. He heard soft voices coming from outside.

Alexander struggled into his boots and got up. Yawning, he went out into the morning light.

The sun had already climbed well above the eastern hills, its warm light flooding through the trees, but a faint chill clung to the air. Alexander saw that Cyril had brought a small table loaded with tea things to Morowyn. As Alexander watched, the apprentice

filled an earthenware cup from the pot and handed it
to his master. Morowyn still had some movement in
his arms. He was able to clutch the cup in his gnarled
hand and bring it slowly to his mouth. The leaves and
twigs that had sprouted along the length of his arm
rustled slightly. He took a sip from the steaming cup,
satisfaction apparent on his brown face.

After a moment Morowyn noticed Alexander.
"Ah," he said. "Good morning, my young prince.
Come and have some tea."

Alexander nodded and went over to Morowyn.
Cyril poured another cup of tea and handed it to him.
Holding it tightly in both hands, Alexander savored
its warmth. He breathed in the fragrant vapors coming
from the cup, then drew a sip. The tea was an herbal
blend, soft on the tongue, but with the suggestion of
an astringent bite.

"Good," he said.

The wizard said, "Yes. It will be a sad day when
I can no longer manage this."

Alexander regarded the wizard from the corner of
his eye. "Have you made any progress toward re-
versing the spell that's doing this to you?" he asked.

"Yes. I could do it now, if I wished. There would
be an unfortunate drawback to it, however."

"What?"

"It would result in my death."

"A serious drawback, that."

"Indeed. The problem is that I have already lived
longer than my appointed years. Without this spell to
sustain me, flawed though it may be, I will die. So, I

have the choice between life as a tree and no life at all.''

"I'm not sure I would find that an easy choice."

"Nor have I found it easy, I assure you."

They were silent for a time. Morowyn drained his cup, then let it drop. Unsupported, the cup hung in the air, then sailed away from the wizard's hand and circled the table twice. At last it dropped down and settled gently next to the teapot on the table.

Morowyn gave a stiff smile. "I may be a tree, but what a tree, eh? What a tree!"

Alexander laughed. "Yes, Morowyn. A most extraordinary tree."

The smile slipped gradually from the wizard's face. "Well," he said. "You two should be on your way soon. Time may be of the essence, if you are to save King Graham."

Alexander felt the laughter die in his throat. "Yes," he said stiffly. "It's time to go. Are you certain that you'll be all right here alone?"

"I can manage."

Cyril picked up the tea table. "I'd better put these away before we go. I'll be ready shortly."

Alexander and Morowyn watched the young man return to the house. When he disappeared inside, Morowyn said, "There is, ah, one thing that I should probably tell you before you go."

"Oh? What's that?"

"It is a small thing, or perhaps not so small. You see, although Cyril is a capable magician, and will soon be more than capable, he is currently at a delicate stage of his magical development. At this time it is best that he refrain from working magic of any kind."

Not quite believing what he had heard, Alexander looked at Morowyn with wide eyes. "You're joking."

"Alas, no."

Alexander managed to restrain himself from saying what first came into his mind, which was: "Then what good is he?" Instead, he said, "Uh, then how can he help my father?"

"Oh, he can help in many ways. Even though he cannot wield magic, he possesses knowledge that may be invaluable to you. I think that you will be surprised at how useful he will make himself."

"I see," Alexander said, his voice more flat and gloomy than he had intended.

Alexander and Cyril labored along the winding forest path, while the increasing warmth of the day filtered down through the leafy canopy overhead. Their feet raised clouds of dust, making Alexander's nose itch and his tongue feel dry.

As they plunged through the forest, Alexander's mood grew increasingly downcast. He found himself becoming irritated whenever Cyril lagged behind and he had to wait for the younger man to catch up. Sometimes it was everything he could do to keep from turning on the apprentice wizard and making an exasperated comment.

Alexander forced himself to be patient with Cyril.

He realized that it was not even Cyril who he was upset with, but rather with the unsatisfying results of his visit to Morowyn. He had hoped for a quick cure for his father, or at least some realistic cause for hope. What he had gotten was an underaged apprentice wizard who was not even supposed to work magic.

What had happened to Alexander's father was not Cyril's fault. Neither was it his fault that he was who he was, and not the great Morowyn. Alexander had good reason to be upset, but not with Cyril. He knew this.

So, as soon as they reached the brook and crossed over the rickety makeshift bridge, Alexander turned to his companion and suggested that they stop for a rest, even though he was eager to push on toward Castle Daventry. Cyril agreed readily, with a look of profound relief.

Sitting on a rocky ledge above the brook, they shared sips of water from Alexander's flask. Cyril's face had turned bright red from his exertions. Perspiration had gathered in fine droplets on the pale fringe of his beard. It was obvious that Cyril was not as accustomed as Alexander was to long marches over difficult terrain, and yet he had done his best to keep up, with not one word of complaint. Alexander had to admire that.

After they had sat there quietly for a minute, Alexander said, "How is it that you decided to become a wizard?"

Cyril shrugged. "It is not something that I decided. I always had the power. When I was four, I could make small objects move through the power of my mind, and I could see things hidden to most mortal eyes. So the decision was made for me, really. It was decided by my parents and the village elders that I should be apprenticed to a wizard lest I become dangerous in my ignorance.''

''It must have been difficult to leave your parents when you were still so young.''

''It was, yes. But there have been . . . compensations. The things I have seen, the things I have learned, these are treasures beyond any estimation.'' He said this with a slight frown, but in a emphatic tone of voice—almost, Alexander thought, as though he was trying to convince himself that the sacrifice had been worth it.

''Do you ever see your family?''

''Sometimes, yes. Sometimes.'' He paused and glanced up to the treetops. ''Not often.''

Alexander looked on Cyril with a strong sense of kinship. He himself had grown up away from the comforts of family and home. While still an infant, he had been kidnapped by the wizard Mannanan; he was eighteen years old before he could escape and return to Daventry. He sometimes wondered how he might be different, had he been allowed a normal childhood.

He knew that he had learned much during his enforced servitude to Mannanan. Beyond the smattering of magical lore that he had managed to wrest from the wizard, he had been forced to learn something of discipline and self-reliance. He had honed the ability to think on his feet. It was possible, even likely, that he had in some ways benefitted from his strange and loveless childhood.

Yet he knew that these lessons had cost him dearly. Where was the balance? Had he gained as much as he had lost? If he could, would he give up what he was, to be that stranger who had grown up safe and secure amidst a loving family? He did not know. He probably never would.

After resting a short while longer, the two rose and continued on their way, emerging from the forest just as the sun was starting down from its zenith. The air was still, and heat shimmered from the surface of the main road. The two strode along wearily, not speaking, breathing hard.

They paused finally at the top of the hill, near the cairn of green stones. Looking down the slope, they could see the end of their road: the great walls, the towers and turrets, the glistening circle of the moat.

"Castle Daventry," Alexander said.

Less than an hour later, Alexander and Cyril arrived at the gates of Castle Daventry. The portcullis was down, Alexander saw, and no fewer than six guards stood behind it. In his absence, his mother must have been attending to the defense of the castle.

"Ho there!" he said. "Open the gate."

A voice from beyond the portcullis called out: "Open the gate for Prince Alexander!" A moment later, the portcullis started to go up, clanking and rattling as it went. When it had been drawn all the way up, and appeared to be in no danger of slipping down again, Alexander stepped through into the gloom. He greeted the guards with a nod, and said, "Has there been any change in the situation while I was away?"

"No," one of the guards answered. "Not that I know of."

"Good. Thank you." Alexander led Cyril into the courtyard. Armed men were drilling there, with sword, with spear, and with lance. When Alexander looked up to the walls, he could see that they were strongly defended by men in bright mail and iron helms. This was all very strange to him. He had never seen Castle Daventry on a war footing before.

As he made his way toward the keep, some of the men drilling in the court noticed him and started calling out his name, in a harsh martial chant. "Alexander!" the chant went. "Alexander, *Alexander*!" This aroused sharply mixed feelings within the prince. He felt pride at having his name called out with such conviction, almost as a rallying cry, but he also felt inadequate to the faith that was being expressed in him. He felt like a fraud.

When he reached the steps of the keep, Alexander turned back to the men gathered in the court and raised one hand above his head, in a simple salute. At this, the men gave out a great cheer. Alexander bowed stiffly, then continued up the steps, brave voices still ringing in his ears.

Alexander found his mother standing in the throne room, talking intently with Roderick, the Captain of the Guard, and Baronet Hanley. When she saw Alexander, Valanice held a hand out to him with a relieved smile. "Alexander!" she said.

Alexander took her extended hand and kissed her on the cheek. "Mother."

"I'm glad to see you home again." She gave Cyril a curious look over the prince's shoulder. "But . . . who is this that you've brought with you?"

"This is Cyril, Morowyn's apprentice. Morowyn was unable to make the journey himself."

"Ah, I see. I am very pleased to meet you, Cyril."

"And I you, Your Majesty," Cyril said, bowing with awkward gravity.

"You are here to help King Graham?"

"I shall do my best, Majesty."

"A moment, then." The queen nodded to Roderick and Baronet Hanley. "Is our business complete?" The two men murmured their assent.

"Good. I'll speak with you again tomorrow, unless there is some reason that you need to see me before then." The two men bowed, backed away a step, and then turned and left the room.

Valanice studied Cyril for a brief moment. If she felt any skepticism concerning his abilities, she was careful not to let it show. "Will you examine Graham now, or do you need to rest from your journey?"

"I will examine him now, Majesty."

King Graham lay as he had when Alexander had last seen him. If anything, his cheeks were more sunken now, and his pallor more alarming. Cyril

looked down upon him with pursed lips, eyes in a
squint of deep concentration. The young wizard
placed one hand on the breast of the fallen king, then
the other on his forehead. He stayed like that for a
long time, not moving. At last he bestirred himself
abruptly, with the disoriented look of a man roused
suddenly from a dream. "Yes," he said, "yes."

Alexander waited a moment, but when no further
explanation was offered he said, "What is it? What
did you find?"

Cyril cast his gaze down at his feet, obviously uncomfortable with what he had to say. "I'm sorry. I'm
afraid that I've confirmed Morowyn's worst fears.
The magician Telgrin has stolen a crucial part of your
father's soul. Without it, this body is but an empty
husk. It will linger for a while, growing steadily
weaker, until it finally dies. No man can live without
a soul."

Though he had thought himself prepared for this,
Alexander felt a terrible chill touch his heart. "Is
there nothing that we can do?"

"Nothing. Unless—"

"What is it? *Is* there something?"

"If his soul were to be returned to him, he might
well recover."

"Is such a thing possible?" Valanice asked.

Cyril cocked his head thoughtfully to one side.
"Possible, yes. But . . . it would be difficult and dangerous. Telgrin has undoubtedly taken Graham's soul
back to his castle. Someone would have to penetrate
the castle, find it, and steal it back."

"But if someone did that, you could put his soul back into his body?" Alexander said.

"Oh, yes. Almost certainly. I think. Probably."

Alexander did not even have to think about it. "That's it, then. I will do it."

Valanice turned a somber gaze on him. "Alexander, are you certain?"

"You heard him. It is the only way."

"But perhaps somebody else . . . ?"

"Who else could we ask to do this thing? Who else would have the same incentive?"

It seemed that Valanice could find no answer to that. She pursed her lips together unhappily and said nothing.

"There is, uh, something else you should know," Cyril said abruptly.

Both Alexander and Valanice looked to the young magician, and he finally continued, in a halting, apologetic manner: "From what Morowyn told me, Telgrin likes to do things to the souls he steals. Terrible things. If you want King Graham to be the same as you knew him, you will need to get his soul back quickly."

"How quickly?"

"As quickly as you can."

·5·

Alone, Alexander stood in his bedchamber, staring down at his bed, where he had laid out the gear that he intended to carry on his journey. It did not amount to much. He planned to move quickly, over difficult ground. His only chance of success, he had decided, was to depend on stealth and surprise. Direct confrontation could only lead to disaster; he knew that he would be no match against a powerful sorcerer and a castle full of heavily armored knights. Therefore his only weapon would be his short sword, his only defense a lightweight shirt of silvered mail. With any luck, he would not need either.

The rest of his equipment was similarly minimal: a set of sturdy clothes, flexible boots, dark cloak, water flask, fire striker, a packet of medicinal herbs, food that could be eaten on the march. As he contemplated these objects, wondering if he had forgotten anything, there came a gentle tapping on his door.

"Who is it?" he said.

After a slight pause, a diffident voice answered, "It's Cyril. May I talk to you for a moment, Alexander?"

Alexander went to the door, opened it, and saw Cyril standing outside in the darkened hallway. The apprentice wizard's face seemed to convey an unspoken apology for the disturbance.

Alexander gave the youth a nod. "Come in."

"Uh, thank you, Prince Alexander."

"Alexander. Just call me Alexander."

"Yes. Yes, I will."

Cyril moved shyly into the room. "It is very good of you to see me at this late hour, Alexander." He gave a quick glance about him. "This is very nice, Alexander. Very . . . comfortable."

"Thanks. It suits me. How may I help you, Cyril?"

"You are leaving for Telgrin's castle tomorrow?"

"I am."

"I want to go with you."

Surprised, Alexander stared at Cyril for a moment. He seemed little more than a boy, but there was a gravity to his gaze that rightfully belonged to no boy. "That's not a very good idea."

"Why not?"

"Cyril, I don't think you realize how dangerous this is likely to be."

"Of course I do. I'm not stupid."

This brought Alexander up short. He hesitated, realizing what he had just said, then murmured, "I know you're not, Cyril. I'm sorry. I didn't mean that the way it sounded."

"I know. I understand how I must seem to you, Alexander, but I'm not a child. I'm really not. I have been to many lands. I have seen many things. I have been responsible for myself, mostly, almost since I was old enough to talk. I know what I'm doing, when I ask to go with you.''

''But why would you even want to?''

''Because you need me.''

''How so?

''Telgrin is a magician. You'll need a magician of your own, if you are to oppose him.''

''But . . .'' Alexander let his voice trail off. He did not want to put this the wrong way. After a moment, he began again. ''Morowyn told me that you have been barred from wielding magic. He also said that one day you will be a powerful wizard, but—''

''In the case of a real emergency, I'm allowed to use my magic. The results may not be entirely optimal, but I'm the best you have. Besides, I can at least advise you. You are searching for your father's soul. Do you know where to look for a soul? Have you ever seen one?''

''No, I haven't,'' Alexander admitted. ''Even so, I can't ask this of you.''

''You don't have to ask it of me. I am asking *you*. Let me do this thing. I want to.''

Alexander searched for some reasonable reason to refuse Cyril, but could not find one. ''If you're certain—''

''I am.''

''Then I would be happy for your company.''

The intent anxiety on Cyril's face melted suddenly into a satisfied smile. ''Thank you,'' he said.

* * *

In that quiet hour of the morning when a fragile glow
limned the eastern horizon and the world was only beginning to resolve itself from a black totality into a suc-
cession of discrete features, Alexander and Cyril stood
before Queen Valanice outside the gates of Castle Daventry.

"Don't worry, Mother. We'll be back before you
know it. And we'll have Father's soul with us."

"May it be so," the woman said, with the softest of
sighs. "Be careful, Alexander."

"I will. If I have my way, Telgrin will not even know
that I've been there until I am already gone."

"Good."

"Have no fear, Majesty," Cyril said. "I will make
sure that your son comes to no harm."

Alexander thought that his mother might break a smile
at that, but instead she regarded the apprentice wizard
with a grave look. "That is well. I am content."

Alexander gave the queen a quick embrace. "Good-
bye, Mother."

"Good-bye."

With that, Alexander and Cyril turned and started
across the bridge. Glancing over the side, Alexander
saw the waters of the moat roil momentarily, and an
instant later glimpsed the scaly back of one of the
moat monsters breaking the surface. Then it was gone
again, vanished beneath the murky waters. The moat
monsters were huge, fearsome serpents first established in the castle's moat as an additional line of defense by an early king of Daventry. They made

crossing the moat, except by way of the bridge, an unappealing option.

When they reached the other side of the bridge, Alexander looked back over one shoulder. He saw his mother, still standing in the same place, a solemn and shadowy figure. He wished that there was something he could do to reassure her, but in fact he was venturing into unknown territory, to face unnamed terrors, and they both knew it. There was nothing he could say, nothing he could do, to remove that burden from her.

"Don't worry about her," Cyril said, as though he could read his mind. "She is a great woman. She can bear it. If anyone can, she can."

"Yes."

The two men started walking south along a narrow dirt road. After breasting the first rise, Alexander glanced back once again toward Castle Daventry. He could still see the great walls and battlements of the castle, even in the faint light, but he could no longer see the gate or his mother. A momentary sadness seized him, but after a while he managed to put it aside. He was finally on his way, he told himself. He was at last doing something. As the new day grew brighter, so did his mood. By the time the sun broke over the horizon, he found himself humming a pleasant tune under his breath.

The birds, which had long since awakened within their green bowers, accompanied him: their wings rustled in the trees above, and their calls—sometimes musical, sometimes merely strident—filled the quiet of the morning. Occasionally Alexander spotted a feathered form winging its way along the ridge before him.

After a little more than half an hour of steady walking, the two men came to a still green pond beside the road. The pond's wide banks were thickly overgrown with delicate green vines. The branches of a willow drooped low over its shimmering surface.

"We leave the road here," Alexander said.

"Where?" Cyril said, glancing around him at the dense foliage that girded the road on both sides.

"Here." Alexander lifted a willow branch with the back of his hand and ducked below it. Under the thick canopy of the willow, a faint trail began, which cut west away from the road. No one who had not already known of the trail would ever have found it.

Keeping his head down, Alexander scrambled up the steep slope that angled away from the base of the willow. He emerged from under the low-hanging branches and, wiping a cobweb from his cheek, continued along the faint path worn into the rocky bank. He could hear Cyril blundering along in his wake.

To the right was a mound of blackberry brambles. Alexander accidentally caught the hem of his cloak on a bramble, freed it with a quick yank, and made his way to the top of the bank. Here he paused, while he waited for Cyril to catch up. They were on the other side of the pond now; Alexander could see it glinting through the tall brush.

"Where does this trail lead?" Cyril said, as he came to the top of the bank. Alexander could hear his breath laboring softly.

"Overland, toward the river. It comes out on the eastern edge of the Old Wood. The way is hard, but it will save us a half day's travel. It will also make it less likely that we'll be spotted by any spies that Telgrin may have."

"Good."

Alexander waited a moment, to allow his companion to recover from the climb. "Are you ready to move on?" he said at last.

Cyril nodded.

"Come on, then."

The trail rose and fell with the broken contours of the land, often overhung by grasping branches and bordered by thorny brush. The two men struggled along valiantly, while the sun climbed ever higher in the sky. As it neared its zenith, the terrain began to change. The sharp inclinations of the ground eased, at last giving way to a series of gently rolling hills. The trail widened, and the trees fell away. Soon the two were hiking through grassy hills spangled with tiny yellow wildflowers.

They paused early in the afternoon, in the fold between two hills, where they shared some of Alexander's bread and cheese. Cyril sat on the edge of the turf and massaged his legs above the knees. When he caught Alexander looking at him, he said, "I'm not used to walking this much."

"Am I going too fast for you?"

"No, no, not at all. I can manage."

Cyril looked very tired already. Alexander wished that he could set an easier pace, but he knew that he had to reach Telgrin's castle as quickly as possible. If Cyril could not keep up, Alexander would just have to leave him behind. That was the hard truth.

After they had finished their meager meal, Alexander got up, dusted himself off, and said, ''It's time that we were going.'' Cyril gave a mute nod and climbed to his feet, a look of grim determination on his face. The two set off once again. The sun beat down upon them with ever-increasing heat. Whatever wind there had been gradually faded away to nothing.

Eventually the trail led them to the top of a ridge that rose slightly above all of the surrounding hills. Looking down from this vantage, Alexander was able to see the shallow river basin spreading before them. He could see one great bend of the river glistening in the light of the late afternoon sun, and the silver pines of the Old Wood. Somewhere beyond the Old Wood was Telgrin's castle, Alexander knew.

Alexander and Cyril reached the floor of the basin when the sun hung just above the western hills and the shadows were gradually lengthening and combining. The trail led to a wider and more prominent road that ran along the edge of the Old Wood, and there it ended. The two men turned onto the road and began to travel along it, as it veered ever closer to the outer margin of the woods.

As they walked, now side by side, Cyril cast a side-long look at Alexander, and said, ''Have you given any thought to how you are going to get us into Telgrin's castle?''

''No,'' Alexander admitted. ''I'll have to see what it

looks like when we get there.''

"That's leaving an awful lot to chance, isn't it?''

"Probably.''

"What if we can't get inside?''

"We'll get inside.'' Alexander knew how cavalier this must sound to Cyril, but there was really no way for him to determine how to penetrate Telgrin's castle until he could see it up close, study its defenses, and watch the comings and goings of its residents.

The sun sank below the horizon. Alexander continued leading Cyril along through the gathering twilight. Soon they would have to stop for the night, the prince knew, but he was determined to take advantage of every last bit of light that the day was able to give them.

The sky turned a somber shade of purple, except for the fading band of yellow that rimmed the hills. Those few faint clouds that streaked the western sky were slowly changing from angry maroon to deepest indigo.

Alexander was just starting to think about where to make camp for the night, when a distant drumming sound reached his ears. He stopped abruptly, almost in midstride, and listened intently.

"What is it?'' Cyril asked. "Is something wrong?''

"Behind us. A horse, coming fast.'' Alexander considered this for a moment. The horse might well belong to an innocent traveler, but what if it did not? He did not want to be caught out on the open road by one of Telgrin's knights.

Alexander swiftly came to a decision.

"*Come on!*'' he said in an urgent whisper. "To the woods, to the woods, quickly!''

He left the road and started running across a wide meadow, toward the fast-darkening wood. After the many miles they had walked that day, his legs felt tight and heavy; they refused to carry him at the rate that he desired. Alexander could hear Cyril laboring along in his wake. The apprentice magician was falling farther and farther behind him. Alexander realized, with a quick surge of desperation, that the horse would catch up with them long before they could reach the shelter of the wood.

The ground before them dropped into a slight depression. Alexander knew that this was likely to be the best cover that they were going to get. "*Get down,*" he called out in a ragged voice.

Alexander slid down on one leg and quickly rolled over onto his belly. Cyril went down beside him. They lay there gasping, waiting for the horseman to appear.

They did not have to wait long. The staccato beat of the horse's hooves grew steadily louder, and after a few moments horse and rider burst into view. The horse was a sinister black charger, its powerful lines glistening softly in the dim light. Its rider was clad from head to foot in black armor, which showed a curiously flat and lusterless appearance. Alexander instantly knew him for what he was. Two such knights had escorted Telgrin to Castle Daventry.

The knight galloped along the road at full speed. When he reached the place where Alexander and Cyril had left the road, he abruptly pulled back on the reins and drew to a halt. Eerily still, only his head moving, the knight appeared to scan both sides of the road.

The knight's featureless helm swung in Alexander's direction. The prince stayed as close to the ground as he could, hardly daring to breathe. He could see two green glints shining where the knight's eyes should be, and this sent a shiver of cold dread down his spine. Whatever Telgrin's knights were, he was quite sure now that they were not human.

The knight's terrible gaze seemed to fix on Alexander and Cyril. The prince felt a dismal certainty that the creature saw them, that at any moment it would leave the road to pursue them. But just as the last shred of hope fled his heart, the knight suddenly turned his blank face away. A moment later, he gave spur to his horse and took off down the road at a gallop.

Alexander did not move until the clatter of hooves had faded away into the distance. Finally, allowing himself to breathe normally, he sat up. Cyril followed his example, and the two glanced nervously in the direction that the knight had gone.

"*That* was a near thing," the young wizard said, hunched and slightly trembling.

"Yes, it certainly was." Alexander could still feel his heart pounding alarmingly. He did not know what would have happened if the knight had seen them. He did not think that he wanted to know.

After a moment, Cyril gulped down a shuddering breath, and said, "What do we do now?"

"I think that we'd better stay off the road as much as we can from here on. It will take longer, but it will be safer."

"Safer is good."

The two men picked themselves up off the ground, shouldered their bags, and wearily resumed their march. The last light of day faded. Before them rose the Old Wood, dark, somber, and mysterious.

·6·

The small campfire fluttered in the soft breeze, casting shadows that lengthened or shortened with each passing moment. Alexander, too tired to sleep, lay on his back on a bed of fragrant pine needles, staring up at the bright patch of stars that showed through the thatch of overhanging branches.

Cyril had no such problem. As soon as he had finished his evening meal, he had wrapped himself in his cloak and promptly drifted off into slumber. Alexander could hear the faint rhythmic hiss of his breathing over the vague stirrings of the woods. He envied him.

They had not gone very far into the woods, only far enough that they could not be seen or heard from the road. Alexander knew that they were still more than a day's journey from Telgrin's castle, so it seemed to him that they would be in no great danger here.

Even though he told himself this, he had a hard time falling asleep. Every time he shut his eyes he felt an alarming dizziness overtaking him, and in the blackness behind his closed eyelids he saw again that

dark knight on his dark steed, green fire burning
where his eyes should be, and then he would be wide
awake again.

At last, however, exhaustion grew so strong that it
could win out over any phantasm, no matter how
frightful. He dropped into a light and troubled sleep.
It was the kind of sleep in which he seemed always
aware of his surroundings—even when dreaming he
knew that he was dreaming. He never lost touch with
the feel of cool air on his face, the acrid smell of the
woodsmoke, the crackling of the fire. And yet, all the
while, he was asleep and dreaming.

At some time in the night he came fully awake
again, with a suddenness that was disorienting. He
perceived a bright light through his eyelids, and his
first thought was that the campfire had somehow escaped its pit and had set fire to the old pine needles
that carpeted the floor of the wood.

Giving out a hoarse cry of alarm, he sat up
abruptly. He saw then that the campfire, far from
spreading, had gone out entirely. The light had to be
coming from somewhere else, but where?

The light had an eerie silver-white cast. It flooded
through the wood, seeming to come from everywhere
and nowhere. Alexander pulled his cloak off to one
side and slowly stood up. What was this light? What
did it signify?

Alexander gave Cyril a quick glance. The apprentice wizard was snoring softly, unaware of the strange
light. Alexander wondered briefly if he should wake
him. No, he decided, not yet. He would see if he

could discover the source of the light first.

Swinging his head from side to side, he determined that the light appeared slightly brighter to his right. He began moving slowly in that direction. He told himself that he would turn back if there was any sign of trouble.

Cautiously, one step at a time, he wove his way through the trees. A faint music came gradually to his ears, soft, lilting, and unlike anything he had ever heard before. It filled his heart and his mind with its soft sweetness, intoxicating in its beauty. Alexander wanted to find its source, so that he might hear it better. Forgetting caution, he began striding along faster and faster.

After passing through a particularly dense thicket, he found himself on the edge of an open glade. The light shone with exceptional brilliance from this place, with the cool clarity of moonlight, but with a dazzling intensity.

Through narrowed eyes, Alexander saw figures moving about the glade. They were tall and slender, and they moved with a supple grace. He could not make out the figures in any detail, but they seemed to be talking and laughing. He could not hear anything of what they were saying. He heard only that sweet, soft music, still oddly muted.

Alexander took one step into the glade. The air itself seemed to shimmer about him for an instant, as though sparks of white fire were blowing wildly about him. He took a second step, and the shimmering was gone. The world had taken on an appearance of flat unreality. A third step, and suddenly it was as if he had opened a thick door and walked into a room where a joyous fête was being held. He was instantly surrounded by sounds of laughter and song. The sounds struck him with an almost physical force.

Alexander looked about the glade in simple wonderment. All around him were bright figures clad in glittering garments of silk and cloth-of-gold. They were male and female, all tall, all slender, all with faces of exquisite, unworldly beauty. They spoke among themselves in light and lilting tones. Although Alexander could hear them perfectly well now, he could not understand a word of what they were saying. They seemed to be speaking a language that he had never heard before.

In the background, musicians were playing on instruments such as Alexander had never seen. The music they played was sweet, but it possessed a fevered, almost frenzied, undercurrent. It made his blood run quick, made his thoughts seem fleeting and chaotic.

Alexander passed among the revelers gathered together in the glade. No one stopped him; no one interfered with him. Indeed, no one appeared to notice him at all, though he felt conspicuous enough, certainly, in his rough traveling clothes and scuffed boots.

Gaps opened and closed between the revelers. Gradually it occurred to Alexander that, although those around him seemed not to acknowledge his existence, they were in fact artfully guiding his steps toward the center of the glade—but for what purpose?

Suddenly apprehensive, Alexander tried to turn and go back the way he had come. He saw then that the crowd had closed in behind him, forming an impenetrable barrier. Little by little, that barrier was moving toward him, seemingly intent on moving him along his original path. The only way that he might get past it was if he were to forcibly jostle his way through, and he somehow knew that this was something he should not do.

After a moment's consideration, Alexander decided to give in and do as he was evidently expected to do. If nothing else, this might allow him to discover the intentions of the revelers sooner.

Squaring his shoulders, Alexander strode through the gaps that the throng had surreptitiously provided for him, and at last he came to the center of the glade, where he discovered a woman seated upon a round-backed gilt chair.

Her hair was the color of wheat, her eyes the limitless blue of a summer sky. She was attired in a gown of shimmering green, and upon her brow was a filet of silver wire, which held within its circuit a perfect blue stone. The woman looked at Alexander with a gaze that seemed to penetrate deep into his soul. She was, he thought, almost heartbreakingly beautiful.

"Greetings, Prince Alexander," she said. "I'm glad that you could join us this night."

Alexander hesitated, uncertain of what to say. At last he said, "I'm afraid that you have the advantage of me, Lady."

"You do not know what I am? You cannot guess?"

He shook his head.

"I am Culatha, a queen of Fairie, and this is my court."

Of course. He should have guessed it before, he thought. He had stumbled onto a fairy fête. He felt very foolish, suddenly.

Knowing that the denizens of Fairie were jealous of their privacy, Alexander hastened to say, "Forgive me, Your Majesty. I did not mean to intrude on your festivities."

Culatha waved his apology away with one slender white hand. "You were intended to come. That is why you were allowed to hear our music."

"Why did you want me to come here?"

"It is said that you are journeying to the castle of the one called Telgrin. Is that true?"

"Yes."

"You intend to oppose him?"

"To the best of my ability, yes."

"It is well," Culatha said. "Telgrin and his castle are blights upon the land. They disturb the order of what should be. They bring ruin wherever they go. However . . . are you not afraid to face him?"

After considering the question, Alexander decided to answer honestly. "Yes. I am afraid."

"But you will not let that stop you?"

"No. I cannot."

Culatha looked at him approvingly. "You are a brave man."

"As to that, I do not know. I only know that this is something that I must do. It is not something that I want to do, or choose to do. I must do it."

"A brave man," she repeated. "We would be pleased to aid you with your quest, which we deem indeed worthy. Is there anything that we can do to ease your way?"

Alexander shifted his stance uneasily. "You are too kind. But no—your good wishes are boon enough." He knew that it was risky to ask anything from a fairy gathering. The inhabitants of Fairie were unpredictable and easily offended. If he should make a request that for some inexplicable reason offended his hosts, there was no telling what they might do.

"No," Culatha said. "Good wishes are not nearly enough. If you have no specific request to make, we shall just have to think of something on our own." She held out her hand, and suddenly someone appeared at her side, a male of her kind, with a pointed greenish beard and arched eyebrows. Giving a secretive smile, he placed an object in her outstretched hand.

"Come forward and receive your boon from our hand," Culatha said. Her manner made it clear that this was a command, not a request.

Alexander went slowly to Queen Culatha and knelt down on one knee before her. Reaching out, he took the object from her hand. It was a large wallet of green leather, of the sort that one might use to keep provisions in. It seemed to contain something.

"This may seem to be an ordinary wallet," Culatha

said, "but I assure you that it is anything but ordinary. It holds a special traveler's bread, wholesome, nourishing, yet also sweet to the taste and remarkably delectable. The wallet will always be full. No matter how much you take from it, there will always be more. At least you will not know hunger on your journey, so long as you keep this by you."

Alexander held the wallet gingerly in both hands, both touched and awed by the gift. "Thank you, Your Majesty. I feel unworthy of your generosity."

"Take it with our warm regards. May it sustain you on your quest."

Still clutching the wallet, Alexander rose to his feet and backed away a step. Queen Culatha's eyes were upon him all the while, attentive and unblinking. "Now," she said, "will you stay and join in our celebration? You may dance until morning's light and for one night at least know the ineffable joy of the immortal."

"It's a tempting invitation, but I've far to travel tomorrow. I really should sleep."

"Ah. Sleep," Culatha said, in a manner that suggested that this was a distant and unimpressive concept to her. "Very well, you may go, and go with the blessing of Queen Culatha."

"I thank you." After giving a slight bow, Alexander turned and started back the way he had come. Dancing, talking, laughing, the revelers parted before him, without ever seeming to notice him.

When he reached the edge of the glade, he again passed through that place where the air seemed to shimmer for a moment. Glancing back over his shoulder, he saw the light that had filled the glade flicker and go out. Everything was gone—the light, the music, the voices, the dancers. Everything. The glade was empty.

Alexander felt weighed down by a sudden, profound weariness. He felt as if he had not slept for days, as though the fairy fête had lasted a small eternity, instead of the minutes it had seemed at the time. His thoughts had become hazy and confused.

Shivering from the cold night air, Alexander looked around him. Now that the light from Fairie had gone, the wood appeared black and threatening. There was only the faint starlight to show him his surroundings. He wondered if he could find his way back to camp.

His eyes open as wide they could go, the prince started retracing his steps, searching for broken twigs, scuffed places on the greyed carpet of old pine needles, any sign of where he had passed before.

It took a long time, or seemed to, but eventually he managed to find the camp, where Cyril was sleeping as soundly as ever. Alexander briefly considered waking the younger man and telling him about his extraordinary experience, but he was just too weary. He threw Culatha's gift down next to the black rectangle of his cloak, then fell to his knees beside it.

Awkwardly, the prince went down on one elbow, thrust his legs out to their full length, and at last settled onto his back. He grasped the edge of his cloak and pulled it over him, as evenly as he could.

He was asleep within the minute.

*   *   *

When Alexander awoke the next morning, he found that a thin fog had invaded both the wood and his own skull, with apparent equality. He opened his eyes, but did not otherwise move for several long moments. The events of the previous night now seemed so unlikely that he could not help wondering if he had dreamed them.

At length he gathered enough strength to sit up, and there beside him was the wallet that Culatha had given him. He picked it up and fingered it pensively. Obviously it was no dream.

"What's that?"

Alexander looked across the blackened fire pit and saw Cyril seated cross-legged at the base of a tree, clutching his cloak to his chest. "A gift," Alexander said.

Mild surprise registered on Cyril's face. "A gift? From whom?"

"Queen Culatha of Fairie." And then Alexander told the other man of his experiences of the night before. After listening to Alexander's tale with ever-widening eyes, Cyril said, "I wish that you'd woken me. I would've liked to see that. I've never been to a fairy fête." There was more than a hint of reproach in his voice.

"Sorry, I didn't know what was happening at the time."

Cyril accepted this with a sullen nod, but a moment later his expression brightened. "Have you tried it yet?"

"What? The traveler's bread? No, not yet."

"Well, let's give it a try."

Alexander hesitated. He had often heard that it could be dangerous to eat or drink anything obtained from the fairies. In this case, however, he had no reason to believe that they meant him any harm. "All right," he said at length. "Let's."

Alexander opened the wallet and removed one of the thin brown loaves he found inside. After breaking the loaf in two, he handed one piece to Cyril and contemplated the second piece himself. He gave it a sniff, then took a tiny bite.

A wonderful taste filled his mouth—sweet, yes, but not cloyingly so. He detected many subtle flavors, each of which contributed to a smooth and harmonious whole. Before he knew it, he had finished the entire piece and was wondering if he should have another.

"*Delicious!*" Cyril declared. "I've never tasted anything quite like it!"

"It *is* good," Alexander said.

Cyril gave the wallet a furtive glance. "I wonder . . ."

"Would you care for another piece?"

"Please."

Alexander split another loaf of the traveler's bread, which the two men shared in silence. When the prince had finished his portion, he allowed himself to bask in the contented glow that it had created in him, but only for a moment. The grey light pervading the wood was becoming less delicate by the moment, he saw. He knew that they needed to resume their journey.

Alexander sealed the fairy wallet and climbed slowly to his feet. He gave a nod to Cyril. "It's time to go," he said.

*   *   *

Alexander and Cyril picked their way through the gloomy, fog-shrouded wood for most of the morning. That sense of well-being which the traveler's bread had brought Alexander stayed with him for a long time. His stride seemed more buoyant than usual; no effort seemed sufficient to tire him. The bread appeared to have had a similar beneficial effect on Cyril. The young wizard seemed to be having far less trouble covering the difficult ground today. Indeed, he almost looked as if he was enjoying himself.

This was well, for the way through the wood proved arduous. There was not the faintest trace of a trail to follow, and impenetrable thickets frequently blocked their progress. The ground sloped this way and that; the footing was uncertain at best.

As they went, Cyril pressed Alexander for details of his visit to the fairy fête. Unfortunately, the prince's recollection of the event was hazy at best. It almost seemed to have occurred in a dream, and now the specifics were quickly fading, leaving only a vague impression. He could tell his companion little more than he already had.

It was Alexander's intent to parallel the main road, where the Old Wood was at its most narrow. They were so often forced to depart from his chosen course, however, that he began to fear that they would lose their way. Whenever the thickness of the forest would permit it, he would look to where the sun, a wan silver disk, hung in the overcast sky and try to adjust their bearing accordingly. Still, he was far from certain that they were where they should be.

It was therefore with some relief that, with the woods thinning, he was finally able to see the road on their right. From this point on, the going became easier, and soon they found themselves at the farthest edge of the wood, at the place where the road curved around toward the river.

They halted here and took sips from the water flask, while Alexander contemplated the next stage of the journey. They would be leaving the shelter of the Old Wood as soon as they resumed their march. A patchwork of small farmsteads began just the other side of the road, however, and Alexander thought that they would be safe enough traveling across the open fields and pasture lands. First, however, they would have to get across the road. After their encounter with the black knight on his black horse the previous evening, this made Alexander nervous.

The prince capped his water flask and returned it to his bag. He said, "I want us to get across the road as quickly as possible. Do you see those two trees on the other side, there at the top of that earthen bank?"

Cyril narrowed his eyes and nodded.

"We're going to head for those trees. Whatever you do, don't stop until you get there."

"I understand."

"Good. Let's go."

The two left the safety of the wood and struggled down the rocky slope. As soon as they reached the road, they immediately crossed it and started up the bank on the other side. The soil was extremely loose here, making it hard for them to keep their footing, as the side of the bank kept crumbling away under them. Eventually, however, they managed to reach the top, where a pair of oak trees gave them shelter while they caught their breath.

From this new vantage point, Alexander carefully scanned the lands they would be traveling over next. To the left was a small pasture, bounded by the curve of the road. To the right, a recently harvested field. Separating the two was a thin line of trees. Alexander decided that they should stay close to the trees for as long as possible, since they would provide some cover.

After climbing down the other side of the bank, they made their way along the line of trees, on the side of the harvested field. Half an hour later, they found themselves passing by an old apple tree. Its limbs were heavy with red, ripe fruit, and the ground under it was littered with yet more fruit.

"Apples!" Cyril said, clearly delighted. He went to the tree and picked an apple from a low branch, then another. He held out one to Alexander. "Do you want one? They look ripe."

Alexander glanced about him. Normally it was poor form to filch fruit on another man's land, but it seemed that these apples were just going to waste. "All right," he said. "Thanks."

The two sat in the shade of the tree. Alexander polished the apple on his sleeve, then bit into it. It was juicy and sweet, with just a hint of tartness.

"Good apple," Cyril said.

"Very good."

"Sweet."

"Mmm."

Alexander finished his apple and flung the core into the brush. While the afternoon warmth made him drowsy, he watched while Cyril did the same. "Ready to move on?" he said.

"Just a moment." The young wizard stood up and pulled several more apples down from the branches, which he tucked into his bag. "For later," he said.

The two started off again. They had only been walking for a few minutes, when Cyril pointed off across the field. "Look!"

"What is it?" Alexander said, frowning.

"There. Do you see? Smoke."

Narrowing his eyes, the prince gazed off in the direction that the other man had indicated. At the far edge of the field there was a small collection of modest structures, barely visible from this distance. These were the farm buildings, he assumed—farmhouse, barn, perhaps a granary or storehouse. From the center of them a dark column of smoke was rising ominously, to blend at last with the overcast sky.

The farm buildings rose before them, a haze of smoke hanging above them. Somewhere a dog was barking, its voice loud and ragged.

As they approached the buildings, Alexander flipped the left edge of his cloak over his shoulder and gripped his sheathed sword. He knew that it would have been safer to avoid this place altogether, but he could not make himself do this. If there were people here who needed help, how could he walk by without seeing if there was anything that he could do? It was all very well to tell himself that he had a quest to fulfill, and that this should take precedence over all else, but other people had fathers, too. And sons, daughters, and wives. In the great scheme of things, they were no less important than Alexander's father. All loved and were loved. All mattered.

Alexander opened a gate and entered the farmyard, Cyril trailing a pace or two behind. Ahead was the side of a large stable, walls half of stone, half of timber. The two men moved to the front of the structure and saw that the big doors were standing open. There was an elusive smell of hay and livestock, but the stable appeared to be empty. Alexander paused by the open doors, scanning the dusky interior. When he saw nothing of interest there, he continued around to the other side.

Here there was a small yard, a stone well in the center of it. A small house, or what was left of it, stood at the far end. The pall of smoke hung particularly thick over the house, though it no longer rose up in a dark column.

The house had been heavily damaged by fire, its open door and windows showing a blackened interior. In one place, the front left corner, the roof had been burned through. It appeared that someone had waged a heroic campaign to extinguish the flames, for the porch and the side of the house were wet. Small puddles glistened darkly in front of the house.

Alexander moved toward the house, but then a sudden voice behind him brought him swinging around. "Go away," the voice said. "There is nothing for you here. The others got everything. They got it all, all."

Alexander saw that a young man and woman sat before the open door of a small shed. The pair looked bedraggled and dispirited, their faces smudged with soot, garments muddy and wet. The man had an angry purple bruise beside his left eye. On the ground before them were two empty pails.

"Go away," the young man repeated. "There is nothing."

"We want nothing from you," Alexander said in his most reassuring voice. "We'd like to help, if there is anything that we can do."

"Help," the woman said bitterly.

"What happened here?"

The man said, "They came, the black knights. They took our whole harvest, everything . . . grain, fruit, vegetables, comb honey, everything. When I tried to stop them, I got this for my trouble." The man touched his bruised temple.

"He fell to the ground senseless," the woman said in a flat voice. "I was afraid that they had killed him, but by the blessings of heaven he was still alive. There was nothing that I could do. I watched them fill their wagons and drive away with everything."

"But what of the house? How did it catch fire?"

"O sir, they are wicked men, the knights of the black castle. After they had taken everything that they wanted, one of them lit a torch and threw it into our house, saying that perhaps next time we wouldn't be so foolish as to oppose the will of Telgrin."

The young man said, "We managed to put out the fire, but . . . there isn't much left."

"I'm sorry for your loss," Alexander said. "Is there anything that we can do for you?"

"No, nothing."

"My friend and I have pressing business elsewhere, but if you want for anything, go to Castle Daventry and ask for an audience with Queen Valanice. Tell her that Prince Alexander sent you."

The young man gave him an appraising look. "You are Alexander?"

"I am."

"You are marching on the black castle, aren't you?"

"Yes."

"Good. It is . . . good. Someone must oppose this wickedness. I must warn you, though . . ."

"Of what?"

"You may have some trouble getting across the river. Telgrin has set an evil kelpie to guard the only bridge. Anyone who attempts to cross the river will be dragged under and drowned."

"A kelpie?" Alexander said. This was an obstacle that he had not anticipated. He knew that kelpies were horselike water spirits, often malignant, who lived in rivers and lakes. No kelpie had been seen in Daventry for years, but Alexander had heard and read accounts of them. They could be formidable, from everything he had heard. "Are you sure?" he asked.

"Yes," the young man said, his voice steady and certain. "Several of my neighbors have seen it with their own eyes—and a murderous, black-hearted creature it is, too. Beware of it, I beg you."

Alexander nodded. "Thanks for the warning. We'll try to be be careful." The prince was troubled. It would not be easy to get past the kelpie. The bridge that it guarded was the only way across the river, which ran swift and deep hereabouts. If they tried to avoid the bridge, it would take at least a day to reach a place where the river was fordable—a day that they could ill afford.

While Alexander considered and discarded several possible plans of action, his eyes fell upon a coil of coarse rope that hung upon the door of the shed. He said, "I hesitate to ask this of you, who have already given up so much, but might I borrow the rope that hangs there behind you?"

The young man appeared momentarily startled by the request. "Of course, but why?"

"I think it may be useful in dealing with the kelpie."

"Hmm. I don't see how—but take it, if you wish."

"Thanks, I appreciate it. It may be a great help." He paused, while he looked upon the weary, soot-streaked couple. He wished that he could do more for them. "Please," he said, "feel free to call upon my mother. She would want you to, really."

"Perhaps we will. The best of luck to you, Prince Alexander. May you succeed in your mission."

Alexander and Cyril stood on the riverbank, perhaps fifty yards upstream of the bridge. The sun was starting to ride low in the sky. Alexander figured that there was about two hours of daylight left. *Time enough*, he thought.

Cyril said, "I don't understand. How do you plan to get past the kelpie? And how do you expect a piece of rope to help?"

Alexander dropped his bag on the bank. "I *don't* plan to get past it, exactly. Do you still have those apples you picked?"

"Ye-es."

"Good. I'm afraid that we're going to need them."

The prince unbuckled his sword belt and let it fall beside the bag.

"A rope, some apples," Cyril said, frowning. "I still don't see what you're planning."

In short order, cloak, coat, and mail shirt joined the bag and sword on the bank. "There is no way to avoid the kelpie, and no way to kill it. From everything I've heard of such creatures, the only thing that we can do is try to break it."

"How do we do that?"

Alexander sat on the bank and started to pull off his boots. "I am going to take the rope and wait near the bridge. When I signal you, you will drop the apples into the river. Kelpies like apples. With any luck, this one will surface, in pursuit of the apples. When that happens, I will leap onto its back and slip the rope over its head. It will try to shake me, but if I can hang on it will have no choice but to deal with me."

Wide-eyed, Cyril stared at him. "Dangerous," he said. "Dangerous. I don't think very much of this plan of yours. There is much that could go wrong."

"Do you have a better suggestion?"

A pause. "No."

"Then we have no choice."

"There must be something else that we can do."

Alexander shook his head and climbed to his feet. "When I signal you, drop the apples into the river. Not too far toward the center. We want the current to carry them under the bridge, but we also want the kelpie to surface where I can reach it."

"Alexander—"

The prince looked at him. "What?"

"Good luck."

"Not too far toward the center, remember."

Alexander took the rope and padded down the bank, limping from the sharp stones on his bare feet. As he went, he made a small loop in the rope and knotted it in place. Inserting the end of the rope through the loop and pulling, he fashioned a bigger loop. He pulled on the knot as hard as he could; the knot held. It seemed strong enough. If it should give way, of course, he was doomed.

After taking his place on the bank near the bridge, Alexander squatted down as low as he could and looked down into the river. The grey-green waters appeared deceptively calm. The untroubled surface reflected the low arch of the narrow wooden bridge. If Alexander were to attempt to cross the bridge now, the kelpie would cause an immense swell to rise from the river and sweep him from the bridge. The kelpie would then seize him and pull him down to the bottom of the river, until he drowned. Everything he had ever heard of kelpies agreed on that point.

Alexander saw no sign of the kelpie; the water was too murky to allow light to penetrate beyond a few inches. This was a problem. He knew that, once the creature surfaced, he would have only a few moments to grab hold of it. He wanted to be positioned directly over it, if at all possible.

Alexander continued to peer down into the river for a long time, trying to pierce the green obscurity.

At last, just when he was about to give up, he saw two small bubbles break the surface. Did they come from the kelpie? Maybe, maybe not. It was the best sign he was likely to get, however.

He adjusted his position slightly, so that he was over the place where the bubbles had surfaced. Holding the loop of rope in both hands, he looked to where Cyril waited upstream. When he caught the young wizard's eye, he gave a slow nod.

Cyril pulled the apples from his bag. Staying as low to the bank as possible, he threw the apples, one by one, into the flood. Bobbing, slowly turning, the apples made their way downriver. As they neared the bridge, Alexander felt his heart start to beat fast. What he was about to do could easily get him killed. And there was still a possibility that the kelpie would not rise to the bait.

Alexander forced himself to breathe deeply and evenly. The first apple approached the bridge, and passed almost directly over the spot where the bubbles had come up.

Alexander tensed, preparing himself to spring. Did he see something stir beneath the surface? Suddenly a long head broke the surface. It was very much like that of a horse, save that it was strangely translucent and shimmering, and its mane was the deep green of an aquatic plant. Its dark eyes were wild and frightening.

Not letting himself think about he was doing, Alexander sprang into the water, aiming himself at where he imagined the creature's back to be. He felt the coldness of the water, and then something solid beneath his legs. He tried to grasp the kelpie's back with his legs, but it proved slippery and elusive.

At the same time, he threw the loop of rope over the creature's head and pulled at the free end. The loop tightened remorselessly around the glistening neck. It became clear by this point that the creature was aware that there was something wrong. It tried to dart back under the water, but Alexander pulled with all his might upon the rope, preventing the kelpie from lowering its head.

Water sprayed from the kelpie's nostrils. Its hindquarters rose and fell in a violent bucking motion, but by now Alexander had managed to scissor his legs tightly around its slick midriff, and he was able to stay with the creature.

Now, unexpectedly, the kelpie tried to roll in the water. Alexander leaned against the direction of the roll, pulling all the while on the rope, and managed to keep his head above water, if just barely.

The kelpie did everything it could to shed Alexander. It rose and fell like a great ponderous wave. It tried to crush him against the underside of the bridge, tried to pull him down into the dark depths. Through it all, Alexander clung stubbornly to the creature, refusing to let it go, countering every move it made. From time to time, he could hear Cyril shouting encouragement from the bank.

This went on for a very long time—how long Alexander did not know. He became chilled to the bone, and his legs began to ache and tremble. His whole world narrowed to a few simple imperatives: hold on, move to the left, move to the right, pull back, lean down low, now move to the right again.

At last the kelpie ceased its struggles. Craning its sinewy neck back, so that one wild eye could look upon Alexander, it spoke, in a high, airy voice: "*Mortal, why do you thus abuse me?*"

"Kelpie, I have heard of how you lurk under this bridge, rising up to drown those unwary souls who try to cross the river here."

"Why, this is in my nature. Do you seek to punish me for that which nature has ordained?"

"No. I do not seek to punish you."

"What, then?"

"I seek to cross the river."

Silence. Then, after a long moment: "If I bear you to the far bank, will you leave me in peace?"

"That would be a start."

"What else?"

"I want your solemn pledge that you will leave this place and nevermore trouble the people of Daventry."

"You drive a hard bargain, mortal."

"I'm not bargaining, kelpie."

The creature snorted, blowing white steam from its nostrils. "I'm of a mind to try your strength again."

Alexander tried not to let the weariness tell in his voice: "Go ahead. Try it. It will profit you nothing."

The kelpie was silent for a long moment. Finally it said, "Very well, very well! I will take you to the opposite bank *and* promise to leave this place, if you will just let me go free. I find this more distressing than you can imagine."

"To the bank, then."

Undulating slightly, the kelpie propelled itself to the riverbank. Alexander forced himself to cling tight to the creature. His strength was nearly gone.

When they bobbed near the rocky riverbank, Alexander said, "Now, swear that when I let you go, you will not attempt any mischief upon my person."

"I swear it."

"Swear that you will never again work violence upon any person, for any reason."

"I swear it."

"Good. I will now release you."

With trembling hands, Alexander loosened the rope and slipped the loop from the kelpie's head. He released the hold his aching legs had on the creature's back, and floated free. One long stroke brought him to the riverbank. He levered himself up onto the muddy margin, slowly got to his feet, and staggered to the top of the bank.

Eyes barely cresting the surface of the river, the kelpie regarded him impassively. After a moment it raised its muzzle, to display its many teeth, in a hideous sort of grin. "I know you. I know you, Alexander. You have mastered me, but Telgrin will master you. You will die—but only if you are lucky."

With that, the kelpie plunged back into the depths. Alexander saw its great body heave ponderously beneath the surface for one instant. Then it was gone.

Alexander looked across the river and saw Cyril on

the opposite bank. He slowly gathered the strength to shout to the other man: "*The way is clear. Come across.*" Cyril nodded, then began to gather up the things that the prince had left on the bank.

Exhausted, Alexander stood alone above the river, in the dying light of day, and shivered.

·8·

Alexander and Cyril camped that night in a small grove of elms, at the base of a high rocky ridge overlooking the river. A sharp wind had come up, moaning down from the heights. They were less than a day's march from Telgrin's castle now, close enough that Alexander would have preferred not to risk a fire; but as it was, after his long struggle in the river, he could not stop shivering. It was better to risk being discovered by Telgrin's knights than to die of exposure, he thought.

Wrapping his cloak tightly around him, Alexander sat beside the small fire. His teeth kept chattering; he could not stop them. No matter what he did, he could not seem to get warm. Even several loaves of the traveler's bread did not help.

Cyril sat on the other side of the fire for a time, watching him with concerned eyes. At length the young wizard got up, filled a small pot with water, and placed the pot over the fire, supported by two flat stones. He rummaged briefly in his bag, coming out with a leather pouch and a tin cup.

When the water in the pot came to a boil, Cyril

took several pinches of a dried leaf from the pouch and sprinkled them into the water. He set the cup under the pot, and used a stick to tilt the pot up on one side, so that a quantity of the boiling liquid spilled into the cup.

Cyril brought the cup to Alexander and held it under his nose. "Here," he said. "Drink."

Alexander sniffed suspiciously at the potion. It had a pungent, slightly astringent smell. "What is it?"

"Drink."

After freeing one hand from his cloak, the prince took the cup from his companion, put it to his lips, and took a small sip. The liquid was hot, almost too hot to drink. Its taste was not unpleasant, though it did make his tongue feel a bit prickly. He held it in his mouth for a moment, then swallowed.

"Is this supposed to help overcome my chills?" the prince asked.

Cyril smiled, and said nothing.

Alexander took another, slightly larger, sip. He began to feel a warmth growing in his belly, expanding gradually outward. The potion did seem to be helping, if only slightly.

"One more."

Tilting the cup back, Alexander swallowed another mouthful of the potion. It was actually quite tasty, in an odd way, he decided.

Cyril ducked down, to take the cup from the prince. "Enough," he said.

"I wasn't finished." Just then, however, Alexander became aware that he had broken out in a light sweat.

His cheeks felt suddenly flushed and hot.

"Have to be careful," Cyril explained. "Too much, and it could become uncomfortable."

Alexander loosened his hold on his cloak. "Yes, I can see what you mean. *Whew*."

"The effect should lessen in a few minutes."

And so it did. The sensation of warmth spread to his limbs, just as the heat faded from his face. A serene sense of well-being overtook him.

Alexander gave his companion a speculative look. He realized that he had continued to underestimate Cyril's skills and potential usefulness. Why? Because of his youth? Or the way he looked? The prince knew that he had been stupid and short-sighted. There was nothing he could do about that. All he could do was to try not to make the same mistake again.

Alexander slept well that night. If he dreamed at all, he could not remember it when he awoke. The morning came dank and gloomy. A cold mist lay upon the land, curling through the trees, entwining itself in the branches. The lowering sky was soft and as grey as slate.

After a modest meal, Alexander and Cyril set off once again, moving through the thin screen of trees that paralleled the river in this place. The ground here was black and damp; it crumbled easily under their feet. A subtle smell of decay was in the air.

Toward midmorning, the two came upon a wide grassy glade, bordered by tall sedge on the side nearest the river. At the center of the glade sat two huge wagons, loaded with numerous barrels blackened with pitch, and bushel baskets overflowing with produce. Four shaggy dray horses cropped the grass nearby.

At the back of one of the wagons sat an immense ogre, a great barbed sword leaning up against the wagon bed next to him. The ogre was fully eight feet tall, with wide shoulders, brawny chest, and long arms thick with muscle. He wore loose grey trousers, ragged at the bottom, and a greasy jerkin of stiff leather. Chest and shoulders were covered with coarse, coppery hair. Two long, yellowed fangs projected from his lower jaw, peaking up over his thin upper lip.

The ogre had an open cask clamped between his thighs, and he was happily munching on a dripping piece of honeycomb.

Alexander started forward into the glade. He felt Cyril's hand catch his arm. "What are you doing?" the young wizard whispered.

"I want to speak to the ogre."

Cyril gave a dubious look toward the glade. "Are you *sure*?"

"I'm sure."

Alexander stepped into the open. "Ho, there! Sir Ogre!"

With a startled look, the ogre looked up. "Who calls?" he said. His fierce eyes found Alexander and stayed on him, suspicious.

"Good day! Whose wagons are those, Sir Ogre?"

"They belong to the magician-king Telgrin, he of the castle that came in the night."

"Then you are stealing from Telgrin?"

"Not so!" the ogre said indignantly. "I am guarding the wagons, until Telgrin's knights return to take them to the castle."

"I see. But . . . you seem to be eating up the wagon's contents. Telgrin doesn't mind this?"

"It is only my due. In exchange for guarding these wagons, I'm allowed to eat whatever I wish. I am the mighty Azakas! My appetite is as great as my strength!"

"It must be very great indeed, then."

"Aye." Azakas squinted at Alexander, apparently thoughtful. "You do not intend to interfere with these wagons, do you? If so, I shall have to take your head."

"No," Alexander said. "I was just . . . curious."

"Curiosity can be dangerous," Azakas said, the unpleasant hint of a growl in his voice.

"I'm sure you're right. Thank you for that warning. Well, I must be going. A pleasant day to you, Sir Ogre."

"Hmmph!"

Alexander rejoined Cyril in the shelter of the trees. The young wizard shook his head disapprovingly at the prince. "What was that all about?"

"The more we know about the movements of Telgrin's confederates, the better," Alexander said.

"Do you have any idea what that ogre could have done to you?"

"A calculated risk. Ogres are not known to be overly ambitious. I didn't think that this one would care to chase after me, unless he had no other choice.''

Cyril shook his head again, and the two men moved on. They continued to follow the river at a slight remove, crossing many trickling brooks and passing increasingly frequent pools of standing water. Sticky mud began collecting on the soles of their boots, until it seemed that they both had gained an inch or more in height.

Alexander could see that the river was getting steadily wider. Stiff-legged wading birds patrolled the shallows, and cattails often screened the bank. The gloomy light of this day glimmered upon the grey waters.

As the two men were passing a fallen pine, Alexander stopped abruptly. ''Hold,'' he said. ''Did you hear that?''

''Hear what?''

''That. There it is again.'' There was a distant rumble.

''Thunder,'' Cyril said. ''I think.''

''Telgrin's castle,'' Alexander said grimly, staring up at the overcast sky. ''We must be getting close now.''

The two journeyed on, increasingly reluctant to speak. The trees became fewer and more widely spaced, and beetle-black ravens croaked at them from the uppermost branches of those few trees there were. Alexander found himself grinding his teeth as he went. They had almost reached their goal. It had taken three long days, but now that they were almost there, he found his patience suddenly running out.

At last the two struggled to the top of a low sandy embankment and were rewarded by their first glimpse of Telgrin's castle, peeking out from behind a drooping willow, curls of mist threaded through its outthrust battlements. It sat on the very edge of the river, one massive corner tower rising from the lapping waters. Its walls were smooth and blacker than night. They glistened softly in the dreary light, as though made of glass. A single dark storm cloud hovered over a high central tower. From time to time, this cloud would light with an internal fire, and a low, menacing rumble would break across the land.

Alexander gave an inward shiver at the sight of the castle. Here it was. Here, at last, it was.

Silently the men crept down from the embankment. The ground below was covered with a glassy film of water, never more than an inch deep. Streaks of bright green algae floated in stippled bands upon the surface. The smell of stagnant water and decay filled Alexander's nostrils.

The two men made their way across this watery waste with curious gliding strides, as they attempted to step from one relatively solid patch of ground to another. They made their way to a sandy bar, scrambled up it, and took shelter behind the pliant green boughs of a willow.

The two edged closer to the castle, while circling toward the front of it. Finally they knelt down behind a curtain of densely woven brush directly opposite the main gate.

Alexander studied the enormous structure before him, with an increasing sense of dismay. Somehow it had never occurred to him that anything that had flown through the air could be quite so imposing. The walls were high and extensive, dominated by crenelated battlements. Round towers bowed out from the wall on either side of the gate, from which any approach could be easily seen. The spade-shaped gate was wide, but it was blocked by a portcullis of black iron. The portcullis was substantial—too heavy to lift without the aid of a capable winch, Alexander thought. Two knights in full armor stood guard on the other side of the portcullis.

Next to the gate on either side was what Alexander at first took to be carved ornamentation. When he looked more closely at it, however, he saw that what had looked like ornamentation was in fact two columns of shallow niches carved into the wall. In each niche was a human skull—some two dozen in all, all staring forward with empty sockets, all grinning ghastly, lipless grins.

Alexander felt a cold chill when he looked upon them, and not just because of the macabre aspect that they presented. He became convinced, for no rational reason that he could name, that those eyeless sockets could look back at him, and that they meant him no good.

''Well,'' Cyril said in a low voice. ''We're here. Now what?''

Alexander studied the castle for a moment more. It was, of course, quite hopeless. There was no way that they could penetrate those walls without being observed.

Or was there?

Slowly a plan began to take form in his mind. "Come on," he said, his heart starting to race. "We have to go back. *Quickly!* I'm not sure how long we have."

·9·

It was late in the afternoon by the time Alexander and Cyril returned to the clearing where the ogre Azakas guarded the wagons eventually bound for Telgrin's castle. Alexander was relieved to see that the wagons were still there and that there were no black knights hanging about them yet.

The ogre, apparently having finished the honey, had started in on a bushel of ripe apples. He was munching on one when the two men arrived, and the ground about him was littered with stripped cores. Alexander could not help but think that there must be a more economical method for guarding supplies.

As he stepped into the clearing, Alexander said, "Ho, Sir Ogre! I've returned."

Azakas swallowed and licked his lips. "So I see."

"May I approach?"

"You don't have any mischief in mind, do you?"

"No, indeed!"

"Approach."

Mustering what nonchalance he could, Alexander made his way toward the center of the clearing. As he went, he said, "I see that those who left the wagons for you to guard have not yet returned."

"No."

"When do you expect them back, if you don't mind my asking?"

"Sometime before dark, they said." Azakas looked up at the prince, dark suspicion wrinkling his brow. "Why do you ask?"

"No reason. It's just that it is already quite late. How long do they expect you to wait?"

The ogre shrugged.

"It is a shame that you must associate with persons so lacking in consideration."

"I . . . suppose."

"That is why I came back."

"Mmph?"

"I got to thinking about your plight. It's obvious that you are an ogre of quality, and yet cruel circumstance has forced you to take a position far beneath your dignity."

"Hm, now that you mention it . . ."

"You should be living under some nice bridge somewhere, in comfort and quiet. Instead, you must linger here, exposed to the elements, where you can be disturbed by any passing vagabond."

Azakas gave a great sigh. "An ogre has to eat."

"Exactly, yes. That's just what I got to thinking about. When I had the means at hand to spare you this terrible indignity, how could I fail to act?"

The ogre was regarding him intently now. "You begin to interest me, human. Say on. What means are those?"

Alexander took out the fairy wallet from his bag. He opened the wallet and removed one loaf of the traveler's bread, which he held out to the ogre. "Here. Take a taste."

Azakas regarded it mistrustfully. "Is this some sort of trick?"

"I swear not."

Frowning, Azakas took the traveler's bread from the prince's hand. He sniffed it, then nibbled at one corner. A beatific smile slowly blossomed on his face. "Good. *Very* good."

Azakas stuffed the rest of the loaf in his mouth and chomped away happily, ruddy cheeks unpleasantly distended. He swallowed, then said, "More."

"Yes, more. All you want. But I want to show you something. See here? I'm emptying the wallet. There's nothing left inside now. Correct?"

"Aye, correct."

Alexander passed the thin stack of traveler's bread to Azakas, who accepted it greedily. He shut the wallet and waited a moment.

"Now, watch carefully," he said, opening the wallet and displaying it to the ogre. It was full once more.

"*Magic*," Azakas said in an awed voice.

"Yes, magic. A most wonderful magic. No matter how much you take from it, it can never be empty. If you had such a wallet, you would never want for food again." He paused a moment. "I give it to you."

Alexander offered Azakas the wallet. The ogre looked as if he wanted to snatch it from his hand, but that he was holding himself back. "Why? What do you want for it?"

"Nothing. It is enough to know that I have been of service."

"Well . . ." Azakas reached out and seized wallet in his big hand. He looked somewhat bewildered by events.

"Now, you'll doubtless want to take that and leave, before the black knights can return. I don't think that they can be trusted with such a prize, do you?"

The ogre hesitated. "I probably should serve out my shift. I said that I would, after all."

"Nonsense. You are much too important to waste your time in such an unproductive pursuit. I will stay and look after things here. And I can tender your regrets to the black knights, when they return."

Azakas rose up very straight. "You're right!" he declared. "I am Azakas, mighty among ogres! I am no one's servant!"

"True, very true."

The ogre tucked the fairy wallet under one arm, picked up his sword and rested the flat of the blade on one shoulder. With a lordly air, he said to Alexander, "I thank you for your faithful service. If there is ever anything that I can do for you, do not hesitate to call on me."

"I will do that, Sir Ogre," Alexander said gravely.

Azakas nodded, wheeled about, and strode from the clearing, humming a discordant tune to himself. Alexander waited for several moments after he disappeared, then beckoned toward where Cyril had hidden himself in the brush.

The apprentice wizard rose, dusted himself off, and made his way into the clearing. "That was remarkable," he said.

"Come on," Alexander said. "We have work to do. The black knights will return soon."

"What do we do?"

"We must get two of those big barrels open and dispose of their contents, somewhere where it won't be seen."

Cyril considered this. "I think I understand, yes. All right, let's do it."

Working swiftly, the two men wrestled two of the great barrels from the back of one of the wagons, pulled off the lids, and spilled out their contents— coarsely ground flour, as it turned out—behind some bushes. They had just boosted the barrels back onto the wagon bed and begun to lash them in place, when Alexander heard the sound of approaching hoofbeats.

"They're coming! Quickly!"

They knotted the ropes holding the barrels in place as well as they could, and then each man climbed hastily into his own barrel. Balancing the barrel lid on the palms of his hands, Alexander settled down. Carefully he lowered the lid into place behind him. As he did so, the daylight faded and was entirely eclipsed.

The prince made himself as comfortable as possible, which was not very. The barrel was cramped and nearly airless. Enough of the flour that had filled it remained inside that a powerful urge to sneeze plagued him.

It seemed that he waited a very long time, with growing impatience. At last, however, he heard the muffled sounds of a horse cantering into the clearing. A few moments later, he heard a second horse approaching from a different direction. They both came very near the wagon, then stopped.

"*Greetings, One-Who-Was-Harold,*" came a flat and uninflected voice.

"And greetings to you, One-Who-Was-Edmund," replied a second voice. It was similar to the first, but different in some subtle way.

"Where is the ogre that we left to guard the wagons while we continued to forage?"

"Gone, it seems."

"Gone!"

"Ogres are not known to be particularly reliable."

"I suppose that's true."

"I see that you have brought the men to drive the wagons."

"Yes. They are uncouth rogues, but they should suffice for our purposes. Should I tell them to harness the dray horses? Our master bade us to return before nightfall."

"Do that. We do not want to fail to follow our instructions."

"No."

One of the voices issued harsh orders, Alexander heard other voices then—these more ordinary and human-sounding, at least. There were hoarse shouts, the complaining whinnies of horses, some small thumps and crashes. After some minutes of this, Alexander finally felt the wagon lurching into motion. He tried not to lean too hard against the side of the barrel, fearful that his hasty knots would come loose and the barrel tip from the back of the wagon.

It was an uncomfortable, jarring ride. The wagon bounced up and down and from side to side. Its wheels struck stones and dropped into holes. Despite his best efforts, Alexander kept banging up against one side or another of the barrel, sometimes with painful force. He wondered how Cyril was bearing up.

The trip seemed to last forever—certainly longer than the short distance from the clearing to the castle would seem to require. Alexander had to remind himself that heavily loaded wagons would be forced to take a more circuitous route.

At long last the wagon drew to a halt. Alexander heard faint voices, but could not make out what they were saying. After several long moments, there was a metallic clanking sound, and the prince guessed that this was the castle's portcullis being drawn up.

At length the wagon started forward again. Alexander felt a strong rush of fearful excitement. They were finally entering Telgrin's castle, he was sure.

The wheels of the wagons rolled more smoothly here. Alexander could feel a series of small, rhythmic jolts, as the wheels caught and surmounted the fine seams joining the stonework. After a few minutes, the wagon rolled to a halt.

"What now?" a voice said. Alexander could tell from the lack of inflection that it belonged to one of the black knights.

"Have the drivers unharness the dray horses and take them to the stables. After that, pay them off and send them away. Tell them that there may be more work for them in a few days."

"I will do as you say, One-Who-Was-Edmund."

"Very good, One-Who-Was-Harold."

"May you know the mercy of our master."

"And you."

There was a brief period of activity, its sounds distorted, echoing weirdly from stone. Alexander heard the hollow clip-clop of hooves on flagstone, which slowly receded and at last vanished altogether.

At last there was silence, but Alexander was reluctant to assume that all had gone. He waited a long time before gingerly placing his hands on the lid above his head and pushing up on it. The vibrations of the trip had caused the lid to seat more firmly, and for a moment it did not want to budge. Alexander battled an instant of irrational panic. Forcing himself to react calmly, he exerted a steady pressure. Eventually unyielding wood yielded. The lid came loose and rose above the top of the barrel. Gloomy light filtered down into the prince's small prison; dank air met his face.

He waited for a moment, listening for the smallest sound. Hearing nothing, however, he attempted to heave his body up through the opening. This proved more difficult than he would have thought. His body had stiffened from its long confinement; it did not want to serve him.

Eventually, though, he managed to rise up through the opening, legs and back complaining from the effort. Twilight had fallen while he had been shut away in the barrel. The sky showed a moody purple, with only the fading traces of daylight upon it.

Alexander saw that the wagons had been left unattended in the castle courtyard beside three similar wagons, near the outer wall. The courtyard appeared empty; there was no one in sight. After carefully setting the lid aside, the prince pulled his legs from the barrel and stood on the wagon bed. He gave each knee a slight flex. His legs still did not feel quite normal.

Alexander tapped his knuckles on the top of the barrel next to his, saying, in a hushed voice, "Come out. It's safe."

There was a faint stirring within. The lid came up, and Cyril's face slowly appeared. Alexander took the lid from him and put it down. "Mmm, not a comfortable ride," the young wizard said. "I'd rather not do that again, if it's all the same to you."

"Agreed," Alexander said, helping the other man from the barrel. The two stepped stiffly from the wagon and stood together in the darkness, glancing uneasily about them, trying to gain their bearings.

The courtyard was vast, its outermost extents shadowy and mysterious. The flagstones were darkly glistening, and a thin damp mist eddied and curled among the castle's massive internal structures. Ahead and to the right was a tall, blocky keep, its castellated crown supporting a strong turret on each of its four corners. To the left of the keep was a high, tapering tower, large windows breaking its topmost story. Above the tower hung the black cloud, a dismal smudge in the evening sky.

Most of the other structures were far less imposing. They were obviously purely functional auxiliary buildings: stable, storehouses, kitchen. There was, however, one other substantial edifice. It appeared to be a two-story house, its roof sharply peaked, several prominent gables projecting from the upper story. A stone wall completely surrounded the house, a stout oaken door set into a central arch.

Alexander hesitated for a long moment, uncertain of where to go next. Where would Telgrin hide his father's soul? The most likely locations were the keep, the tower, and the walled house, but Alexander could not decide among them. He asked Cyril if he had any idea, but the young wizard merely shook his head.

Alexander glanced furtively about him. One thing was certain: they could not just stand around and wait for inspiration. The longer they were in the castle, the greater their chances of being spotted.

Not quite at random, Alexander chose to start with the walled house. It was obvious to him that the wall was intended to guard something of importance. Was that something Telgrin's magical workshop? It seemed a reasonable assumption.

After giving Cyril a quick gesture, Alexander started across the courtyard. He clutched his dark cloak to him and hunched his shoulders, hoping to make himself as small and inconspicuous as he could. In the deserted courtyard, the slithering sounds their boots made on the flagstones seemed appallingly loud.

When they reached the wall surrounding the house, Alexander stopped to study it. It was quite tall, so tall that even if he were to stand on his toes, he would not be able to reach the top of it. It was constructed of finely dressed stone, with no seams that could be used for climbing. They would need either a ladder or a grappling hook to get over it, neither of which they happened to have. There were several iron grates set low on the wall, probably for drainage purposes, but these were far too small for a man to squeeze through.

Alexander circled the wall for part of a circuit, until he came to the single door that pierced its thickness. The door was recessed into a deep arch. Above the arch, a grotesque face had been carved into the stone-work. The face was extremely round, with prominent ears, a snoutlike nose, wide mouth, and fleshy lips. Its huge eyes appeared to be closed.

The door itself was obviously thick and well made, of clear oak reinforced by strips of black iron. The hinges had to be inside the wall, since there were none that Alexander could see on the outside. He supposed that it was too much to hope that it would be unlocked, but it seemed worth a try.

Alexander stepped to the door. There was an iron handle beside the lock plate. The prince grasped it and pushed. Nothing. The door did not move. He pulled, and the door still did not move. It was locked.

Cyril plucked at the prince's sleeve. "Alexander, *look!*" His voice was little more than a whisper, but it conveyed a sharp urgency that instantly commanded Alexander's attention.

Cyril was pointing at a place just above the door. When he looked there, Alexander was shocked to see that the carved stone face had somehow lifted its heavy eyelids, revealing a pair of glassy bloodred eyes. The eyes had neither iris nor pupil, but the prince had the unsettling impression that they were staring straight at him, that they saw him.

The face's stone lips quivered and began to part, showing a grey tongue and two rows of peglike teeth. The tongue uncoiled sluggishly over the lower teeth. Alexander thought for one moment that the face was going to speak, but it did not. It began to scream.

·10·

The scream came so shrilly from the mouth of the stone face that Alexander had to clap his hands to his ears and turn away. Even so, the sound was painful. It made his jaw tighten and his nerves shriek. It penetrated his hands, his ears, and filled his brain.

Cyril shouted something and staggered away from the door. Alexander followed him, feeling that he would die if he did not get away from the screaming face.

Alexander was dimly aware that lights had come into the gloomy courtyard, but it was several moments before he could afford them any attention. At length he saw that the lights were torches carried by a number of Telgrin's dark knights, who had apparently come from the keep and the gatehouse. They were coming at him with long, swift strides.

Still clutching his hands to his ears, Alexander changed direction slightly, in an effort to avoid the knights. For a moment it appeared that he might be able to escape toward the tower, but as he neared it he saw still more knights coming from the base of that lofty edifice.

Alexander quickly saw that they were nearly surrounded. The only avenue left was toward the outer
wall, and he doubted that there would be anywhere
to hide there. Still, it held out a slender hope at least.
He veered off in that direction. Cyril was close beside
him.

After a few more steps, the prince risked lowering
his hands from his ears. The sound from the stone
face was still blaring, but it seemed to be receding to
tolerable levels now.

They reached the wall. A few yards to the left
bulged the base of a squat tower. Hoping that he
might find an open stairway there, Alexander moved
quickly toward it. He could tell, from their voices and
the sounds that their armor made, that the knights
were closing in. The prince ran as fast as he could.

It was not fast enough. As he neared the tower, a
dark shape stepped in front of him: another of Telgrin's knights. Alexander knew that the only prospect
for escape lay in getting past this knight without delay. The prince dropped his bag and drew his sword
as he ran.

Two more steps, and he could see his enemy plain,
black armor showing with a soft luster in the vague
and shifting light. The knight had his sword out and
at the ready. Its reach was considerably longer than
the prince's sword, he noticed.

As Alexander reached the knight, he turned slightly
and tried to get his back to the wall, which he hoped
would make the superior reach of the knight's blade
a liability.

"Surrender," the knight said in the hollow voice of its kind. "Surrender. You cannot prevail."

Alexander did not answer with words. Instead, he aimed a slashing blow at his opponent's head. The knight parried, sweeping his blade off to the right, and then riposted with a vicious downward cut.

By now, however, Alexander had managed to maneuver close to the wall. He dropped down into a crouch, and the knight's blade scored the wall, striking bright sparks. Alexander rose up slightly, driving himself forward, sword extended and aimed at the knight's middle. The tip of the blade struck home, but could do no damage against that black armor. It turned harmlessly to the right, and Alexander had to struggle to catch himself lest he stumble into the knight's arms.

The prince sensed more than saw the next blow descending upon him. He managed to get his sword up in time to block the knight's blade. Swords clanged violently together. By turning his wrist and exerting a steady pressure, Alexander kept the blades locked together long enough for him to push the knight back half a step. Sword blades released and slipped past each other with a ringing sound.

From the corner of his eye, Alexander saw that the other knights were closing in rapidly. He knew that he had to best his foe now, or not at all.

The knight aimed a quick, low thrust at Alexander. The prince beat it down and, without pausing to wonder if he was leaving himself open to another attack, made a backhanded upward cut at his opponent's head. The knight could not counter in time, and Alexander struck him on the helm with the full of his blade, at a place just above the neck.

The helm flew off and crashed to the ground several yards away. Alexander paid little attention to that, for his attention was at that moment riveted to the knight himself.

Floating above the knight's shoulders, where the helm had been, was what seemed to be a face of green fire. Wavering slightly in the wind that was sweeping down from the wall, it dazzled the prince's eyes. He could see well enough to know that it represented a noble and well-favored face, with a high forehead, straight nose, and strong jaw. Only the eyes were not comely, for they burned with a tormented madness that was awful to behold.

The face hung there for only an instant, then suddenly it flared upward into the night sky and was extinguished. Still feeling the touch of that unnatural radiance on his cheeks, Alexander watched the knight's armor totter and fall to the flagstones. The armor burst apart, arms and legs falling away from the torso. The prince saw that it was empty, save for a single curl of black smoke drifting up from the vacant neck hole.

"Behind you, Alexander!"

Warned by Cyril's outcry, Alexander tried to turn, but two viselike hands suddenly grasped his arms just above the wrists. "That was ill-done," a hollow voice said in his ear. "Drop the sword. Drop it."

The hands began to exert a bruising pressure, persuading Alexander to do as he was instructed. He opened his hand and let his sword clatter to the flagstones.

''Now, you will come with us.'' One hand released him, while the other spun him around violently. Alexander saw that there were black knights closing on him from two sides, green lights glinting from their featureless helms. He supposed that they resented what he had done to their comrade, but it was hard to tell by looking at them.

Cyril was in the hands of one of the knights. The two men exchanged nervous glances. ''I think that we'd better do as they say,'' the wizard said.

''Yes.''

The knights slowly gathered about the two men, until they were all around them. ''Come,'' said the knight who held Alexander.

Alexander narrowed his lips and allowed the knights to impel him forward. It would be futile to resist, he knew. If he was going to escape them, it would have to be later. For now, the best that he could do was play for time.

The sound of cold metal ringing all around them, Alexander and Cyril marched dutifully across the vast courtyard and into the heart of Telgrin's mighty keep.

The throne room of Telgrin's castle was a vast and shadowy hall, its high ceilings obscured by blackness, its grey walls pierced by darkened arches leading to obscure side chambers. Drapes of ancient velvet hung at intervals upon the walls, stiff, sooty, their color long since leached away.

At the far end of the room was a circular dais, flanked on either side by a hideously ornate iron brazier, in each a sluggish flame burning. A knobby ebon throne occupied the center of the dais, and upon the throne sat a tall man in somber robes, his pallid face showing brighter than the flames in their braziers.

Telgrin.

The assembled black knights marched Alexander and Cyril the full length of the hall. When they came at last to the foot of the dais, they cast the two men to their knees beneath the baleful stare of their dire king and retreated a pace.

Alexander rubbed his bruised wrist and stared resentfully at the castle's master. He did not see any point in trying to rise to his feet just then. He knew that he would only be forced down again, and he did not especially want to give them that satisfaction.

Telgrin gazed down upon the two men. A peculiar dark passion seemed to animate his sharp features. "Well," he said, voice thick. "These are the miscreants, are they? Were they alone?"

One of the knights spoke: "Yes, your Majesty."

"And they did not succeed in penetrating the wall? Princess Lydia is still secure in her quarters?"

"Yes, your Majesty."

"That is well." Telgrin returned the full force of his scrutiny to Alexander and Cyril. "Hmm. It seems that we have two hot-blooded young men with mischief on their minds. Out for an amorous adventure, were we? What a shame that we had to spoil it for you.''

Alexander frowned. "I beg your pardon?"

"Come, don't think to play the innocent with me. I know very well what you were about."

"Which was . . . ?"

Telgrin let his breath out with an exasperated sigh. "Where did you hear about her? Is her presence here widely known in the vicinity? Will we soon have other adventurers following in your footstep? Tell me what I want to know, and I may even let you go."

"Where did we hear about *who*?" Alexander said helplessly. "I have no idea of what you're talking about."

Turning his glance to Cyril, Telgrin said, "What of you? Your companion has already sealed his fate. Will you admit your guilt? You may save yourself considerable anguish."

"I'm sorry. This conversation is meaningless to me. What is it that you think we were doing?"

Telgrin stroked his chin pensively. "I almost believe you. Almost. But why have you come here, if not to steal away with my lovely Lydia?"

He looked from Alexander to Cyril and back again, but the two men compressed their lips and said nothing. At length he said, "You there, the tall one, what is your name?"

"Alexander."

"I know you, don't I? I've seen you before."

"I was in the throne room of Castle Daventry when you came."

"I *see*. Perhaps this begins to make sense, then. You are from Castle Daventry, are you? And your little foray here is—what—an attempt to save your beloved Graham? A feeble try at revenge? Both?"

Telgrin threw back his head and gave a harsh, contemptuous laugh. "Oh dear, perhaps I *will* let you go. Certainly you are harmless enough. You could serve as living examples of the futility of resistance."

Suddenly one of the assembled knights spoke: "The person who calls himself Alexander fought with One-Who-Was-Harold and dispatched his soul unto the night."

The amusement drained from Telgrin's face. He scowled darkly. "What is this? Did you do this thing to King Harold?"

"*King* Harold?"

"Oh, yes—king. All of my servants are kings, or were. That one there is King Louis, that one King Saul, that one King Balthazar, and that one . . . King Michael, isn't it?"

"Yes, Majesty."

"Wherever this castle has brought me, I have taken the soul of the local king and, employing such arcane devices as I command, turned him to my will. Now all serve me. I am a king of kings."

Alexander regarded the magician-king with pure revulsion. The man actually seemed proud of his monstrous actions. The prince thought that he understood now. The black knights were nothing more than tormented souls that Telgrin had magically bound to suits of armor. When Alexander had knocked the helm from that one in the courtyard, he had inadvertently set its soul free, leaving behind nothing but empty armor.

"And soon," Telgrin said, "there will be a King Graham to serve me."

"No. He will not. Never."

"He will. Of course, he will not be quite the same Graham that you knew by that time, but into every life must come change. Is that not so?"

"You are an evil man."

"So it has been said." Telgrin shrugged. "Personally I've always found that such abstractions do not apply well to life in the real world. They make matters that are by their very nature complex seem rather too simple, don't you think?"

"Evil," Alexander repeated.

Telgrin sighed. "I can see that you're really not up to a probing and dispassionate philosophical discussion. So be it. The question, then, is what am I going to do with you? I can't let you go free, not after what you did to poor Harold. It might make my other servants restless, and it might encourage others to try to repeat what you have done. I think—yes, I really do think—that we should just give you to the barikar."

"The barikar?"

"A most interesting creature, one that I collected in my travels. It should be hungry again about now."

Telgrin rose and stood looking down at the two men, his face remorseless and cruel. "Take them."

Two knights came forward, grasped Alexander and

Cyril by their shoulders, and lifted them to their feet. As they were leading them from the room, Telgrin said, "Farewell, my young stalwarts. I must say that I do not envy you your last adventure."

·11·

The knights led Alexander and Cyril along the gloomy corridor, roughly propelling them forward whenever their pace flagged. At length they came to a narrow stairway that descended into darkness, and here they paused. "Down," commanded one of the knights.

The two men exchanged quick glances. It seemed that they would have to do as they were told. All along, Alexander had been looking for an opportunity to break away from their escort, but none had presented itself. Now it might be too late.

The knight who had spoken grasped the prince's right shoulder, exerting a painful pressure. "*Down.*"

Alexander pulled away from the knight and started down the stairway, Cyril following behind. The knights came after them, their armored bulk blocking out most of the light from above.

The stairs were worn from long use, and awkwardly spaced. The prince had to make his way down them cautiously, or risk tumbling down into the blackness below. The stairway curved as it descended, rough walls rising on either side.

The stairs finally ended in a small, vaulted chamber. The chamber was empty, its walls and floors of crudely dressed stone, damply glistening in the light of a single torch set into a crumbling iron sconce.

It was here that Alexander made a nearly fatal mistake. Troubled by the situation in which he found himself, knowing that he and Cyril were about to be fed to what sounded like a highly dangerous beast, without arms or any means of escape, he began to consider options that were perhaps bolder and more desperate than he normally would have.

So, as he and Cyril stepped down from the stairway, it occurred to him that this was the moment to strike. The knights were coming down behind them, and it seemed that this was one place where he could use their armored weight against them.

Letting Cyril pass him, Alexander hung back at the foot of the stairs. When the first knight reached the second stair from the bottom and started to step from it, the prince suddenly reached out, grabbed the knight by his arm, twisted about, and pulled with all his strength. He hoped to unbalance the knight and send him plummeting to the stone floor. After that was done, he could turn on the second knight, perhaps sweep his legs out from under him, and then flee up the stairway.

Unfortunately, the first knight proved more difficult to topple than Alexander had hoped. He resisted the prince for a crucial second, and when he was finally pulled from the stair, he was more nimble than ex-

pected, staying upright and crashing into the wall
rather than the floor.

When Alexander turned back to the stairway, he saw
that the second knight, having received ample warning, had stopped several steps up, far out of reach.
With a sinking heart, Alexander looked up at the
knight, his hands outstretched and twitching uselessly.

He had failed.

A metal-clad arm suddenly came around from behind and locked around his throat. It tightened, forcing Alexander to stagger back against the knight's
iron breast. Alexander gasped, finding it increasingly
hard to catch his breath. If this kept up, his windpipe
would soon be crushed.

"Don't kill him," said the knight on the stairway.
"The barikar likes his food alive."

At last the pressure on the prince's throat relented.
A voice from behind him said, "Come, you have an
appointment to keep."

The knight spun him around and pushed him toward the door. Alexander stumbled and nearly fell,
but managed to stay on his feet. He looked with dread
upon the door that was before him. It was a massive
construction of seasoned oak bound by black iron. A
thick metal bolt secured it.

The knight on the stairway came down and went
to the door. He drew the bolt back loudly, then pulled
the weighty door open. There was darkness beyond
the door—darkness and an unpleasant smell. It was
partly the smell of damp, stale air, but it was partly
something else, also: a musky, almost sweet smell.

It made Alexander wrinkle his nose with disgust. Without meaning to, he took a step back from the door.

The knight behind the prince pushed him forward again. "Inside."

Alexander went reluctantly through the doorway. Cyril followed a moment later. The door shut behind them with a heavy thud, and the prince could hear the bolt being slid home.

At first it was too dark to see. Gradually Alexander's eyes began to adjust to the gloom, however, and he was able to make out the vague outlines of where he was. It appeared to be a large vaulted chamber, from which three corridors led away into the deeper darkness, each framed by a crude stone arch.

"What now?" Cyril whispered.

"*Shhh!* I think I hear something." There *was* something: a faint slithering sound—or maybe a hissing. It seemed to be coming from the corridor to the right, and it seemed to be getting closer.

Alexander touched Cyril's shoulder. "To the left," he said.

Three shallow steps led down to the chamber floor. The two men descended them as quietly and carefully as they could and moved toward the left-hand corridor. The chamber floor was of uneven stonework, slightly slick with moisture. No matter how delicately they walked, their feet made wet whispering sounds on the gritty stone.

Alexander wondered where the light was coming from, thinking that perhaps it could lead them to some hidden way out. He soon abandoned that thought, however. The light seemed to be directionless, coming from everywhere and nowhere. He guessed that it originated from a multitude of tiny vents and shafts in the high ceiling.

Alexander saw an indistinct patch of white on the floor ahead, close to the wall. He opened his eyes as wide as he could, but there was not enough light to make out what it was yet.

The noises emanating from the right-hand corridor had grown louder and more definite. The prince thought that he could hear breathing now, a slow rasping sound. That sickening musky smell was growing stronger. He glanced apprehensively at the corridor, but saw nothing there.

Alexander drew even with the patch of white. It seemed to be a collection of scattered objects. As he passed by them, he bent and felt over the floor. His fingers touched something, and his hand closed around it.

The prince brought the object up before his face and looked at it. A thrill of horror communicated itself down his spine. There was no mistaking it. It was a bone, certainly human, probably a femur. It looked as if something had been gnawing on it, something with extremely large teeth.

Alexander lowered the bone, but did not let go of it. It was the only weapon he had.

The entrance to the left-hand corridor was very near now. A few more steps would see them there. Alexander did not know what they would find there, but he knew that the chamber they were in now was a deathtrap. Likely, the corridor would be no better, but it was the best chance they had.

Suddenly Alexander heard a new noise from the right-hand corridor. It sounded like a low growl, reverberating softly from the chamber walls. He gave a quick look in that direction, and saw something.

Eyes. Eyes that glistened faint silver in the dim light. Judging by their spread and elevation, the creature they belonged to had to be huge, both taller and wider than a man.

Fear making his heart pound, Alexander pushed Cyril past him and into the corridor. The prince weighed the bone in his hand. It would be quite useless as a weapon against a creature of that size, he knew.

The creature made a moist snuffling sound, and its eyes bobbed up and down and from side to side. This made Alexander think that perhaps the creature was as blind as he was in this light, that it depended on its other senses to find its prey. He found this slightly encouraging. It was a small thing, but maybe he could make use of it.

Stopping in his tracks, Alexander turned back in the direction of the door and carefully lobbed the bone across the chamber and against the wall. The bone spun in the air, struck the wall, bounced, and thudded to the floor.

In an instant, the creature darted from the blackness of the corridor, to where the bone had landed. The prince caught one brief glimpse of the creature as it

went. It was huge, with a long ratlike snout, but with
fangs that appeared more nearly canine, though much
longer. It went forward with an odd hopping motion,
driven by powerful hind legs. There was something
about it that made it look vaguely wet and shimmering. Alexander realized with a start that the creature
was covered with fine silver-grey scales, except for
the tangled ruff of hair about its neck.

The barikar.

Seizing upon the bone, the barikar brought it up to
its mouth with front paws that were almost hands—
hands tipped with wicked three-inch claws. The creature shattered the bone into bits with one bite, then
looked around, snuffling, disappointed. It made an unhappy growl.

Alexander saw most of this over one shoulder, for
he took advantage of the creature's moment of distraction to make his way to the corridor entrance. Just
as he reached it, he saw the barikar turn its gaze in
his direction and he felt a sudden wave of giddy fear
sweep over him. It saw him, he knew.

Abandoning stealth, Alexander turned and ran, ran
with every bit of speed that he could muster. The
corridor embraced him, the walls dark and dripping.
Cyril must have heard him coming, for he too began
to run.

Alexander heard the barikar emit a high-pitched
screech, and he knew that the chase was on in earnest.
He caught up to Cyril a moment later, and the two
sprinted down the corridor, heedless of what might
lurk before them in the concealing darkness.

The corridor turned sharply to the right. As Alexander went around the corner, he glanced back and saw a huge shadowy shape loping after them, moving swiftly. The prince doubted that they could long outpace the creature.

The corridor turned again, then narrowed slightly. Alexander hoped that it would continue to narrow. If it did, the barikar's size would eventually prevent it from following.

Unfortunately, after one more turning, the corridor widened again and entered a long chamber. Alexander immediately noticed that one wall of the chamber appeared to be of a more recent construction than the rest: the stone lighter in color, the masonry more finely wrought.

The only exit from the chamber was a wide corridor directly opposite the new wall. The two men went directly for this corridor. As they entered it, Alexander gave a quick glance back and saw that the barikar was just entering the chamber. It was mere seconds behind, now.

The two men had gone only a few yards, when Alexander was dismayed to see that the way ahead was blocked by an iron gate. They reached this obstruction a few seconds later. Grasping the iron bars, Alexander attempted to open the gate. It would not move. It was locked.

With mounting urgency, Alexander exerted all his strength against the gate. Cyril came beside him, seized the bars of the gate, and tried to help. It was no use. The metal was corroded and crumbling, but it would stand long enough for the barikar to reach them.

Alexander turned from the gate. He saw the barikar's eyes shining at the entrance to the corridor. All realistic hope had fled, but the prince could not give up. He flexed his hands, tightened them into fists, and took a step toward the creature. "Get behind me, Cyril," he said. "Perhaps I can occupy the creature long enough for you to get away."

"No," Cyril said firmly. "You get behind *me*. It is time for me to try my magic. If this isn't an emergency, I don't know what is."

The young wizard moved past Alexander. He raised his hands above his head, and his sleeves fell back from his wrists. A fragile radiance shone from those hands, making the darkness seem less oppressive.

"*Cyril*—" Alexander said, his voice coming as an urgent whisper. In his mind, the prince saw the barikar reaching Cyril and tearing him apart before he could work his spell.

The wizard ignored him, taking several more strides toward the creature. Alexander could see the barikar plainly now. It crouched at the end of the corridor, eyes tracking Cyril, batlike ears poised, haunches shifting slightly, as it prepared to spring. If Cyril's magic should fail him . . .

Cyril seemed somehow larger and more substantial now. He continued to walk slowly toward the barikar, hands raised high. Alexander thought that he could hear the wizard muttering one phrase over and over again, but he could not make out what he was saying.

Suddenly, uttering a horrifying hiss, the barikar launched itself into the air, claws outstretched. At almost the same instant Cyril threw his hands forward. A loud clashing, like the sound of receding thunder, rumbled through the corridor.

Alexander was not entirely sure what happened next. A terrible stinging light abruptly engulfed the barikar. Still in mid-leap, the creature was almost entirely consumed, as if by fire. The prince saw the creature reduced to a smoking skeleton in that one instant, bones a black silhouette against a background of blazing yellow. The skeleton blew apart, bones scattering everywhere. It all happened so quickly that the barikar probably never knew what hit it.

Alexander let out his breath, which he had kept a close captive in his breast. His relief lasted only the span of that breath, however, for suddenly he spied a great fireball boiling up the corridor at them. Some portion of Cyril's spell must have struck something at the other end of the corridor and rebounded.

"Get *down!*" Alexander shouted, as he threw himself forward. He caught Cyril from behind and, using the full weight of his body, swept him to the ground and held him flat. A moment later, he heard a muffled roar pass overhead, and felt a great heat across his back. The iron gate rattled violently, then all was quiet.

It was a moment before Alexander dared move. Finally he stuck his head up cautiously. The gate was glowing cherry-red where the fireball had struck it.

There was the smell of smoke in the air—which a moment later he discovered was coming from his cloak. Uttering a short squawk, he leapt up, tore off the cloak, and commenced beating it vigorously against the wall.

Cyril sprang up, seemingly energized by the success of his spell. "Did you *see* that? Amazing. I've never worked one of the major spells before. I know them all, of course, but I've never worked one before. It went better than I'd hoped. *Whew!*"

Alexander's cloak appeared to have quit smoldering now. He examined it ruefully, finding many holes where the fabric had been scorched through. "It was an astounding spell," he agreed. "Rather more powerful than was strictly necessary, I thought."

"You may be right. I haven't quite got the control thing down yet. That's why Morowyn doesn't want me to use magic. But *still*. Amazing."

The apprentice wizard went to survey the remains of the barikar, and Alexander followed. The creature's bones were blackened and smoking; a few had tiny tongues of flame coming off them. A sickening smell hung in the air.

Alexander found it almost impossible to believe that the creature had been so thoroughly consumed in so brief a time. If he had not seen it himself . . .

"Look at that!" Cyril said, as he walked past the barikar's skeletal remains and into the chamber beyond.

Alexander glanced up and looked in Cyril's direction. At first he did not see what the young wizard was talking about; then he saw it plain. "By heavens, Cyril!"

Not only had the spell incinerated the barikar in an instant, not only had the backlash heated the iron gate red-hot, but it had also burned a gaping hole through the wall of the outer chamber. It was a miracle that they had not been killed. The prince could well see why Cyril was normally prohibited from working magic, if all his spells were as uncontrolled as this one.

"You have no idea what it's like to command such power, to feel it coursing through you," Cyril said wildly. "Working such great spells is supposed to take a toll on one, but I've never felt better in my life. It's like my mind is on fire!"

Alexander gave the man a sidelong glance. It appeared to him that Cyril was becoming overly excited. He seemed almost irrational. "I understand your excitement," the prince said in a soft voice. "But perhaps you should just take a moment to relax. You've performed an awesome feat. You don't want to let it overwhelm you."

"I appreciate your concern, Alexander, but I'm fine, fine. Relax! How can I relax?"

Alexander shrugged and went to examine the hole blasted into the wall. It was remarkable: the stone itself had been melted completely through, in an almost perfect circle. It was still extremely hot. He could feel the heat radiating onto his hands and face, as he stooped to get a closer look.

There was something behind the wall, he saw. It

appeared to be a small chamber, a single narrow corridor leading away from it. Curious. It looked to him as if this wall had been put here for the sole purpose of sealing off this corridor from the rest of the dungeon. Certainly the wall was of a more recent construction than anything else he had seen here.

Alexander thought that the corridor might lead to a way out of the dungeon, and that this was perhaps the reason why it had been walled off. There was only one way to be sure, but it would be some time yet before the hole cooled enough to allow them to go exploring.

"Do you see something interesting there?"

"Yes, I think so." Alexander rapidly told his companion of what he had seen through the gap in the wall. Cyril did not seem especially impressed. He took in the prince's words with little more than a nod. "Interesting," he said.

"I suggest we rest here while the hole cools."

"Yes, yes, all right." Cyril still seemed excited, but Alexander thought that he could detect a certain fatigue about his eyes now.

"Come, let's sit over here and wait." After putting his back to the wall opposite the hole, Alexander slowly slid to the floor. A chill dampness quickly communicated itself through the seat of his trousers, but he was prepared to ignore it.

Cyril took his place next to him. The wizard yawned, and said, "Once we get out of here, what then?"

"The plan hasn't changed. We will find where Tel-

grin has put my father's soul, and try to take it back.
At least we now know one place where it *isn't*.''

"Hmm? Where's that?"

"The house. The house behind the wall. I'm ab-
solutely certain that Telgrin wouldn't put the soul in
the same place as Princess Lydia."

"Oh. Yes. There." He yawned again. "Who is this
Princess Lydia, do you think? Telgrin was awfully
disturbed when he thought that we had come for her."

Alexander frowned. "I don't know. It may be that
she is someone Telgrin kidnapped from another place,
perhaps a great beauty. Telgrin did seem jealous of
us."

"Maybe we can use her against Telgrin,
somehow."

"Maybe."

Cyril yawned a third time. "*Mmph.* If you don't
mind, I think I'll close my eyes for a moment."

"Go ahead."

Stretching his legs out straight, Cyril shut his eyes
and let his facial muscles go lax. He gave his nose a
slight twitch. By and by, he began to snore.

·12·

Alexander awoke with a start. Disoriented, he had to take a moment to put his world back together. Where was he? *Yes.* Who was this beside him? *Yes.* How long had he been asleep? *No way of knowing.*

His body had stiffened and begun to ache while he slept. He felt a strong desire to get up and move around, but he did not want to disturb Cyril, who still slumbered beside him. Slowly and carefully, he shifted away from his companion, then struggled to his feet, grimacing.

It was cold, and the darkness and the damp were oppressive. Clasping his arms tightly to his breast, he marched up and down the length of the chamber. Eventually his blood started flowing again, the feeling returned to his extremities, and he went to the hole in the wall and squatted beside it.

The stone seemed to have cooled now. Cautiously he touched the inner edge of the hole with one finger, finding only a slight residual warmth left.

Alexander glanced back at Cyril. The apprentice wizard was obviously deeply asleep. It did not seem likely that he would be waking soon. The prince decided that there was no reason not to explore beyond the wall while he slept.

He put a leg through the hole, ducked his head, and brought the rest of his body inside. Looking around, he saw that the chamber was much like the one he had just left, containing nothing of interest.

As quietly as he could, he made his way to the corridor leading from the chamber. He did not know what he might find. For all he knew, another of Telgrin's monsters might lurk here. It was unlikely, but not entirely out of the question.

Alexander began to wonder if he was doing the right thing by coming here alone, instead of waiting for Cyril to awake. He decided that there probably would be no harm to poking his head into the corridor for a moment. If there was any suggestion of danger, he would withdraw at once.

He came to the corridor entrance. It looked safe enough, so he stepped inside. He noticed that a faint greenish radiance filled the corridor, which appeared to be coming from somewhere toward the other end.

He hesitated, considering whether or not to turn back. Curiosity finally got the better of caution, and he began making his way quietly down the corridor.

The way turned, and then turned again. The green glow grew steadily brighter. The corridor entered a narrow chamber, and he saw that there were a series of arched vaults set back into the wall. Some of these were separated from the main chamber by rusted iron bars. All were dark and apparently empty.

The chamber extended for quite some distance, occasionally broken by rough stone pillars. Finally, as he neared the end of it, he passed the final pillar and discovered the source of the green light.

There was another vault here, little different from all the others. It too was sealed off by bars, but these bars glowed with an eerie light, shedding a sickly green radiance. There was something about those bars that filled him with dread, but he was also strangely drawn to them.

He crept closer to the vault, and looked beyond the glowing bars. What he saw there caused him to stop dead in his tracks, frozen by wonderment and horror.

It appeared to be a large man seated upon a chair, clad in garments that had once been fine, but which were now filthy and disintegrating, hems frayed, seams puckering and coming apart.

What was most remarkable about the man was that he had no head. No, that was not true. He had a head, the prince saw, but it was not where it ought to be. The man held it tucked under one arm, rather like a soldier might hold a helmet. The face was ghastly pale, and the light coming from the bars gave it a greenish cast. It had a long beard and a high forehead. Its cheeks were gaunt. Its eyes were open.

Those eyes were staring at Alexander. They did not blink.

As soon as the first shock subsided, the prince recovered his power of motion. He started backing away, scalp prickling with horror.

Suddenly the head spoke: "O sir, do not be afraid. I mean you no harm. Even if I did mean you harm,

I fear that I would be helpless to effect it, now.''

Alexander stopped where he was. "Wha— Who are you?''

"I am the unfortunate Owen, who was once master of this castle.''

"Master? What . . . happened to you?''

"Ah, that is an unhappy story. I am as you see me now as the result of treachery and my own trusting nature.''

"Treachery. Does this story perchance involve the one called Telgrin?''

Owen's expression darkened at that name. "Oh, aye. It involves *him* most especially.''

"Tell me. Tell me what happened.''

"If you have the heart to hear the story, I will tell it,'' Owen said dolefully. "You see before you a man who had everything, once. I was a king, a magician, and a scholar. I had the love of a beautiful and gracious woman. But when she died—the result of an accident that even I could not forestall—I lost heart, and could no longer tend to the affairs of my kingdom. I caused this castle to be built, then, investing it with a powerful and singular magic, enabling it to sail from place to place on the wind. I then set forth with my dear daughter, intending to spend the rest of my life exploring the length and breadth of the world.''

Owen took a brief pause, while Alexander reflected on the fact that he was getting used to carrying on a conversation with a beheaded man. It was starting to seem almost normal. Almost.

At length Owen said, "Telgrin was a lad from the scullery when I first became aware of him."

"The *scullery*?" Alexander almost laughed.

"Yes," Owen said, his expression mournful. "He was an unusual youth, bright, ambitious, and seemingly interested in everything. I decided to take him as my apprentice. I taught him everything, showed him the ways of magic, and the secrets of the castle. He was an apt student. He learned everything I cared to teach him."

Owen paused again, then said, "And what was my reward for six years of effort on his behalf? How did he choose to repay me? I'll tell you. He came upon me one day while I was hunched over a volume of obscure lore, struck off my head, and took from me my staff of power. He expected me to die, of course, but I had gone far in my arcane studies, and had strengthened myself with powerful magic. I did not die, could not die. So he locked me away here in this cell, behind bars reinforced with potent spells, and sealed behind a solid wall. I, who set out to roam all the world, have spent ten long years in this small cell, alone. Until you came."

"A terrible tale," Alexander said with heartfelt sympathy. "I am saddened to hear of what you have endured."

"I have told you who I am," Owen said, his voice turned sharp and commanding. "Now, who are you? How is it that you have come to this place?"

"I am Prince Alexander of Daventry. I have come to save my father from Telgrin." Alexander quickly told Owen of the events that had brought him to this point. Owen listened gravely, then said, "Telgrin's sins have grown even darker than I had imagined. It may be that I can help you, if you will help me."

Alexander considered this for a moment. "How?"

"It will not be easy," Owen said. "It will not be easy at all. It is fortunate that I did not tell Telgrin *everything* before he usurped me. I've a trick or two yet that might serve."

Owen rose and began to pace the length of his cell, still holding his head under his arm. Seeing him up and moving around renewed Alexander's uneasiness. Somehow a beheaded man on his feet was infinitely more alarming than a beheaded man quietly seated.

"The mirrors," Owen said.

"Beg pardon?"

"The mirrors. There are three of them. They are magic mirrors, but Telgrin doesn't know that. One is located in my—or rather Telgrin's—study, which is located here in the keep. It is likely that your father's soul can also be found there. The second mirror is in the great tower, in a small chamber on the first story. That would be your best bet, I'll warrant. If you can get to it . . ." Owen let his voice trail off, suddenly pensive.

"And the third?"

"Hmm?"

"The third mirror. You said that there are *three* magic mirrors."

"Ah. The third mirror—and this should not concern you—is in the quarters of Princess Lydia."

"*Lydia!* Telgrin mentioned her. Who is she?"

"She's my daughter. What did Telgrin say about her? Tell me."

"It was rather strange, really," Alexander said, and then he told Owen what he could remember of what Telgrin had said.

Owen listened intently to all he had to say. Finally he shut his eyes, and said, "That is good. That is well. It does not sound like he's done it yet."

"Done what?"

"Married her. Overreacher that he is, Telgrin hopes to make legitimate his rule of this castle by marrying my daughter, when she comes of age."

"Ah, I see." Alexander understood why Telgrin would react sharply to someone trying to gain access to Lydia's quarters.

Owen thoughtfully tapped his right temple with one finger. This simple gesture had a remarkably eerie effect, given that he was holding his head in one hand, while doing the tapping with the other.

Owen said, "Now, back to the mirrors. They are rather special. I devised them myself. If one knows how, one may not only see through one mirror and out one of the others, one may move from one mirror to another."

"Physically?"

"Yes, physically."

"You mean, one can actually walk through one of the mirrors and out another?"

"Yes."

Alexander considered this. "Useful."

"Very. I designed them in order to enable me to keep a watch on Lydia. For some reason, I never told Telgrin about them. Some lingering shred of native cunning, I suppose."

For a moment Owen seemed lost to idle remembrance, but then he appeared to rouse himself. He said, "If you can get to the mirror in the great tower, you can use it to spy on Telgrin in his study. It is then likely that you will be able to discover where he is keeping your father's soul."

"All I'd have to do is wait until Telgrin is out of the room, step through the mirror, reclaim my father's soul, and return through the mirror." Alexander liked this plan.

"No."

"No? What am I missing?"

"Telgrin's staff—*my* staff. I want it. You must bring it here to me."

Alexander pulled dubiously at his lower lip. "That would greatly complicate matters."

"I know it. I don't care. I will require that you give me your solemn word to do as I ask before I tell you how to use the mirrors. I'm not entirely devoid of my old powers, so I can tell that you are not one to give your word lightly."

"Why do you want it?"

"Can't you guess? I am helpless now, locked as I am within this warded cell. The staff will give me the power to break free from here, so that I may attempt my revenge on Telgrin. I have waited ten years for someone to find me here, and I will not be denied."

Alexander thought about it for a long moment, then said, "Very well, I will promise."

"Good. I thought that you would."

"There's one more thing, though," Alexander said. "I don't know how to get out of these unholy dungeons."

Owen gave him a thin smile. "I will tell you how."

·13·

When Alexander returned to where he had left Cyril, he found the apprentice wizard awake and waiting for him. "Where did you go?" the young man asked aggrievedly. "I was beginning to think that I had been left alone in this dreadful place."

"Sorry," Alexander said. "Sorry. I was caught up in a most interesting conversation."

"A conversation? With whom? About what?"

Alexander told him.

"Well," Cyril said at length, "that changes things, doesn't it? I'm not sure that I like the idea of trying to steal Telgrin's staff. A magician never lets his main object of power far from his side. It will be very risky."

"I'm not particularly happy about that part, either. Unfortunately, I had no choice but to promise. We'll just have to do our best."

"I suppose." Cyril glanced thoughtfully at the hole burned into the wall. "I guess it's a good thing that my spell turned out to be so powerful."

Alexander nodded, then said, "How . . . are you feeling now?"

"Drained. I have a nasty headache. Right *here*. I guess working that spell was more of a strain than I had thought."

Alexander grinned. "I guess."

Cyril was silent a moment. "And I guess I'd better not try working another spell, unless I have no other choice."

"That sounds sensible."

"Well, how do we get out of this place?" Cyril asked brightly. "Truly, it begins to oppress me."

"This way." Alexander led the other man back in the direction from which they had come, to the chamber where they had first entered the dungeons. There they once again confronted the three corridors. "That one," Alexander said, indicating the right-hand corridor.

The two men slowly entered the corridor. At first it did not seem much different from the other corridor. Soon, however, it began to slant sharply downward, and the ceiling lowered, forcing them to keep their heads ducked while they walked. Oily puddles collected on the cobbled floor, and the walls became stippled with a faintly luminous moss.

The slant of the floor eventually leveled off. Shortly after that, a low stone beam crossed their path, square, massive, and finely worked. Alexander braced himself with one hand on the beam, as he ducked beneath it.

When he came out from under the beam, he found himself in another chamber, one several times larger than any of the others they had visited. The entire center of the chamber was filled by a murky pool, its flat surface glimmering faintly in the dim light. A delicate stone bridge spanned the pool, apparently the only way across it.

Cyril came into the chamber behind Alexander and started forward. The prince grabbed his arm, stopping him.

"Not yet," Alexander said. "It's not safe."

Cyril looked at him askance, raised an eyebrow, but did not attempt to go farther. Alexander moved cautiously to the right and found the stone obelisk that Owen had told him about. Atop the obelisk was a crystal sphere, made nearly invisible by the gloom.

Alexander gingerly put both hands on the sphere, tenting his fingers. Slowly, carefully, he lifted the sphere from the obelisk and carried it toward the pool. The sphere felt strangely warm to the touch. It seemed to give off a dark energy, which the prince fancied he could feel tingling faintly on his face.

He halted several yards short of the pool, raised the sphere before him, and spoke the word that Owen had taught him. It was a long word, lilting and almost impossible to pronounce. Saying it made Alexander feel oddly giddy.

Suddenly a bright light grew within the crystal sphere, bathing the chamber in its clear white radiance. After he had been so long in darkness, the light hurt Alexander's eyes, causing him to squint and avert his gaze.

Even though partially blinded, the prince was able to see the vast shape that lay just under the surface of the water, and the round, dark eye that for an instant peered malevolently from the center of the pool.

As soon as the light struck it, however, the eye screwed itself shut and moved ponderously under the murky grey water. Alexander heard a splash, and saw a glistening tentacle momentarily break the surface before vanishing with a slight flutter, leaving an expanding circle of gentle whorls in its wake.

"Come," Alexander said. "It's safe now. Just be careful not to slip while crossing the bridge."

Still holding the bright sphere aloft, Alexander led the way across. The bridge was not at all wide, and there were no rails, so he went with prudent deliberation, one slow step after another.

He was greatly relieved when he reached the other side and stepped down. Turning, he waited while Cyril crossed after him, arms held out from his body slightly, for balance. After a few moments, the young wizard stepped down next to Alexander, and he was able to breathe easier.

There was another obelisk, exactly matching the first, but on this side of the pool. Alexander told Cyril to move away from the pool, then he set the crystal sphere on top of the obelisk. As soon as he took his hands from the sphere, the light gradually faded and died. For a moment a silver spark lingered at the heart of the sphere, then it too was gone.

For a short but disquieting time, Alexander was completely blind. The blackness was impenetrable. He stood very still, listening to the faint churnings of the water. At last his eyes began to readjust, and the chamber once again became a place of vague grey shapes.

"Can you see all right?" Alexander said.

"Yes. Sort of."

"This way, then."

Slowly, Alexander made his way to the far end of the chamber. Here he found a stone stairway hidden by a fluted column. He made his way up it, until he came to a small landing. There was a small brass grille set high up on the wall here, and a soft light showed from it, sketching its duplicate in light and shadow upon the opposite wall.

A little beyond the grille was the entrance to a long, confined corridor. Alexander entered the corridor, noticing as he did so that the stonework here was far more artfully done than it was below.

Partway down the corridor he came upon a small face carved into the stone, then another, and another. The faces were highly stylized, rendered with the minimal detail needed to make them recognizable as faces. Alexander counted each one as he came to it, until he reached the fifth face in the series. He paused before this one, and pushed upon it with a direct and steady pressure. He felt it sink into the wall slightly, and heard a metallic *click*.

Continuing down the corridor, Alexander counted three more faces, stopped and pushed, then two more, stopped and pushed again. A short distance beyond that point, the corridor appeared to end in a wall paneled with dark, lusterless wood.

A thick strip of matching wood ran all along the

top of the panel. After confronting the paneled wall at the point where he judged the center to be, Alexander reached up and felt along the top edge of the wood strip.

A moment later, his fingers found a shallow depression, and in it a small metal rod. He pushed the rod to one side, while at the same time pressing against the wall with his shoulder. He felt the wall give with a sudden lurch.

Alexander stepped back. He saw that a dark gap had opened in the wall. One section of the panel had sprung inward.

Standing at the prince's side, Cyril said, "Ingenious."

"Yes."

"Where are we now?"

"Right now, somewhere under the great tower. This should take us into the tower's basement."

"And then?"

"We'll make our way to the first story and try to find the mirror." He paused. "We will have to be very quiet from here on out. There's bound to be a few of Telgrin's knights about."

Cyril nodded.

Alexander pushed the panel the rest of the way forward and stepped through the opening, finding himself in a small space, at the end of which was the start of a stairway, framed by wavering cobwebs hanging from the stout beams crossing overhead.

Alexander moved to the stairway and began to climb. The stairway did not strike him as particularly safe. Though it was built of heavy stone, many of the steps rocked perilously as he moved up them—and once he thought that he could feel one start to slip. "Watch out here," he said in a low voice. Cyril responded with a soft grunt.

At last the stairway ended, in a small, square room. The ceiling here was so low that Alexander could not stand upright, although Cyril could. Alexander searched the ceiling, until he found the round metal plate that Owen had told him of.

He hesitated. The next step had a certain degree of peril attached to it. Alexander had to lift the plate and move it aside, which would allow them finally to enter the basement of the great tower. The problem was, if there was anyone in the basement, they might see or hear the plate move. The prince had no way of knowing when it was safe, or when it was not.

Alexander drew a breath, then let it out with a sigh. There was nothing for it. He had to take the risk.

After putting both hands flat on the bottom of the plate, Alexander pushed up, trying to judge exactly how much pressure to exert. The plate made a grinding sound as it started to come free from the stone that surrounded it, making Alexander grimace. Slowly the plate cleared the stone, and the prince moved it to his right as far as he could, then let it down.

Yellow light flooded down from the crescent-shaped opening overhead. There was not yet enough of a gap to get through. He would have to slide the plate at least six more inches to the side. There was no way to do this silently. He would just have to hope that there would be no one nearby to hear it.

Gritting his teeth, he gradually worked the plate to his right. The noise that this created was even worse than he had expected, but he did not stop until he had cleared enough of an opening to climb through.

He paused a moment to catch his breath and rub his perspiring hands on his trousers. He did not hear any cries of alarm or approaching footsteps. So far, so good.

Reaching above him, he grasped the edge of the opening with both hands and pulled himself up. First his head, then his shoulders cleared the top of the opening. He shifted his grip, and laboriously levered himself the rest of the way out of the hole. After he managed to get one haunch safely down on the edge, he gave a quick glance about him.

He was in a large chamber bounded along one side by a curving wall. Many massive pillars rose to meet the high ceiling, and in their shadows were many crates and barrels, piled up in great mounds. Obviously this space was used primarily for storage. It appeared to be deserted at the moment.

Alexander swung his legs from the hole, then knelt beside it. Looking down, he saw Cyril's upturned face. He extended his hand to the young man. "Here, grab hold. I'll pull you up."

Cyril nodded and grasped his hand. Alexander pulled him up and partially out of the hole, then got a good grip on the back of the young man's belt and hauled him onto the stone floor.

Cyril lay there on his stomach for a moment,

breathing hard. "*Oof*," he said. With the look of a man nearing the end of his strength, he pushed himself up and struggled to his feet.

"You know what I'd like?" the young wizard said softly. "A nice hot cup of tea."

"Sounds good."

"And a bath. Definitely a bath."

Alexander could not think about that. Everything that yet remained to be accomplished stretched oppressively before him. First, he had to get to the magic mirror, then he had to try to get it to function for him, then he had to spy on Telgrin and find his father's soul, all the while hoping that he was not discovered. *Then* all he had to do was take back his father's soul—and Telgrin's staff—and make his way somehow to Owen's cell. . . .

He already was so tired. He did not know if he had enough strength left for all that needed to be done.

After allowing himself to wallow in depression for a short while, he pushed his mood aside with a firm effort, squared his shoulders, and said, "Well, the sooner we get going, the sooner you'll get your bath and your tea."

"Yes, I suppose. Where . . . do we go now?"

"The stairs are this way."

Alexander led the way around a huge stack of barrels and crates, and then past a rough-hewn and purely functional pillar. Ahead he could see a high iron fence, behind which was a curving stairway of dark grey stone. Mounted in an iron sconce near the base of the stairs, a sputtering torch cast fluttering shadows across the floor.

Alexander approached the gate in the fence with some trepidation, afraid that he would find it locked. He was relieved when it swung open at his touch. At least *something* had gone easily.

Alexander held the gate open, while Cyril passed through, then closed the gate gently, making sure that it made no sound. "Let me go first," he said, his voice little more than a whisper. "There's a chance that we'll meet someone on the stair."

"Very well."

Alexander went up the stairway with a careful, quiet tread. The stairway curved around the wall as it rose. Whenever the prince looked down into the gloomy basement, it made him feel distinctly giddy. He was careful to keep his hand firmly on the iron balustrade to his left, as he moved steadily upward.

At last he reached the top. There was a small landing here, at the end of which was a narrow door. Alexander went to the door and stood with his ear to it, listening, for a moment. He heard a few sounds, the occasional clunk or clank, but none of them seemed to come from anywhere nearby. It sounded as if they had filtered in from elsewhere in the tower.

Aware of Cyril standing at his back, Alexander slowly and cautiously opened the door a crack. He saw a small room, windowless and unfurnished, from which two other doors gave exit. It was unoccupied.

Alexander opened the door the rest of the way, wincing when it made a soft creaking sound. He moved into the room, and gestured for Cyril to follow.

Fear and exhilaration battled within the prince's breast for a moment. He was exhilarated to finally be out of that gloomy underworld beneath the castle; afraid, because he knew that the danger of being discovered was never greater.

One of the doors leading from the room was slightly ajar, so that a wedge of yellow light marked the floor before it. Alexander went to this door, flattened himself against the wall beside it, and peered through the opening.

He saw a short hall, its walls hung with faded tapestries of green and gold. At one end was an open doorway. At the other, the start of a steep stair. Between the two, there was a door, and what appeared to be the entrance to a vestibule, there near the foot of the stair. If he remembered what Owen had said correctly, the magic mirror was in the vestibule.

The sounds of the tower were louder here. He could hear voices, doors opening and closing, ponderous footsteps, spurs ringing on stone. For a moment Alexander could not force himself to move from where he was. In the end, he had to tell himself that whatever safety he felt in this place was illusory, that the longer he hesitated, the greater his chance of being found out before he could use the mirror.

Jaw clenched tight, scarcely daring to breathe, Alexander slipped through the opening. A few wary, rather mincing steps brought him to the vestibule.

The vestibule was a small, square space. On one

wall hung a scarlet drape, and against the opposing wall a tall brazier of black iron stood, a tiny yellow flame dancing from the center of it.

At the far end of the vestibule, Alexander saw it: the mirror. It was set into a shallow niche in the wall, an object at the same time beautiful and dreadful.

It extended from floor to ceiling, its wide frame of some lustrous black substance, numerous strange figures and glyphs etched upon it. The mirror itself showed him his own person—gaunt, disheveled, dirty, dark circles under his eyes, and lips firmly compressed—and yet he thought that he could detect some hidden depth to it, something that lurked beneath the mundane image.

That something frightened him. It made his mouth go dry and his heart quicken. It spoke of things no man should know. It was a feeling that was totally unlike what he got from the magic mirror hanging in Castle Daventry. That mirror normally gave off an aura that was lucid and bright, while this mirror seemed dark, obscure, and melancholy.

Alexander saw Cyril join him in the mirror's reflection, and this roused him from his momentary reverie. He moved quickly to the mirror and studied the arcane glyphs rimming it. On the right side there was a symbol that looked something like a trident; on the left, two interlocked diamonds; above, a trio of wavy horizontal lines.

Touching the symbol on the right, the left, and then above, Alexander said, "You are a window through which I can see. You are a door through which I may walk. You are the way between the High and Low Kingdoms. Open, as Owen bade you.''

Alexander could detect a subtle change within the mirror. It seemed that a dark haze had come over the images it reflected. If he concentrated as hard as he could, he could just make out a deeper image, which was coming slowly closer to the surface.

It was the image of another room, at first dim in outline and faint in detail, but becoming increasingly real, specific, and solid the harder he concentrated on it. There was a terrible pressure at the front of his skull, an aching behind his eyes. He had the sensation of overcoming a tremendous resistance, a resistance that was as much inside as outside him.

At some point Alexander lost all touch with his surroundings, so tightly was his attention affixed to the mirror. On some level, he was aware of the approaching footsteps, the soft chiming of spurs, but it meant nothing to him. Suddenly he felt Cyril's hands on his shoulders.

''There's someone coming!'' came the young wizard's voice. ''Can you hear me? *Alexander!*''

Alexander tried to shrug his companion off. He was almost through, had almost opened the way. For an instant he could see the distant room as clearly as if he stood within it. It was a workroom, ceilings high, bookshelves covering one entire wall, tables piled with books, scrolls, and many curious artifacts occupying the center of the room.

One of the artifacts was a shimmering sphere, delicate in appearance, small enough to hold in one hand.

There was a faint blur of movement within it, which immediately attracted his attention. When he looked closer, he saw that movement came from a disembodied face floating within the sphere, tiny but recognizable.

Alexander felt a chill seize his heart. "*Father!*" he said.

He started to step through the mirror and into the scene that it portrayed, but at that instant something seized him roughly and pulled him back. A voice said, "What are you doing here? You will come with me." He recognized the voice by its dry and dispassionate tone. It was one of Telgrin's knights.

Unwilling to give up when he was so close, Alexander tried to pull free. As he did so, however, he lost his concentration. Helpless, he watched while the scene before him dissolved with a sudden rush.

Abruptly he saw his own face reflected in the mirror, and the black knight looming over him, grasping his shoulders with an iron grip.

A prisoner. Again.

·14·

The black knight spun Alexander around and pushed him toward the hall. From the corner of his eye, the prince saw Cyril standing by helplessly, a look of uncertainty on his face.

"You will come with me," the knight said. "Both of you."

Frustrated anger welled within Alexander's breast. He had been so close, so close. He was determined that it would not all come to naught now. Twisting suddenly, he managed to break the knight's grip on his shoulders; then he slammed his right forearm against his opponent's metal breastplate with all his might.

The knight staggered back a step, as numbing pain sparked through Alexander's arm. It felt as if he had tried to punch through a solid stone wall. Now his fingers did not want to close, and his elbow did not work quite right. He blinked back tears, hoping that he had not broken his arm.

The knight recovered quickly. "There is no point in resistance," he said, starting toward the prince again.

Right arm hanging useless, Alexander stooped to grasp the leg of the iron brazier with his left hand. He lofted it and swung it in an awkward backhanded movement, sending red-hot coals showering at his opponent.

Apparently startled, the knight put up his arms and rocked back on his heels. Alexander swung the brazier again, this time striking the knight square in the chest. There was a sharp clang of metal against metal. Already off-balance, the knight tottered and fell backward, coming down hard on his back. Alexander let the rebounding brazier go. It crashed against the wall, bounced, and then hit the floor.

Alarmed voices echoed in the hall. Hearing footsteps coming their way, Alexander caught Cyril's arm. "We've got to get out of here!" he said.

Alexander staggered out into the hall, hoping that they could make it back to the basement before the pursuit could close on them. His heart sank when he saw two of Telgrin's knights entering the hall at the far end, effectively cutting off their escape.

"You there," said one of the knights. "Stop where you are. You will come with us."

Alexander gave a quick, desperate look about him. He saw that the first knight was starting to get up from the floor. In a moment, they would be facing three armed knights, with more to come. There was only one place left to go.

"The stairs," Alexander said.

Cyril nodded, and they started for the stairway. This time Alexander let the younger man go first. He himself would fight the rearguard action—although he very much hoped that it would not come to a fight. Lacking any sort of weapon, with one arm crippled, he knew that he could not achieve much in a conflict.

The two men raced up the first flight of stairs, then paused on the landing and listened for the sounds of pursuit. That pursuit was not far behind. The sound of ringing footsteps on the stair echoed from below: steady, methodical, relentless.

"Up," Alexander said. "*Again.*" He was happy to discover that he could work his fingers a little again, though the arm still tingled and throbbed.

Wearily, the two launched themselves up the next flight of stairs. When they came, gasping, to the next landing, they again heard the remorseless pursuit below. It did not seem to have fallen much behind.

Alexander realized that matters were not heading in an ideal direction. The knights would not slow, would not tire. How could they? They were merely suits of armor animated by disembodied souls. Sooner or later, they would trap him and Cyril. If the pursuit continued up the stairs, it would happen on the top story. If he and Cyril tried to break off and hide on one of the intervening floors, the knights would certainly realize it, cut them off from the stairway, and corner them at their leisure. Either way, there would be the same depressing result.

Still, they had to try *something*.

"Fast as you can, on the next one," Alexander said, voice rasping harshly.

It was Alexander's intention to try to lose the

knights on the next story. He was not wildly optimistic about their chances of succeeding at that, but he knew that it was better than simply continuing to race to the top of the tower.

When they reached the next landing, Alexander gestured frantically toward the hall. Cyril understood what he was trying to say, and the two went quickly for the hall.

And nearly ran into the waiting arms of another of Telgrin's knights.

The knight was trying to go from the hall to the stairway at precisely the same moment that the two men were trying to go from the stairway to the hall. They met at the entrance to the hall, not a yard away from each other, when both parties stopped. "What are you doing here?" the knight said. "You will come with me."

Alexander wished they would stop saying that. It was beginning to get on his nerves.

As one, Alexander and Cyril took a step backward, turned, and made for the stairway. As they reached it, the prince could see the knights from below coming up. They were only a few steps behind now.

The two men sprinted up the stairs, taking them two at a time, afraid that at any moment a metal-clad hand might reach out and grab them from behind. When they came to the next landing, they did not pause at all before launching themselves up the next flight of stairs.

That worked well, Alexander thought dourly. Now there were *four* knights chasing them.

By the time they reached the top story, they had managed to put a little distance between themselves and their pursuers. They had some time to work with, but not much.

The two men went into the hall and moved swiftly down it. The hall was punctuated by many doors. The men tried each one. All were locked.

The hall turned just ahead. As the two men reached the corner, the first of the pursuing knights came into the hall at the other end. "Stop!" the knight said. "You will come with me."

Alexander was dismayed to see that they had almost run out of hall. It ended in a solid wall a few yards ahead. There was only one more door to try.

Alexander tried it. It was locked. Listening to the clanking, chiming approach of the four knights, he tried to think of what to do next, but he was out of ideas.

The prince threw himself against the door several times, hoping to break through, but it was no use. The door was stoutly built, of thick oak. He had little strength, and no time, left.

Desperate, Alexander said, "Cyril, do you think that you can use your magic on this door?"

The young man frowned. "I don't know. It's . . . dangerous, you know."

"Just give it a little nudge."

"A nudge?"

"Just a nudge."

"I'll . . . try."

"Hurry."

"Step back." Cyril turned to face the door. Closing his eyes and drawing a long, deep breath, he pressed the palms of both hands against the dark wood. He muttered a word that held no meaning for the prince. The door trembled, rattling within its frame, then was still. The wizard stepped back a pace, spoke another low word.

The door trembled again, more violently this time. Alexander could hear a distant roaring arise from nowhere, growing louder all the time. The door seemed ready to give way at any moment.

Cyril spoke a third word.

The tower shook with sudden violence, and the door blew inward—as did the door frame, a sizable portion of the wall, the furniture behind the wall, and the wall behind the furniture. Nearly deafened by the force of the explosion, Alexander was thrown back against the opposite wall, striking his head with such force that for a moment everything went hazy and he thought he would lose consciousness.

The air was thick with dust. Head reeling, Alexander moved toward the jagged hole that had been blasted into the wall. Little remained of the room beyond, save for rubble and ruin. The blue of the sky showed through the shattered outer wall, and a heavy oaken bench hung halfway out the breach, covered with plaster dust and shards of broken masonry.

Cyril stood in the midst of the room that his powers had demolished. He was laughing, his face showing a manic elation. "By heavens!" he said at length. "Look at what I've done. Just *look*."

At this moment the knights came clattering around the corner, all four of them, in close formation. Apparently they had not been much slowed by the violent spasm that had shaken the tower. They were coming at the same steady pace. Two of them had their swords out.

"Impressive," Alexander said. "Unfortunately this room will not make much of a refuge, now. They've got us cornered." The prince started looking around for something that he could use as a weapon.

"Cornered?" Cyril said. "Not so! The power is still upon me."

"If you use your power again, you'll bring the roof down on top of us."

"Do not fear. I'll not do anything destructive. I'll simply fly us out through the breach in yon wall." The young wizard raised his hands, fingers spread. A bright, flickering aura surrounded him.

"Cyril, I really don't think—"

"*Enough.* There's no time for discussion. Prepare yourself."

"No, Cyril, I— *Aieee!*"

Cyril reached out and grasped him by the left forearm. Alexander felt a strange tingling sensation, as the aura spread to encompass him. Suddenly he was floating above the floor and being dragged through the air at great speed by the young wizard.

They sailed out through the gap in the outer wall and soared high over the castle's courtyard, buffeted by winds, while exhilaration and vertigo battled wildly for control of Alexander's senses. They circled

the tower for one dizzying circuit, then flew out over
the top of the keep, nearly colliding with one of the
turrets. At the last moment they veered sharply over
the outer wall, dropped abruptly lower—then rose
again, when it appeared that they were about to become ensnared in the upper branches of a tree.

Alexander called out in alarm. It seemed to him
that their flight was becoming increasingly erratic and
dangerous.

"This is no good, Cyril!" Alexander cried out.
"We must get back to the castle."

"I'm *trying*. This isn't as easy as it looks."

They curved back toward the castle, paralleling the
contours of the land and gaining speed. As they glided
in over one of the castle's great corner towers, Alexander called, "Too fast, too fast!"

"I *know*."

They began to slow, but it was already too late.
The courtyard flashed beneath them, then the keep,
and the opposing wall. They were out over the river
in an instant, and dropping toward its grey and un-
inviting surface.

"I'm losing control!" Cyril shouted.

"You can't, not yet!" A plunge in the river here
would not be a good thing, Alexander knew. The current was strong, and there were dangerous rapids not
far downstream. They might not survive such an adventure.

"I'll try." Gradually they leveled off, though they
ended up skimming the surface of the river at a level
far too close for comfort. They turned slowly back

toward the castle, wheeling over glistening, marshy land. Ahead in the distance was a line of trees, rising dark and tangled in the gloomy light of the gathering dusk.

Alexander noticed that the aura surrounding them was growing patchy and dim. He did not know how long it could last. Certainly not long enough to get back to Telgrin's castle. He prepared himself for the inevitable landing.

A moment later the aura flickered out, and they plummeted headlong from the sky.

·15·

Perhaps three feet of water covered the ground where Alexander came down. He struck it with stinging force, then found himself facedown in the murky mess, his hands buried to the wrists in soft, silty mud. The force of the impact had knocked the wind from him; his body responded by sucking up a mouthful of stagnant water and aspirating most of it into his lungs. He began to cough.

Several minutes later, he was still coughing, but no longer with such violence that he was rendered physically helpless. He was able to pry his hands out of the muck and, with difficulty, get to his feet. He was dripping wet, cold, and his face stung as if it had been pierced with a thousand tiny needles and immersed in salt. He could barely see through the blur of tears and muddy water.

"Cyril," he croaked. "Cyril . . ."

After a few more moments, his eyes began to clear. To his horror, he saw that Cyril was three or four yards ahead, floating facedown and motionless in the grey-green bog. Alexander began slogging awkwardly toward the apprentice wizard, afraid of what he would find when he reached him.

Progress came hard and slow. The water impeded his every step, his sodden cloak pulled on him, and the soft mud kept seizing his feet and refusing to let go. As he pressed on and finally neared the young man, he saw that he had come down on a sandy bar, which the water barely covered. Cyril's legs were floating, but his torso was well grounded. His head was cocked slightly to one side, the bar supporting his chin. His mouth was only partially submerged, except when the water lapped up particularly high. The prince could see the young man blowing shimmering bubbles from the side of his mouth.

He was alive, at least.

Relieved, Alexander struggled forward three more steps, climbed up onto the bank, and stooped to catch Cyril under the arms. After dragging the young wizard farther onto the bank, he turned him over onto his back and then pulled him up, so that he was sitting upright.

Cyril immediately began to cough, and a rivulet of murky water flowed down his chin. Taking this to be a good sign, Alexander pounded him on the back and encouraged him to breathe. Cyril coughed, gagged, and coughed some more. At last his eyelids fluttered open. He stared ahead blankly, apparently dazed.

"Huh? Wha— Where am I?" he said with a sudden start.

"Take it easy. We are in the bog outside Telgrin's

castle. We landed here after you lost control of your spell. Remember?''

''I . . . remember. I used it all, everything I had. There's nothing left.''

''Listen, Cyril. We have to take cover. Telgrin might be sending his knights to look for us at any moment. Can you travel?''

The young man made a feeble effort to rise, then subsided heavily. ''No. Sorry. Nothing left. So tired. So tired.''

''That's all right,'' Alexander said in a flat voice. ''You rest. I'll take care of it.'' He did not give voice to the ''somehow'' that was in his thoughts.

Alexander gave an apprehensive glance in the direction of Telgrin's castle. The great edifice was a little more than half a mile away, he estimated. A white mist shrouded it, softening its harsh lines, so that he felt he was looking at it through a milky glass. He thought, but could not be sure, that he could see dark riders coming through the gate. If Telgrin had sent his knights to find them, he did not have much time. Somehow he would have to get Cyril to cover.

There were trees and land that appeared solid, to his right, perhaps sixty yards away. He wondered if he had enough strength left to haul his companion that far.

There was only one way to find out.

''Just relax, Cyril,'' Alexander said. ''I'm going to try to get us out of here. Do you understand?''

There was no response. The young man appeared unconscious.

With a slight sigh, Alexander again grasped Cyril under the arms and pulled his limp body from the sandy bar and into the bog. He tried to lock his fingers together around the man's chest, but this proved difficult. His injured right arm still did not work quite right; its fingers kept losing strength and releasing the fingers of his left hand.

Alexander was forced to walk backward, dragging Cyril's body along at an awkward angle, pulling first one foot and then the other from the sucking mud. His arms hurt, his legs hurt, his back hurt. He came close to giving up with every step, but somehow managed not to give up. The world slowly dissolved into an endless blur of effort and pain.

In subtle increments, the level of the water went from the middle of his thighs, to below the knees, to the middle of the calves, and then to just above the ankles. Small islands of raised land appeared around him, some supporting barren, leafless trees, with ragged streamers of sickly green moss festooning their branches. Small marsh plants pricked the surface of the water; tall sedge lined the shores.

Soon the islands began to converge and join, and the water was reduced to a multitude of shallow streams, some wide, some only faint rivulets wearing away slowly at the bank. Alexander pulled the unconscious Cyril along one of these streams for as far as he could. At last, when he was nearing collapse, he piled the young man up on the bank and promptly fell down beside him in the shining, stinking mud.

It was a long time before he could move again, but when his lungs finally stopped working like a great overburdened bellows, he sat up and took a look around. He saw that there were several gnarled trees growing behind him on the bank. One of them had an ample hollow in its massive trunk. Alexander decided he could not hope for better shelter than that.

With difficulty, the prince got to his feet and seized hold of Cyril once again. Slipping and sliding, his wet boot soles finding little purchase on the damp, crumbling earth, he pulled the young man up the slope leading to the trees.

When he neared the tree with the hollow in it, he tripped on the raised loop of a root and nearly fell over backward. Fortunately he was able to catch himself, but this insignificant event raised within him an unexpected fury. He cursed the poor root to withering, black perdition, cursed it deeply and sincerely, cursed it with all his soul. He let loose on it all the anger he felt toward Telgrin, his frustration at finding himself once again outside the castle, the anxiety that had been growing at the back of his mind ever since his father had been stricken.

After he had given full vent to his rage, and was already beginning to feel foolish about it, he began to regain control of himself. He told himself that this was not doing any good—though in fact it made him feel remarkably better—and that he still had much to do before he could allow himself the luxury of uncontrolled emotion.

After drawing a deep, calming breath, Alexander continued dragging Cyril to the tree, proceeding more carefully this time. When he finally reached it, he inspected the hollow for wild animals and wasps' nests. Finding neither, he installed Cyril within, legs outstretched. That done, Alexander dragged himself wearily into the hollow beside the other man.

Night was fast approaching. The sun, an indistinct white circle behind the pale overcast, was sinking below the horizon. A strong breeze had come up, bringing with it the noisome smells of the marsh: standing water, mud, and decaying vegetation.

Alexander shifted, trying to make his aching bones more comfortable. As the heat of his exertions faded, he was becoming chilled, and the dampness of his garments felt increasingly unpleasant.

He was so tired, however, that he merely noted these discomforts, as if from a distance. He was not capable of trying to do anything about them.

He could hear the rhythmic sound of Cyril's breathing, and found an odd comfort in it. His thoughts were rapidly becoming as hazy as the sky. He let them go, let them fade, let oblivion come.

It was night when awareness returned to Alexander. A bright half moon shone down from a gap in the clouds, tattered shreds of mist blowing across its face. Silver glints danced upon the black surface of the marsh.

Alexander rubbed a hand over his eyes. How long had he been asleep? he wondered. Was the night almost over, or just beginning?

He very much hoped that it was almost over. He was shivering from the cold, and he knew that he could not risk a fire, even if he had the means to light one. Sighing, he shifted uncomfortably. He was cold, wet, hungry, and tired. There was not one part of his body that did not hurt.

And that was not the worst of it. The worst of it was the certain knowledge that he was now farther from his goal than ever. He had almost done it. He had *seen* the vessel containing his father's soul. It had been right there before him. All he would have had to do was step through the mirror and take it.

Now, however, he found himself again outside Telgrin's castle. He had nothing, no weapon, no resources to draw upon, nothing. He could not imagine how he could even enter the castle again, let alone find his way undetected to one of the magic mirrors. This was it, the nadir. It could not get any worse than this.

Try as he might, he could not stop running down the list of all the reasons he had to be depressed, over and over again, in an endless loop. As he did so, his situation kept seeming darker and darker.

It took an hour or more for him to spiral to the bottom of his depression, and another hour to start to talk himself out of it. At least he was still alive and at liberty. He had escaped both the barikar and the black knights. He knew what he had to do, and how to do it. Somehow he would find a way to get back into Telgrin's castle.

Shivering, Alexander clutched his arms tightly to his chest and waited for the dawn. And waited. He could hear Cyril snoring softly beside him, and the occasional wild animal moving stealthily through the brush, and the frogs in the marsh. "*Ribbet*," they said. "*Ribbet, ribbet.*"

He must have fallen asleep again, for the next thing he knew it was grey dawn. A thick white mist lay upon the marsh, flowing and curling with the wind. There was a growing brightness in the east, behind a dense copse of trees.

Grateful for the daylight, gloomy as it was, Alexander roused himself and crawled from the tree hollow. He stood, and surveyed the marsh, seeing nothing there to gladden his heart. The mist was omnipresent, making the limbs of the trees droop and drip. The water had an unwholesome oily sheen to it, and the shores were stippled with a yellow-green moss. There was a large mud flat off to his right, its gelatinous surface cracked and curling. The occasional dragonfly darted above the water, seeming to have places to go. Somewhere a raven croaked ominously.

Alexander went to the water's edge, intending to get a drink. He was not looking forward to partaking of that greasy-looking water, but it was all that was available to him. He knelt on the muddy bank, and for a while watched the minnows making their way furiously along the bottom of the stream. Cupping one hand, he prepared to scoop up some water.

He saw, reflected in the water, something close behind him. For a moment he thought it was a tree, one of those clad in long strands of hanging moss, but he knew that there were no trees that near. He looked more carefully at the reflection, and realized that in fact it was a person.

Surprised, he quickly rose and turned. The person stared at him without apparent emotion. Was it a man or a woman? After a moment's consideration, he decided that it must be a woman.

She had been tall once, he guessed, but her back had acquired a permanent crook, forcing her to look up at him with her neck bent back at an angle that looked painful. Her sharp face was as brown as the mud, as was her hair, which hung down far past her shoulders. Her garments, such as they were, appeared to consist of numerous tattered strips of mossy green crudely woven together. In one hand she held a tall staff of twisted wood. A raven rode on her right shoulder, and it gazed at the prince with shining black eyes.

"I have been watching you," she said in a high, harsh voice.

Alexander did not know how to answer that, so he said, "I did not hear you approach."

The woman chuckled. "You wouldn't, would you? This is my marsh. I make my way through it as I like, and no one knows of my passing, unless I will it."

"Who are you?"

"They call me Sinofas, that do talk of me."

"I've heard of you." And so he had. Sinofas was reputed to be a solitary and powerful witch. She had lived in this marsh for as long as anyone could remember. Some said that she had lived here since the beginning of time. There were stories, terrible stories, of what happened to those who had the misfortune to annoy her.

Alexander said, "I hope you will forgive my trespass here. It wasn't planned, or even desired."

"You have nothing to fear from me, Prince Alexander." Sinofas gave him a searching look, cocking her head to one side. "It *is* Alexander, isn't it?"

"I am Alexander, yes."

"I have been watching you. I witnessed your extraordinary departure from the black castle. Would you care to tell me about that?"

Alexander studied the witch's face for a moment, wondering why she was interested. He did not want to say the wrong thing.

"We had an urgent need to leave the castle."

"You could have left by the front gate."

"No. We couldn't."

"Ah. You did not leave on good terms with the one called Telgrin, I take it."

The prince hesitated before responding. For all he knew, Sinofas was allied with Telgrin. He decided to risk it. "No, not on good terms."

The witch gave a twisted smile. "I am glad to hear it."

"You are not . . . on friendly terms with Telgrin?"

"No, not friendly. He has set his accursed castle down in the middle of my little realm, without asking permission. He has refused to move it, though I've asked—politely, and not so politely."

"He lacks all courtesy," Alexander agreed.

"What of you?" Sinofas said. "What brought you to his castle?"

"Telgrin has stolen something of great value. I was trying to get it back."

"What?"

"My father's soul."

"I *see*. Yes, I think I understand now. Did you succeed in recovering it?"

"No."

"Then you will have to go back."

Alexander felt a scowl come to his face. "Yes, I'm afraid so."

"How do you intend to get inside the castle again?"

"I'm not sure. I haven't figured that out yet. I will have to look for an opportunity."

"You don't have much time to waste. Your father cannot long survive without a soul."

"I *know*."

The witch stroked her pointed chin thoughtfully. "Hmm. It may be that I can help you get back into the castle. Yes, I think I may have a way."

"I would appreciate any help that you can give me. But . . . what did you have in mind?"

"I will show you." Sinofas raised her arms, and the raven that rode upon her shoulder lifted its dark wings and flew off. A swirling wind came from no-where. The mist eddied about the witch, entwining her arms with ghostly tendrils.

"Wait," Alexander said, alarmed. "Why don't you just *tell* me?"

Sinofas did not answer. She kept her arms raised, and shook her staff vehemently to one side. A strange white light played upon her face.

Alexander felt an odd prickling on his flesh. At first he thought that this was merely his apprehension at work; then he realized that in fact it was the power of the witch's spell touching him. A sudden dizziness overtook him. He felt a rising urge to flee, but he seemed rooted to the spot. He could not move.

Sinofas loomed huge before him, growing larger and larger. . . . But, no, it was not she who was getting bigger; it was he who was getting smaller. He was shrinking. Soon, it seemed, there would be nothing left of him.

Alexander found himself being forced into an odd crouch. His arms and legs seemed to articulate differently than they had before. They felt strange, foreign, not a part of him.

At last Sinofas lowered her arms. She leaned heavily on her staff, and gazed down upon him with the appearance of satisfaction. "There," she said. "That should do the trick. It will take the kiss of a princess to change you back. Remember that—the kiss of a princess."

With that, the witch gave a wild cackle and spun

quickly about. The mist closed around her, and she was gone.

Alexander felt very odd, in a way that he could not define. With some difficulty, he moved to the water's edge. Perched on a flat rock, he gazed down into the smooth surface of the water. He saw reflected there a round snout, a lipless mouth, and a pair of bulging eyes.

With a sense of profound shock, he realized that he had been transformed into a frog—a rather large and handsome frog, it's true, but still a frog.

The enormity of this disaster seemed at that moment crushing and insurmountable. He had thought that he had problems before, but *this*— Had Sinofas really thought that she was being helpful, or was this her idea of a joke? How could he do anything useful in this form? Despair filled his frog breast and clouded his frog eyes.

At length he realized that there was something he wanted very much to do. He resisted it for a long time, but at last he knew he had to give in.

"*Ribbet*," he said. "*Ribbet, ribbet.*"

·16·

In its way, the marsh was lovely. The mist was soft on the skin, the mud soothing to the feet. The water concealed many interesting things, some of which darted along the bottom, stirring up pretty little plumes of silt. The dragonflies that skimmed the surface looked fat and tasty.

Alexander stayed in the shallow water, submerged up to his eyes, lest a passing bird look upon him as breakfast. It was rather pleasant, really—the cool water lapping against his skin, the softness of the mud upon the webs of his feet. He drowsed while he waited.

At last Cyril stirred within the hollow tree. He sat up straight, looked about him with a bemused expression, and shifted himself from the base of the tree. "Alexander," he said, slowly climbing to his feet. "Are you here? Alexander?"

Alexander ventured from the comparative safety of the water and took several long hops in the young wizard's direction. He was starting to get the hang of moving about as a frog. Now, he wondered, could he still speak in some recognizable fashion?

"Here. Cyril. Over here." To his ears, at least, the words made sense, though they came out somewhat faint and oddly formed.

Cyril frowned and looked about him. "Alexander?"

"Here, Cyril. Look down."

The young wizard appeared to follow the sound of his voice. When his eyes met Alexander's, his frown became more profound. "Did you speak, Sir Frog?"

"That's Prince Frog, to you."

"Alexander! Is that you?"

"Unfortunately, yes."

"What . . . happened to you?"

Alexander told him. By the time he finished his story, his voice was getting tired. He was surprised that he could speak at all, since he did not have any lips worth mentioning. He guessed that it was part of the spell.

Cyril listened carefully, and when the prince finished, he said, "Interesting. Sinofas must have had a reason for what she did. I don't *think* that she could have been acting out of sheer caprice. What is it that she said—something about the kiss of a princess being necessary to change you back?"

"Yes, I think so."

"And where might we find a princess nearby?"

"Princess Lydia!"

Cyril smiled. "Princess Lydia."

"*Of course,*" Alexander said. "Lydia." It was so obvious now. That he had not thought of it himself he blamed entirely on his frog brain.

Still smiling triumphantly, Cyril said, "It seems to me that a frog would have an easier time entering Telgrin's castle unobserved than a man would."

"Yes, I expect it would." The prince sighed. "It's not a disguise that I would have chosen for myself, but it was not given to me to choose. We'll just have to use the means at hand."

It was hardly an ideal way to travel. Cyril had made a loop in his cloak, supporting it with his forearm, into which he had placed Alexander. The coarse fabric irritated the prince's amphibian hide, and he could not help but have horrified visions of the young man tripping and falling on top of him. He did not especially want to end his days as a stain on an apprentice wizard's cloak.

Cyril took a cautious path back to Telgrin's castle, staying behind the trees wherever possible and avoiding any place where he might come unawares upon one of Telgrin's knights. Finally he came to a place where a thin screen of trees overlooked the castle's main gate and stopped.

Cyril said, "Here we are. I don't think that I can get much closer without being seen."

"*Ribbet.*"

"Beg pardon?"

"Uh, this is fine."

"All right, don't be alarmed. I'm going to pick you up and set you down on the ground now."

"Very well."

An enormous hand entered Alexander's place of

concealment and closed on him. He felt himself being lifted up and brought from the folds of the cloak. As he was held out before Cyril, he had to fight back an irrational feeling of panic. Nothing in his experience had prepared him for being dangled over the ground by a giant, no matter how gentle the giant.

Bending over, Cyril set Alexander down on the ground and let him go. Once free of the confining hand, the prince felt a strong sense of relief.

"Good luck," Cyril said. "I'll wait here for you."

Alexander had been giving this some thought. "That is probably not a good idea."

"What?"

"Staying here. I may be gone for days. You have no food, no blankets, no tools. You can't even make a fire, this close to the castle. You could die of exposure and hunger, if you stay." The last of this came out sounding a little hoarse. His voice was getting tired again.

"I can't just go off and leave you."

"You must."

Cyril hesitated, appearing to consider the matter. At length he said, "If you insist, I will go off and find some supplies. But, after that, I will come back and wait for you."

"That really isn't necessary. You've done well, Cyril, but your part is done. You have done all that you can do."

"I will come back," he repeated stubbornly.

Alexander would have shaken his head, if he were still able. "Well, I can't stop you, if that's what you want to do. I . . . thank you for your dedication to the pursuit of this quest.''

Cyril flushed slightly. ''Please don't thank me. I've done little enough. I wish . . . I wish I could do more.''

Alexander gazed with dread toward the castle. It seemed that a vast stretch of open ground separated them from it, but he knew that this was mainly because of his current small size. It was actually quite near.

''I must be going,'' he said at last.

''I would that I could go with you, Prince Alexander, but you will instead have to take my good wishes.''

''Thank you, Cyril. I do appreciate it. Farewell.''

Alexander began hopping toward the castle, leaving the shelter of the trees and starting across the open ground. His main concern at this point was not that he would be seen by Telgrin or his knights; it was that he would catch the attention of some large predator. He wanted to reach the castle as quickly as he could.

He hopped, landed, gathered his hind legs under him, and hopped again. As he went, he began to get the hang of this method of locomotion, and his hops got longer and longer. He found an odd exhilaration in the process. He was doing what his present body was designed to do, and doing it well. There was a certain joy to be had in that.

As he neared the castle gate, he slowed and became more circumspect. He did not think that Telgrin's knights would think much about an approaching frog, but he could not be certain. He did not want to do anything to arouse suspicions.

The portcullis was down, sealing the gate, but that meant nothing to Alexander, in his present form. He could go right between the iron bars, with room to spare. Of more concern, however, were the two dark knights who stood guard behind the portcullis. If they should see him attempting to enter the gate, they might try to catch and forcibly eject him. If they should fail to see him, they might accidentally step on him. This last was an especially unpleasant possibility.

Alexander carefully approached the gate from the side, hopping along the side of the wall. There were numerous small pools and puddles scattered along the outer margin of the wall. The prince plunged through these happily, enjoying the sensation of the cool water on his skin.

When Alexander reached a point where he could see through the bars of the portcullis, he stopped. He watched the two knights who stood within the gate for a long while, noting that they did not move around much, if at all. They stood quite still, staring straight ahead. This made Alexander's task easier, since it meant that he did not have to worry much about a stray foot coming down on his back.

Several short, careful hops carried Alexander to the portcullis, and another carried him through the bars. As soon as he got past the two knights, he increased the length of his leaps, eager to get through the passage before he could be spotted.

At last he entered the courtyard. He was starting to get tired. Even so, he decided not to take the most direct route to the walled-off house where the Princess Lydia lived. The center of the courtyard was not safe. He could be easily seen there, and it was possible that some crossing knight or horse would crush him, without even seeing him. No, he decided, it was best to stay near the wall.

Alexander made his way along the base of the outer wall, slowly working his way to the walled-off house. From time to time, he would see or hear one of Telgrin's knights striding across the courtyard, and he would congratulate himself on his good sense.

It took a long time to work himself around to the wall that surrounded Lydia's house. The combination of the physical effort and the strain of his need for stealth had exhausted him long before he reached it. His webbed feet burned from the constant movement over the rough stone of the courtyard. He was definitely starting to tire of being a frog.

Alexander slowly circled, looking for one of those iron grates that he had noticed in the wall when he had been here before. Eventually he found one. After a brief inspection, he decided that there was enough space for him to squeeze through between the bars of the grate. On the other side of it there was the suggestion of a stone ledge, then a dark opening, which he thought to be a drain.

Not wanting to end up falling down the drain, Alexander was extremely cautious when going through the grate. He moved first his head, then his thick middle between the bars, and stood on the ledge.

The drain loomed before him, a yawning black opening. Beyond it was a row of bricks, then the start of what appeared to be an extensive and well-tended garden, at the center of which the house rose. The only way to get past the drain was to jump over it, a prospect that did not delight the prince.

After a long hesitation, Alexander carefully positioned his hind legs, making sure that his feet would not slip. Then he jumped, using every bit of strength his legs could deliver. He sailed over the dark chasm of the drain, and came down on the row of bricks. Without thinking, he jumped again. This time he landed on a small patch of grass, near a dense hedge. He paused there a moment, shivering slightly from the sudden release of suppressed tension.

As soon as he recovered, Alexander ventured under the hedge. He saw a curving garden path to his left, and followed it. He passed borders of sweet herbs, flowering hedges, and well-pruned roses. Eventually he came to a wide grassy area, at the center of which was the house.

It was a small two-story dwelling, with sharply peaked eaves and ivy climbing the sides. Before it stood a fountain of white marble. Its spout was in the shape of a pair of leaping dolphins, from whose mouths flowed a constant trickle of water. The trickling water splashed into the round pond below, where water lilies bloomed.

Alexander knew that it would be next to impossible

to gain admittance to the house in his current form, so he decided to take refuge in the fountain, at least until he could figure out what to do next. He hopped up onto the smooth marble ring surrounding the collecting pond, then slid into the green and inviting water.

The water was soothing on his skin. He swam around for a bit, before climbing out onto a lily pad and shaking his feet dry. He found it strange that he should have come to this. Here he was, Prince Alexander of Daventry, squatting on a lily pad. Life had certainly wrought its changes on him recently.

Alexander decided that he would try waiting where he was. With such a beautiful garden as this to wander in, the house's occupant would surely venture out soon.

In this, he was proved correct. After less than an hour had passed, the door opened and someone came out. It was, he saw, a girl of perhaps fourteen. She was quite pale, with masses of blonde curls framing her round face. Her gown was of pale blue, sewn with satin bows and many tiny pearls. Wearing a dreamy expression, she came down the steps and started past the fountain.

Uncertain, Alexander said, "Princess Lydia?"

She stopped, frowned, and looked around her. "Who's there?"

"Here. In the fountain. Yes, here."

Her eyes lighted upon Alexander, then widened perceptibly. "A talking frog!" she exclaimed.

"Not really. I am Alexander, Prince of Daventry.

I was transformed into what you see before you by the witch Sinofas.''

"How unfortunate!''

"It was necessary, that I might come here to see you. You *are* Princess Lydia, are you not?''

"Yes. Yes, I am. You have undergone this change, just to see *me*?'' The thought was agreeable to her, Alexander could tell.

"I have. I will explain, by and by. But first, I must ask a favor of you.''

"What is it?''

"It is, ah, rather a big favor.''

"What? Tell me.''

"I need for you to kiss me.''

She laughed. "No, you're joking.''

"I fear not. It is the only way for me to break the spell that Sinofas laid on me and regain my proper form.''

Lydia wrinkled her nose dubiously. "It is the only way? Are you certain?''

"I'm certain.''

"Well.'' She appeared to consider the matter for a moment, before saying, with reluctance in her voice, "Very well, I'll do what you ask. Come over where I can reach you.''

"A moment, Princess Lydia.'' Alexander jumped from the lily pad, splashed through the water, and pulled himself up awkwardly onto the pond's marble border. "How's this?''

"It will do, I guess.'' Carefully arranging the skirt of her gown, Lydia knelt by Alexander. She brushed her hair back over her shoulders, then hesitated. "This better not be a trick," she said in a dire voice.

"I assure you, Princess."

"All right, then." She leaned over Alexander, blotting out the sky. She screwed up her face in an expression of distaste and closed her eyes. It was all rather unflattering, the prince thought.

Lydia touched Alexander on the top of his head with her lips, as briefly and as lightly as she possibly could. Alexander felt the change beginning almost immediately, an odd quivering deep inside him, followed by the sensation that his limbs were starting to lengthen. There seemed to be an increasing weight upon him. He felt dizzy.

After a moment, Alexander looked down and saw that his hands looked like human hands again, though they had a slightly greenish cast. A moment later, they had resumed their normal color.

Alexander gave a small gasp. He was facedown on the edge of the pond, one elbow and one leg dangling in the water. Retrieving his errant limbs from the pond, he sat up and flexed one hand before his face. "Praise be," he said.

"Goodness!" Lydia said, still on her knees. "You were telling the truth. But . . . you're *beautiful!*"

"Uh, thank you."

The princess flushed bright red, and she clapped one hand to her mouth. "Did I say that aloud? *Oh.* It's just that I haven't seen that many men in my life. Hardly any, actually. I'm sure that you're really very ordinary."

"Uhm—"

"I'm not making it any better, am I?"

"It's all right. I . . . understand."

"Do you?" She beamed. "I'm so glad."

Alexander climbed to his feet, then helped Lydia up. It felt good to be standing on two feet again.

A thought appeared to occur to Lydia, for her eyes suddenly got very big, and she cast an anxious glance in the direction of the house. "But we must hide you," she said, her voice sounding urgent. "Lorell must not see you!"

"Who's Lorell?"

"I can't explain now. Come with me. *Quickly!*"

·17·

Princess Lydia opened the door and stuck her head inside. After a moment, she withdrew her head and stepped back. "The way is clear," she said quietly. "Follow me. And say nothing. We're going upstairs."

Alexander nodded. He followed the princess through the door, and found himself in a sedate foyer, its walls paneled with dark wood oiled to a soft luster, its floor of blue tile. Several open doorways led from the foyer. A wide staircase was straight ahead.

The princess went on tiptoe to the staircase, put one hand on the curved banister, and gestured with her other hand for Alexander to join her. Taking two long, gliding steps, he came to the bottom stair, as Lydia started up.

Alexander proceeded in her wake, as quietly as his booted feet would allow. When they reached the top of the staircase, they stepped out into a long corridor. Their steps here were muffled by an old, patterned rug that had been worn almost to gauze in spots.

Lydia led the way past two closed doors, then turned to enter the third. She motioned urgently for

Alexander to follow. He did, and she shut the door behind them.

Alexander glanced about him. He saw a bedchamber of generous proportions, walls of white plaster, one of them rising only half as high as the others before following the slope of the roof. The furnishings were modest. There was a small bed, its frame square and of stained oak, a big wardrobe with a bit of carved scrollwork above the doors, a trunk, two high-backed chairs, and a small desk, which stood before the window.

Lydia said, "It should be safe to speak now, if you keep your voice down."

"Is this your room?"

"Yes."

"Who is Lorell?"

"She . . . is the one who watches out for me. And just plain watches me. She must not find out that you are here."

"What would happen if she were to find me here?"

"I expect that she would tear your head off, then go to inform Telgrin."

Alexander did not like the sound of this. "She sounds formidable."

"She is. Fortunately, she is also lazy. She rarely ventures upstairs. Climbing stairs is difficult for a creature of her size."

"Creature?"

"She's not entirely human."

"Uh, in what way is she not human?"

"To begin with, she has two heads, no hair, only

three fingers on each hand, and is fully seven feet tall.''

"You're right. That doesn't sound entirely human.''

Lydia took Alexander by the hand and pulled him over near the desk. "Come, sit with me. You can't imagine how nice it is to talk with another person. I have been shut up here alone for as long as I can remember.''

The princess sat on one of the high-backed chairs, and Alexander pulled the second chair from behind the desk and sat opposite her. "Is there no one that you can talk to?''

"Well, there is Lorell, but she isn't much for conversation. And there is Telgrin, when he comes to visit, but I would prefer not to have to talk to him. He's a bit creepy, really. He says that he means to marry me, and very soon now. I'd rather marry Lorell, if it came to that. I'd rather marry the frog that you were.'' She stuck out her chin defiantly.

Alexander could well understand her feelings. In her place, he would have preferred to wed a frog, too. "Is there no one else?'' he said.

"Sometimes one of Telgrin's knights, but they rarely have anything interesting to say.'' She paused a moment, then said, "There used to be someone else, long ago. I can barely remember, now. I . . . think it was my father. He died a long time ago, but I used to dream that he would come and take me away from here.''

Alexander opened his mouth to speak, but then

stopped himself. He did not think that it was his place to tell Lydia in what gruesome state her father still lingered—at least, not without asking Owen first.

Lydia gave the prince a beatific smile. "But now you have come, and it will be you who will take me away. It's very romantic, just like in the books."

This brought Alexander up short. "What . . . do you mean?"

The princess frowned. "There's no need to be shy, Prince Alexander. I know that you have come to steal me away. It is what Telgrin has always feared. It is why he has walled me up here, and why he set Lorell to watch me. I always knew that someday someone would come."

Alexander tried to choose his words carefully, but there was no easy way to say what he had to say. "Princess Lydia, you are charming and beautiful young woman, and a man would be very lucky to steal away with you. But . . ."

"But?" she said with a frozen expression.

"But that is not the reason I came here. I did not even know of your existence before I came to this castle. I'm . . . sorry if I have disappointed you."

"I see," she said, a distinct arch to her brows. She looked away with a frown, and did not speak for a long time, while Alexander watched her uncomfortably. At last she returned her gaze to him. "If that is so, why *did* you come here?"

Alexander drew a deep breath, then told her, omitting any mention of her father and of how he had learned about the magic mirrors. She listened intently.

When he was done, she said in a flat voice, "I see. You have come to make use of my mirror. Well, this might be difficult. The mirror you described is downstairs, in a room that Lorell frequents."

"That *is* unfortunate," he said dully. It no longer surprised him when some new complication arose.

"Perhaps something can be done about that. We'll see." The princess got up briskly. "But first, you look hungry. Are you hungry? You look hungry."

"It's been a while since I've eaten," he admitted. At the mere mention of hunger, his stomach growled and his saliva started to flow.

"I'll get us something to eat. Stay here. Don't leave this room, upon your life."

"As you say, Princess Lydia."

Lydia opened the door, peered into the corridor for a moment, then went out. The door closed softly behind her.

Alexander leaned back in his chair and closed his eyes. He felt a rolling wave of fatigue washing over him. It occurred to him that it was possible that Lydia was going to betray him, now that he had disappointed her expectations. He hoped that that was not the case, but there was not much he could do about it, in any case. At this moment, he did not think he could move from this spot to save his life.

For a time, Alexander occupied that twilight area between wakefulness and sleep, his thoughts centered on nothing at all. The sound of the door opening brought him back to full awareness.

Alexander opened his eyes and saw Lydia coming

into the room, burdened with a wooden tray loaded with foodstuffs. She shut the door behind her with one foot. He started to rise, but she brusquely told him to sit.

The princess set the tray down on the desk. "Come," she said. "Eat."

He did, with considerable zeal. She had brought cold roast chicken, good brown bread, soft cheese, stalks of crisp celery, pears, and a flask of sweet cider. Lydia hardly ate at all, he noticed. Instead, she devoted herself to urging him to eat more. It seemed that, now that she knew he had not come to spirit her away, she had decided to behave toward him as a bossy younger sister.

Finally he was forced to put up his hands and say, "No more! No more! You will make me fat."

Lydia put down the platter that she had been offering him. She sat in the chair across from him and fixed him with a pensive gaze. "I have been giving some thought to your problem. It may be that I have a solution. First, though, I need to know something. When you leave this castle, will you take me with you?"

Alexander gave her a steady look and said, sincerely, "If you wish to leave this castle, I will help you. I will take you to Castle Daventry, and see to it that you are treated in a manner such as befits your station, when I've finished my task here."

"Do you promise?"

"I promise."

Lydia gave a quick, decisive nod. "Good."

"Now, what is this about a solution to my problem?"

"Yes, the mirror. How long will you need in order to do what you have to do?"

"I'm not sure. I'll have to wait until the vessel containing my father's soul is unattended before I can step through the mirror. This could take some time. Why do you ask?"

"We'll have to get Lorell out of the house while you use the mirror. I have an idea of how to do this, but I'm not sure how long I can keep her occupied."

Alexander gave the matter a few moments' thought. "We could just wait until Lorell is asleep. This should give me more than enough time."

"No," Lydia said. "We can't."

"Why not?"

"I told you that Lorell has two heads. What I didn't tell you is that one head is always awake whenever the other head is asleep. Telgrin left little to chance when he chose my guardian."

"It would seem that he has been uncommonly thorough," Alexander said, shaking his head.

"We will wait until tonight before we try my plan. I've noticed that Lorell's nighttime head does not seem to be quite as clever as her daytime head. It should be easier to trick. And the darkness will be an added help."

When the last of the day's light had faded from the window and the sky beyond showed a somber purple, Lydia rose from the side of the bed where she had sat for the better part of the last hour. "It is time," she said.

The princess went to the wardrobe, opened it, and knelt down before it. She shifted a stack of folded garments from one side to the other and, reaching under a layer of paper, brought out a large leather-bound book.

Tucking this volume under one arm, she rose and went to the desk. She placed the book on the desk, opened it, and began turning the heavy pages, scanning each in turn.

She said, "Once, when Telgrin let me visit the keep, I took this from his study. He would not be pleased if he knew that I had it."

"What is it?"

"It is a volume of ancient spellcraft and arcane lore. I've been secretly studying it and practicing the spells that it contains."

Alexander said, "I've heard it said that it is extremely ill-advised to attempt to learn magic without a master."

Lydia shrugged, unconcerned. "Magic is in my blood. My father was a very great magician, or so I've been told."

"Even so."

"Do you want my help or not?"

Alexander sighed. "Forget that I said anything."

The princess continued to page the book for some minutes. Finally she stopped on a page about midway through the book and studied it at length. "Yes," she said. "This should do very nicely."

"What will? What are you planning?"

Ignoring his questions, she said, "I will need your cloak. And your hat."

Frowning, Alexander took his hat and cloak from the back of the chair where he had put them. He handed them to the princess. He suppressed the urge to ask yet more questions. She seemed determined to do this her own way. There was nothing to be gained from irritating her.

With a meticulous air, Lydia put the cloak on the floor before the desk, then placed the hat on top of it. She came around behind the desk, and studied the book again, by the flickering light of a single white taper.

Alexander stood to one side of her. He tried to read the spell that she had turned to, but it was inscribed in a curious script that he could not make any sense of. Even so, there was something about that page that brought a chill to his heart, as though the symbols set down there had some power independent of their meaning.

Lydia closed her eyes and held her arms out before her, palms down. In a low voice, she began intoning a guttural phrase from a language that the prince did not understand. She seemed to repeat the same phrase over and over again, her tone increasingly fervent.

Alexander felt the power of the spell rising within the confines of the room, making the hairs on the back of his neck prickle and start to rise. The air stirred softly. The cloak and hat on the floor appeared strangely luminous.

Lydia made a sudden gesture, sweeping her arms to either side. The hat and cloak gave a twitch, were still a moment, then twitched again. Slowly they began to rise. The hat floated up first, and the cloak followed, spreading as it rose, until it almost appeared that a person occupied it. The hat seemed to perch upon an invisible head.

Lydia lowered her arms with a sigh. Fatigue showed clearly on her young face. "Now, we shall see," she said.

·18·

With a firm gaze, Princess Lydia faced the hat-and-cloak that floated before her in the dimly lit room. "Come here," she commanded.

The disembodied hat-and-cloak dutifully shambled over to her, neatly avoiding the intervening desk. "Good," she said. "Now back a step."

The hat-and-cloak did as it was told. Alexander could almost swear that a man inhabited it, for it stood like a man, moved like a man, and even appeared to possess the attitude of a man. He would say that it cocked its head attentively to one side while waiting for its next instruction, except of course that it had no head to cock.

"Walk around the room for a while," Lydia said. The hat-and-cloak began patrolling the borders of the room, the cloak billowing out from where ankles should be.

"Interesting," Alexander said. "But how is this supposed to help me get past Lorell?"

"We need a distraction, something to get her out of the house—and keep her out. This should do nicely, as long as she doesn't get too close."

"I see. Yes, I think I do see. How do you propose that we proceed?"

"Try to open that window there. Careful, it sometimes sticks."

Alexander went to the big double window, turned the latch, and pushed. As Lydia had warned it would, the window resisted for a moment. He kept a firm pressure on it, however, and at last it gave way with a shudder.

Lydia turned to the hat-and-cloak. *"Stop,"* she said. "Come here." The hat-and-cloak ceased its aimless roaming about the room and went to the princess.

"Listen carefully," Lydia said. "I am about to give you your instructions. When I am done, I will tell you to go, and you will then follow those instructions exactly. But not until then."

The princess squeezed her eyes shut for a moment, then opened them again. "When I tell you to, you will go out the window and into the garden below. You will then retreat beyond the first hedge, where you will stay until the two-headed woman comes out of the house. She will try to catch you, but you must not let her. You may go anywhere in the garden, but you must not return to the house."

She paused a moment, then said, "All right. *Go.*"

Eerily silent, the hat-and-cloak went to the window and flew out of it. Alexander watched it drift to the ground and then start away from the house. As it receded into a garden touched only with the silvery light of the moon, the illusion became more convincing. He could have sworn that it was a man out there, and not merely a pair of enchanted garments.

As soon as the hat-and-cloak reached the first hedge and went behind it, Lydia said, "It is time for me to talk to Lorell. Stay here until I return." The princess went to the door, opened it, and stepped through into the corridor beyond. She closed the door behind her.

Alexander waited by the window for several moments. Finally, however, his curiosity got the better of him. He made his way quietly to the door, opened it a crack, and stood there listening.

At length he heard voices coming from below. The first belonged to Lydia. It sounded excited and concerned. "Lorell, Lorell, come quickly! There is a man in the garden! Do you hear? A *man*!"

There was a ponderous stirring. Heavy footsteps made the downstairs floorboards groan. A rough, growling voice said, *"What?* Where? Show me!"

"There. Behind the hedge. Do you see?"

"A man," Lorell said in a voice full of hostility and contempt. "I will take care of him, Princess. Stay inside. I will make this *man* regret his trespass."

"Oh, hurry, hurry, hurry! I am so frightened."

"I'm going. Bolt the door behind me."

When he heard the front door open and close, Alexander went back to the window and gazed out, careful to make sure that he could not be spotted from the outside. He saw a great bulky shape start to cross the garden, which he assumed to be Lorell. She was not much to look at. Neither of her two heads had any hair, and each came to a definite point. One of the heads lolled to one side, apparently asleep. From what he could see of the features of her two faces, they were extremely blunt and unpleasant.

Lorell was very broad across the shoulders and hips. Her arms were brawny, and in one hand she held a knotty cudgel of dark wood. She wore a skirt and bodice of a coarse, colorless fabric. As she went, she called out, "Come here, come here, man, man, man! Come to Lorell, my pretty man."

Before Lorell could clear the fountain, the hat-and-cloak started away along the line of the hedge. In the darkness, it looked just like a fleeing man. When it reached the end of the hedge, it turned toward the outer wall.

"Come back!" Lorell cried. "Come to me, little man!" She hastened after the retreating hat-and-cloak, taking long, lurching steps, and holding her cudgel aloft. "You have nothing to fear from me, man, man, man!"

Face flushed, breath coming shallow and fast, Lydia returned to the bedchamber. Standing in the doorway, she said, "It's done. Come quickly. I don't know how long this will keep Lorell away."

Alexander followed the princess into the corridor and down the stairs. They went from the foyer into a gloomy room filled with dark, stolid furniture: a big griffin-footed desk, tall bookcases heavy with dusty tomes, a sideboard, several chairs upholstered in murky green fabric, and a low, ugly sideboard.

The princess led Alexander to a shallow niche set

into the wall to one side of the desk. There, hanging on the wall, was the exact mate of the mirror in the tower. It had the same lustrous black frame, inscribed with the same strange symbols. The mirror gave the same impression of unnatural depth.

As soon as he saw it, the prince felt his heart start to race. Here it was, the means for regaining his father's soul. For a time, he had thought that he might never come this close to it again.

"Do what you must do," Lydia said. "But do it as swiftly as you can."

"I'll try."

Alexander faced the mirror. Each in its turn, he touched those three special symbols impressed upon the mirror's frame, saying, "You are a window through which I can see. You are a door through which I may walk. You are the way between the High and Low Kingdoms. Open, as Owen bade you."

As before, when he had so manipulated the mirror in the tower, it seemed that a haze had come over the images on the surface of the mirror, and other, deeper images began to drift to the fore. Alexander concentrated on these, willing them to appear fully.

With agonizing slowness, the image of another room began to appear from the depths and solidify. He recognized it. It was Telgrin's workroom.

There was a shadowy figure moving about the room. When Alexander focused his full attention on it, he realized that it was Telgrin himself. The magician-king was standing beside the shimmering sphere that Alexander knew contained the soul of his father, and regarding it with an intent expression. He was saying something, but it came to Alexander only as a muffled and distorted murmur. He concentrated on the words, and suddenly he could hear them plainly. It was as if a thick door had suddenly been thrown open.

"... *must relent,*" Telgrin was saying. "You cannot continue to resist me for very much longer. Why do you not give in to the inevitable? At the very least you will save yourself a great deal of pain and unpleasantness."

Alexander saw the pale, flickering facsimile of his father's face floating within the sphere. That face looked exhausted, in pain, but there was a grim resolve in its eyes. A faint, heartbreakingly familiar sounded from the sphere: "*Never.* I will never surrender my will to you, Telgrin."

"You must. Eventually you must."

"No."

"You have already resisted me for longer than any of the others. You have *proved* yourself. No one could expect more. It is time, time to put an end to the pain. Let it go, and you will find rest. Wouldn't that be a relief? Rest. An end to your misery. All you have to do is surrender yourself to me. It is such a little thing."

"I will not."

"Your will is strong, King of Daventry. Truly, you will be the greatest of my servants, when I finally break you. And break you I will. Sooner or later, I will. I have all the time in the world. Don't you understand? Forever. I have forever. Can you resist me forever?''

"I can, I will, I must."

"Now you are just being stubborn. There is no virtue in being stubborn, after all hope has fled. We know, both of us, what your future will be. The only question is when that future will begin, isn't it?''

"You may think that you know my future, but I certainly do not."

Telgrin sighed. "Graham, Graham, Graham, I thought we had already established what your future will be. Don't you remember? You will become mine, and serve me in all things. That is your only possible destiny. So, again I ask you—will you relent?''

"No."

"I begin to weary of this. Your conversation lacks all subtlety and depth. Do you want to taste the power of the Jewel of Orkae again?''

"Of course I don't.''

"You can avoid it. It really is up to you. Surrender up your will to me now, and you need have nothing more to do with it.''

A pause. "No."

Telgrin threw up his hands. "So be it! You have made your choice. I hope that you will be happy with it.''

The magician-king moved a peculiar device into place beside the sphere containing Graham's soul. The device consisted of a weighted base of polished brass, from the center of which rose a round post. At the top of the post was affixed an articulated metal arm, which had at its end a heavy iron loop. The loop held a faceted gem of somber purple hue. As Telgrin positioned the gem above the sphere, it glinted with a malignant gleam.

Telgrin said, "A last chance, Graham. Will you change your mind?"

Graham did not answer.

"As you wish, then." Telgrin took up his staff and touched it briefly to the gem. A murky glow blossomed within the gem, and a beam of purple light shot from it, striking the sphere containing Graham's soul.

Graham cried out. Bathed in that evil light, the image of his face became distorted and strange. It was obvious that the beam flowing from the gem had begun to inflict a terrible torment upon him. His pain filled the room with an almost palpable presence— like heat, like light, like sound.

Alexander had to fight back his desire to step through the mirror and put an end to his father's agony. His head told him that to attempt to do so now would be a doomed gesture. Telgrin was there, staff in hand. The prince could not hope to escape the room with his father's soul while that was so; he would have to wait, wait for the proper moment. That was what his head told him.

His heart, however, told him something altogether different. It said that to delay was cowardice or worse, that practical considerations did not matter, that all that was important was stopping his father's pain.

Head and heart continued to wage their war all the

while he watched, with the counsel of his head narrowly winning the battle. Alexander remained frozen at the threshold of the mirror, helpless.

With apparent satisfaction, Telgrin looked down upon Graham's tormented face. "I'll just leave you to enjoy the kiss of the Jewel of Orkae now, Graham. Perhaps when I return—if I return—you will think better of your stubbornness."

With that, humming a cheery tune and swinging his staff as he went, Telgrin strode from the room, leaving the gem to inflict its agonies on Graham's soul.

Alexander had never felt such temptation before in his life. The room was empty and unguarded. All he would have to do was to step through the mirror and take the sphere that contained his father's soul. There was no one to stop him. He could do it now, do it easily.

But he had promised Owen that he would not take the soul until he could also get Telgrin's staff. He had given his solemn word. At this moment that seemed a small thing, lacking all weight and substance, and yet he could not escape the knowledge that in the end it was everything. If he were to leave Owen to his solitary suffering when there was a chance that he could help him regain his liberty, was he really any better than Telgrin?

His father's pain spoke powerfully to him, making abstract considerations of good and evil, right and wrong, trust and betrayal seem as nothing. But he knew. He knew that they were *not* nothing, and so he remained poised where he was, his heart full of bitter conflict.

After long minutes had passed, Telgrin returned to the room, still humming, still cheerful. Alexander could not help feeling that he had missed an opportunity, one that might never come again.

Telgrin went over to the sphere containing Graham's soul and peered into it for a moment. Then, chuckling to himself, he propped his staff against the side of the table and busied himself with various other articles that he found there. He inspected a bell-shaped vessel filled with a churning liquid, consulted a brown and crumbling scroll, took a pinch of a yellow powder from a dish and sprinkled it into the liquid. After watching the liquid foam and change color, he shook his head and went to the desk in the corner. He stood hunched over a thick leather-bound book, slowly turning pages and muttering to himself.

Alexander watched this activity with a rising excitement. Telgrin had left his staff unattended. The prince wondered if he could reach it before Telgrin could. It seemed likely that he could, but he could not be certain. He knew that he might never have a better chance, though.

There was one other question that made Alexander hesitate: how much of Telgrin's power was bound up in the staff? Once he had the staff and the sphere in his possession, it would take him several moments to reach the mirror again and go through it—enough time for Telgrin to stop him with a spell of some kind.

Indecisive, the prince bit the inside of his lip. If only he could think of some way to keep Telgrin occupied for a short while . . .

As he looked from Telgrin, to the staff, to the sphere, an idea occurred to Alexander. He was not sure that it would work, but he knew that he had to try.

It was time to act.

Alexander took a step forward. For an instant he felt a yielding resistance on his flesh, but then it was gone. His foot came down in a different room than the one it had risen in. He found himself in Telgrin's workroom, battling a churning sense of disorientation.

Telgrin must have heard him, or caught some glimpse of movement, for he began to look up from his book. Knowing that he did not have a moment to spare, Alexander dashed for Telgrin's staff.

Uttering a harsh cry of alarm, Telgrin started for the staff himself, but he was too late. Alexander closed his fingers on its dark shaft, and he held it aloft. The staff communicated a peculiar sensation through the prince's fingers and down his arm, a subtle vibration, which made his hand feel numb.

"You!" Telgrin cried. "What are you doing with that? Give it here!"

"I think not," Alexander said, edging toward the sphere that held his father's soul.

"It will do you no good. You don't know what to do with it, you fool."

"It's enough to know that I have it—and you don't."

"It's a mere inconvenience to me. Do you think that I was so foolish as to invest all of my power in the staff? Even now, I can kill you where you stand."

Telgrin raised one hand ominously, and his sleeve fell back from a thin, white forearm. "Farewell, Alexander!" he said.

At that instant, Alexander swung the tip of the staff

to one side, striking the device that held the Jewel of Orkae and causing it to turn. The beam of purple light left the sphere on which it had been focused and flashed about the room, until it finally centered on Telgrin's breast.

The magician-king gasped and fell back against the wall. For a moment he appeared to be pinned there, transfixed by the power of the Jewel of Orkae, but then he slid slowly down the wall, and fell beneath the level of the purple beam.

Gingerly Alexander grasped the sphere containing his father's soul and hurried for the mirror. When he reached it, he could see the reflection of Telgrin gathering himself together and staggering to his feet, careful to avoid the purple beam.

Alexander leaned the staff against the wall, to free one hand, and quickly performed the actions needed to activate the mirror. As he took up the staff again, he concentrated on the mirror, attempting to bring the room in Lydia's house back into focus. It was easier this time, either because he was learning the trick of the mirrors, or because he knew well what the room he was trying to reach looked like.

He saw the room take shape, going from dim to bright, hazy to sharp, and he prepared to step through. At that moment he caught sight of a flash of movement in the residually reflective surface of the mirror. It was large and bright, and it was moving fast.

Alexander plunged through into the room beyond, almost tripping and falling in his haste to escape the mirror. At the very instant he entered the room, he heard a hiss and a shudder behind him.

He turned, and saw that it appeared that a fireball had struck the other side of the mirror. Its face was sooty black at the center, and silvery fracture lines ran in all directions from the blackened area.

Alexander let out a soft sigh. That had been a very near thing.

"Goodness!" Lydia said, staring wide-eyed at what was left of the mirror. "What happened?"

"I'm not exactly sure. All I know is that Telgrin came uncomfortably close to killing me."

Lydia's gaze went from the mirror, to Alexander, and then to the staff. "You have Telgrin's staff!"

"Yes."

"Let me see!" Lydia reached excitedly for the staff.

"Sorry, no," he said firmly. "I have plans for it, and I don't intend to let it out of my possession until those plans are realized."

Frowning, the young woman let her hand fall. "Small wonder that Telgrin wanted to kill you."

Alexander was not sure to what degree peevishness had inspired that observation, and at that moment he did not care. He sat on the edge of one of the chairs, leaned the staff against his shoulder, and held the sphere before him.

"Father," he said. "Can you hear me? It's me, Alexander."

Movement flickered within the sphere. Slowly he saw Graham's frowning face take form. The king's voice sounded very faint: "Alexander? How? Where?"

"I've stolen the vessel containing your essence from Telgrin. We are still in his castle, but I hope to escape it, after I do one last thing here."

"How is your mother? And Daventry? How fares Daventry?"

"Both are well, as far as I know."

"And *you*, my son. How are you?"

"Relieved. You have no idea of what I've gone through, to get you back."

"I can imagine. I'm . . . relieved myself. I don't know how much longer I could have borne Telgrin's treatment. It was very . . . hard on me."

"I know. I had to watch while Telgrin used the Jewel of Orkae against you. Listen, Father, I don't have much time. It won't take Telgrin long to figure out what I did and track me down. I must be on the move again soon. But . . . I was wondering if you know how fragile this vessel is? I wouldn't want to break it."

"I don't think that you *can* break it. When Telgrin was tormenting me, he said that magic had created it, and that only magic could open it."

Alexander nodded. "That's good to know. I won't worry about it, then." He drew a deep breath and let it out slowly. "Well, it's time for me to go now. Is there anything that I can do for you, before I put this vessel away?"

"No, nothing. Good luck, my son. I wish that I could help you, somehow."

"Thank you, Father."

Alexander opened the front of his jerkin and put the sphere inside, tucking it down near his belt, which he thought would keep it from falling out. Closing his jerkin, he stood up and glanced at the ruined mirror.

"Well," he said, "it doesn't look like I'll be going anywhere through *that*. I'll have to go out through the garden."

"You can't. Lorell is still out there."

Alexander gave a sudden frown. He had forgotten about Lorell. "I'll have to risk it," he said at length.

"I'm going with you."

"It would be better if you didn't."

"You said that you would take me with you. You *promised*."

"I know, but—"

"Anyway, you *have* to take me. I have something that you need."

"What's that?"

"The key to the garden gate."

They left the house and closed the door behind them. The garden was dark, but there was enough of a moon that Alexander knew that they would not pass entirely unobserved, if Lorell happened to cast a glance in their direction. He heard thrashing and cursing off to the left, so he pointed Lydia toward the right.

Lydia went first, since she knew the garden better than Alexander did. She led the way past the fountain, then behind the first hedge, to the right, behind a second hedge, to the left, until they came to a stone-rimmed circle planted with roses. The roses were red,

Alexander supposed, but in the darkness they looked black. Here Lydia paused for a moment.

"Which way?" Alexander whispered.

"That way. No, that way. No—"

"You don't *know*?"

"I don't often come out here at night. Yes, it *is* that way, after all. Come on."

They went through a narrow gap in a hedge, to the right, along a patch planted with fragrant herbs, around the side of another hedge, and then to the left. Here they found a gravel path, which led them along the inside of the wall.

"The gate is there," Lydia said.

"Where?"

"*There.*"

Finally he saw it. It was only a few yards away. They were nearly past the first danger.

They were mere feet from the gate, and Lydia had her key out, when Alexander heard something behind him. He turned just in time to see his hat and cloak come running by, pursued hotly by Lorell.

Apparently seeing Alexander and Lydia, the two-headed woman suddenly stopped short. She was, if anything, even more hideous up close. She scowled at the two, fingering her big cudgel. "Lydia!" she said. "What are you doing out here? And who is this *man*?"

·20·

Lorell held Alexander steady in her gaze, lofting up her nasty-looking cudgel. "Come here, man, man, man," she said. "I wish to speak to you."

"I can hear you from where I am."

"*Come here!*" she commanded sternly. At that moment her second head, which had been lolling drowsily to one side, appeared to wake. It opened its eyes, blinked, and said, "Hmph. What's happening? Where am I?"

"It's all right, dear," the first head said. "Go back to sleep. I'm just going to kill this man here."

"Oh, that's all right, then."

Lorell started moving menacingly on Alexander, when Lydia suddenly shouted, "Wait! Come back here." Lorell frowned, perplexed, obviously not able to see the hat-and-cloak behind her stop and start back toward Lydia.

"Throw yourself over her heads," Lydia said. "*Now!*"

The hat-and-cloak obeyed, sailing up and engulfing Lorell's heads. She uttered a startled exclamation and tried to tear the cloak from her, but it resisted her fiercely, twisting itself around her throats.

"Come on," Lydia said. She put her key into the garden door and turned. The door swung open, and Lydia and Alexander hastened through it. Lydia paused to lock the door behind them. "Where do we go now?"

Alexander considered the question for a moment. He had to get the staff to Owen, and there were two ways that he could do that. One way was to go through the keep; the other was to go through the tower. All in all, the tower seemed the better choice.

"This way. The tower."

Alexander worried as they walked. He had no doubt but that the tower would still be full of Telgrin's knights. He did not know if they ever slept; he thought not. How were they to get past the knights and into the basements below the tower?

The two reached the base of the tower and circled around to the main entrance, which was at the top of a short flight of stairs. They climbed the stairs and stood on the cramped platform at the top. Alexander hesitated before the oaken door, afraid of what he might find on the other side.

"I wish I were invisible," he muttered.

"What did you say?" Lydia frowned. "Where are you? Where did you go?"

"Very funny. I'm right here," he muttered.

She looked dubiously at him—or seemingly through him. "No," she said. "You're not."

Alexander still thought that she was having a joke at his expense, until he chanced to look at his hand,

and saw that it was not there. "By heavens! I'm *not* here!"

"What happened to you?"

He wondered about that himself. *Could it be . . .* "The staff," he said. "Telgrin's staff. I wished that I was invisible. It must have carried out my wish."

He looked at Lydia. "I wish that you were invisible, too." With that, the princess's form shimmered, distorted slightly, and abruptly vanished.

Alexander said, "Amazing. It worked. Well, well, this should make things easier." He turned to put his hand on the iron ring set into the door, and found that this was surprisingly difficult and disconcerting when one's hand was invisible.

He said, "Wait a minute, I've got it. I wish that we were both invisible—to everyone except ourselves."

The air flickered oddly for a moment, and then Lydia suddenly reappeared to Alexander. He saw, too, that he could again see his own hand. "That's better."

Grasping the ring, Alexander turned it and pushed the door open. Red-gold torchlight spilled out onto the platform. The prince hastily ushered Lydia across the threshold. As soon as he was inside, he saw one of Telgrin's knights coming down the hall toward him, and it suddenly occurred to him to doubt whether the spell of invisibility would fool such a supernatural creature.

He was therefore relieved when the knight walked right past him, on his way to the door. A flat voice from deep within the tower said, "One-Who-Was-Douglas, who's that at the door?"

"No one," the knight said. "It must have been the wind."

"Well, make sure the door is latched this time."

"Aye." The knight shut the door, checked to see that it was latched, then turned and went back in the direction from which he had come.

"He didn't see us," Lydia whispered, after the knight had gone.

"*Shhhh.*"

Alexander stood where he was for a moment, while he looked around and tried to get his bearings. There was a central corridor and two smaller side corridors leading from this antechamber, and he was not quite sure of which way to go. "To the right, I think," he said softly.

He led Lydia into the right-hand corridor, and found that it did not look familiar. At the far end, on the left side, there was a narrow arch, however, and he decided that they should investigate it before giving up on this way.

When they reached the end of the corridor and looked through the arch, Alexander was happy to see that he recognized this place. It was the short hall that led to both the stairs and the vestibule where the remaining undamaged mirror hung. On the right was the door to the small room that gave access to the tower's basement.

Alexander made his way quickly to this room. After stepping inside and waiting for Lydia to follow, he shut the door behind them. He crossed to the door on the other side of the room, opened it, and went through. Here he paused and looked down the long staircase that descended into the gloom of the tower's basement.

Lydia joined him, and the two went slowly down the staircase, then through the iron gate at the bottom. Alexander hesitated here for a moment, as he tried to recall where the hatch leading down into the lower dungeons was. It seemed as if it had been a long time since he had been here before, though in fact it was only a day.

After finally remembering the way, Alexander led Lydia past massive stone pillars and the mounds of barrels and crates, until they came to the dark gap in the floor. It was as he had left it, with the metal plate that normally covered it off to one side.

After a brief consideration, he said, ''I think it would work best if I took you by the hands and lowered you down.''

Lydia stared down into the darkened hole and wrinkled her nose. ''Where does it go?''

''Into the dungeons under the castle.''

''Is there some concealed way out of the castle down there?''

''Not that I know of.''

''Then why . . . ?''

''There's someone that I must see,'' he said evasively.

''Who?''

Alexander shook his head. "There's no time to discuss this now. Come on."

Lydia made her mouth a thin line of dissatisfaction, but she did not persist. Alexander leaned his staff against the wall, took the princess by the hands and supported her while she backed awkwardly into the hole. He held her suspended in the opening for a moment, then slowly lowered her down. Eventually her feet touched the floor below, and he let go of her hands.

After reclaiming the staff, the prince sat with his legs dangling into the opening. He carefully slid his bottom from the floor, caught himself with his elbows, then let himself drop. He took the landing with flexed knees, staggered slightly, then finally caught his balance.

Alexander looked about the small, square room and located the stone stairway. "I'll go down first," he said. "Watch out. Some of the steps are loose."

The two made their way to the bottom of the stairs without incident. Alexander felt the wooden panel that bounded the small space in which they stood, found the catch, and pushed on it. With a faint click, the panel opened inward. The prince held it while Lydia went through, then followed.

As Alexander went down the corridor with the carved faces on the wall, he realized that he was starting to feel extremely tired. No, not tired, exactly—enervated, drained. He felt as though the vitality of his body were being drawn away. The hand that held the staff felt numb and cold, and that sensation extended all the way down his arm and into his chest now.

It suddenly occurred to him that he had never canceled the spell of invisibility, and he wondered if it was the effort of sustaining it that was draining him. It was a definite possibility, he decided.

"I wish that we both were visible again," he said. He saw Lydia's form flicker slightly, then grow steady. After a few moments, he decided that, although he was not feeling immediately better, at least he was not continuing to feel progressively worse.

Alexander believed that what he had just experienced must be similar to the exhaustion that overtook Cyril each time he used magic, though perhaps not as strong. This gave him more of an appreciation for the price that the apprentice wizard had paid in order to work his spells.

The prince was still surprised that the staff had worked so well for him. He had not even consciously tried to cast the spell of invisibility over himself and Lydia, and it had worked anyway. Simply wishing was enough. The staff seemed almost to possess an intelligence of sorts, which worked to carry out the desires of the person who held it. No wonder Owen and Telgrin prized it so.

Alexander and Lydia came to the end of the corridor, passed the lighted grille set high on the wall, then went down the stone stairway that descended into the chamber with the dark pool in the center. "Wait here," Alexander told Lydia, once they reached the bottom. "Don't come any farther yet." He started toward the obelisk that supported the crystal sphere, then stopped. Something was not right.

A ghastly green light had suddenly filled the chamber. It was coming from a point a few yards ahead of him and slightly above his head, from the middle of the empty air. At first it showed as a bright, tightly confined mote, but then a wide beam stabbed forth from it and swept over the chamber.

The beam overtook Alexander before he could avoid it, and there it stopped. He could feel its unnatural energies prickling his flesh, potent and with the unmistakable touch of evil. Raising one hand to screen his eyes, he peered up into the green mote of light.

The mote had a shape, he suddenly realized. As he studied it, that shape resolved and became plain. The shape was the shape of Telgrin's face—a bleak and scowling face. An angry face.

Alexander heard the magician-king's voice, as if from a great distance: *"So, I have found you.* I don't recognize this place. Where are you?"

"What do you want, Telgrin?"

"What do you think? You've stolen my staff. I want it back."

"That's too bad. I'm fairly sure that I don't want to give it to you."

"I suggest that you think better on that. You'll never escape this castle alive without my permission. Return my staff to me, and I will let you take the soul of your precious Graham and go. I promise you."

"What assurance do I have that, once you have the staff in your hands again, you won't conveniently forget all about this conversation?''

"You have my word."

Alexander laughed bitterly. "And how much do you think *that* is worth?"

"Give me the staff, or I will simply kill you now and take it."

"No."

"Perhaps you don't fully appreciate your position. I could kill you now, if I wanted."

"I don't think so," Alexander said defiantly. He wished that he was actually as confident as he tried to sound.

The magician-king made an exasperated sound. "Is *everyone* in Daventry this obstinate? Very well, I suppose that I'll just have to show you."

The beam of light that held Alexander transfixed flashed suddenly brighter, striking the prince with a terrible force. He gasped and rocked back on his heels. It felt as if the light were burning slowly through his flesh. The pain was almost unbearable.

Somehow, without even thinking about how to do it, Alexander raised the staff and called upon its power. The small crystal that topped the staff burned with a dazzling light, and a jagged bolt shot from it, striking the glowing face that floated above him square in the eye.

"*Aieeee!*" Telgrin shrieked, as his image was shattered into a thousand streaming shards. An instant later there was a thunderous explosion, which threw Alexander back a pace, shielding his face with his arm. The castle's very foundations trembled, sending

down showers of rock and powdered mortar. The
stone obelisk tipped, sending the crystal sphere that
had sat atop it crashing to the floor, where it was
dashed into tiny pieces.

Alexander glanced behind him, to where Lydia
stood, obviously paralyzed with fright. The great column at her back rocked ponderously and began to
topple. Seeing that Lydia was about to be crushed,
Alexander dropped the staff and grabbed hold of her,
spun her about, and flung her out of the way. Then,
afraid that he was himself now in a position to be
crushed, he threw himself at her feet and rolled to the
side.

The column came crashing down, its great length
instantly fracturing into several shorter segments
when it struck the floor. Small bits of rubble rained
down from the jagged hole it had left in the ceiling,
and then this ceased.

All was quiet, for a moment.

·21·

The darkness was almost complete. Apparently the magically induced tremor had sealed off some of the hidden sources that had provided whatever light there had been. Either that, or Alexander's eyes had still not recovered from staring into the green light. It took a few moments for him to be able to discern anything but the largest of shapes.

Nostrils burning from the falling dust, Alexander climbed wearily to his feet. It seemed that working whatever spell it was that had destroyed Telgrin's image had taken most of his remaining strength. His thoughts were hazy with fatigue.

Alexander saw Lydia's dark shape before him. "Are you all right?"

"Yes," she said. "I think so. How about you?"

"I'll live, I think."

Alexander kept looking around him. The darkness did not seem to be getting any less pervasive. "Can you see where the staff went?"

"I can't see *anything.*"

"Hmm. I think it rolled over this way." Hunched over, eyes straining, Alexander searched the floor a little beyond the princess. *Where was it?*

"Uh, Alexander," Lydia said, in the nonchalant tone of one trying very hard not to show alarm. "Is that your hand on my knee?"

"No. Why would you think that I have my hand on your knee?"

"Because— *Waugh!*" Abruptly she flew up into the air, then came down again, landing hard on her bottom. She began sliding toward the pool in the center of the chamber, almost as if she were being dragged.

Dragged. In the excitement, he had forgotten all about the creature in the pond! Uttering a hoarse cry, he leapt for the princess, reaching her just before her feet met the water.

There was something sinewy and darkly glistening wrapped about her knees, he saw. He grabbed hold of the tentacle—for that was what he knew it to be—and attempted to pry it off, but it was as if it were glued to her. He tried pounding it with his fist, to no better result.

Lydia's feet entered the water, and then her calves. She began to thrash about and screech, while Alexander wrestled vainly with the tentacle. In another moment or two, Lydia would be dragged into the water, and there was nothing that he could do about it.

Then he saw it, there at the edge of the pond, the small crystal on its end glimmering faintly: Telgrin's staff. Reaching out, he seized the staff and held it aloft. "Light! Light! Light!" he cried.

The crystal atop the staff abruptly blazed with a searing blue-white light. Alexander caught one fleeting glimpse of the creature in the pool—its round eye, lustrous grey flesh, and curved beak—before it recoiled and slid beneath the greasy surface of the water.

The creature, however, had not released the princess. She was almost up to her hips in the pool, and was still being drawn in. In what was an automatic reaction, Alexander thrust the head of the staff into the water, where he knew the tentacle to be. The water boiled angrily around the staff, and there was a loud hiss.

The tentacle suddenly uncoiled from around the princess and flipped up into the air—long enough for Alexander to see the red welt that the staff had inflicted—then it quickly slid down into the dark pool.

Alexander pulled the glowing staff from the water, then went to help Lydia up. The princess clasped herself to him with alarming fervor, shivering and gasping. "*Thank you,*" she said at length. "I thought that it had me for sure."

"It's all right, it's all right, it's all right," he kept saying, until eventually she stopped shivering and pulled away. "Well," she said, in an obvious attempt to rescue her dignity, "what now?"

"We cross the bridge."

"Oh." She cast a look of loathing at the murky pool. "If we must."

"Careful, then."

"You don't have to worry about that!"

The princess gingerly crossed the bridge, one slow step after another. Alexander followed, with scarcely less caution. Once on the other side, they entered the narrow corridor leading away from the chamber and followed it for a short time, until they came to that chamber where Alexander had first encountered the barikar.

Alexander hesitated here. He turned to the massive oaken door through which he had first entered this chamber. Holding the staff before him, he said, "Bolt, slide. Door, open."

The door shuddered. Alexander could hear the bolt on the other side draw back, and suddenly the door sprang open. A faint light showed through the narrow opening.

Alexander lowered the staff, utterly exhausted. He realized then that he had left the light burning in the crystal, and that it was draining away his life force. He said, softly, "Light, off." The blue-white radiance faded and died away.

Alexander turned to Lydia. He said, "Wait here. There is something that I must do. You should be safe enough here until I get back. If you should feel threatened, though, that door leads up into the keep."

"Why can't I go with you?"

Alexander shook his head slowly. "Just . . . wait. Please."

Alone, he went to the entrance of the corridor that eventually led to Owen's place of confinement. As he came within the rough walls, he clutched the staff tighter, and said, "I wish she would do as I ask."

Alexander trudged down the corridor, until he came to the chamber with the hole blasted in one wall. The repulsive smell of incinerated barikar still lingered in the air here, though it was not as strong now. After ducking through the hole in the wall, the prince made his way along the length of the chamber and into the corridor beyond, where the greenish glow again became perceptible.

At last he came to the narrow chamber with the darkened and barred vaults set into one side. He went to the vault with the green, glowing bars and stood before it. "Owen," he said.

Alexander saw the shadowy figure within the vault rise and step forward. Although he had known what to expect this time, and had thought that he had prepared himself, the sight of the beheaded man still filled him with supernatural dread.

"*You did it!* You got the staff away from Telgrin!" Owen said. The obvious extent of his joy was terrifying to see. There was something about it that struck Alexander as almost indecent. The prince could well understand how, after ten years locked away alone in that small cell, Owen would be overjoyed to finally see the key to his deliverance—but there seemed more to this than that. There was an edge of madness to his happiness.

"Yes," Alexander said, after a moment's hesitation. "It wasn't easy, but I got it."

"Give it to me!" Owen thrust a thin and clawlike hand out through the bars at Alexander. Despite himself, the prince recoiled slightly.

"A moment. We've got to talk, first."

A dire shadow seemed to come over Owen's face. In a suspicious voice, he demanded, "*What?* What's there to talk about? Have you not come here to fulfill your promise? You want to keep the staff for yourself! Is that it? *O betrayal*—''

''No,'' Alexander said firmly. ''I don't want the staff for myself. I said that I'd give it to you, and I will, but—''

''But?''

''Matters did not go as smoothly as we had planned. I had to . . . improvise.''

The beheaded man appeared to gain control of himself, though it was apparent that it cost him a great effort. ''What does that matter to me? What are you trying to tell me?''

''I wasn't able to use the mirror in the tower. I had to use the other one, the one in your daughter's quarters.'' Alexander said this with some reluctance. He did not think that Owen would be happy to hear that he had involved Lydia in his quest.

''*Lydia!*''

''Yes.''

''What did you do to her? Did you do anything to harm my dear, sweet Lydia?''

''No, no,'' Alexander said, trying to calm the beheaded man. ''It's just that she insisted on coming with me. She is tired of being shut away alone, you see. She's here, in one of the outer chambers.''

Owen appeared dazed for a moment. In a soft, feverish voice, he said, ''Lydia, here. My little girl, *here.*''

''Yes. She's . . . not quite such a little girl anymore, of course.''

"No, no, she wouldn't be, would she? Ten years. How . . . is she?"

"Well. Healthy and well."

"That is good. I'm . . . glad. She deserves that much. She deserves the best, only the best."

"Yes," Alexander said with a nod. "She does." He felt uncomfortable, knowing that he had come into the middle of something that he had no proper part in.

Owen came abruptly closer to the bars, and Alexander thought that he detected something desperate and wild in his expression. "You didn't tell her about me, did you? You didn't tell her that I was alive, here, like this?"

"No, I didn't think that it was my place. Not without your permission."

The beheaded man appeared to relax a little. "*Praise be*. She must not know about me. She must not know, do you hear! Let her remember the man I was."

"Are you sure? You could be a father to her again. Together you could be a family."

"Like *this?*" Owen said bitterly. "As this *thing* that Telgrin has made me? No. As I am, I could only be a morbid influence on her. Let her think me dead. For, in almost every important way, I did die on that day long ago. There's so little left of me now, so little. You must take Lydia away from this evil place. She should find a place where there is sunshine, where there are trees and flowers, and the sweet fruit of summer."

"But . . . what of you?" Alexander said quietly. "What will you do?"

"There is but one thing left for me now, the act I have dreamed of for all of these last ten years. I must see to it that Telgrin pays full measure for his crimes. When that is done, I will allow myself to die. Perhaps the dreams that may come when I am finally no more will wash away my suffering and hate."

Alexander shook his head, jaw tight. "Are you sure that you can overcome Telgrin? He has had ten years to practice his Art. He must be stronger now than when you knew him."

A chilling smile came to Owen's bloodless lips. "I look forward to finding out."

Alexander looked long upon the poor, filthy, shabby, beheaded, half-crazed man, and he found his revulsion replaced entirely by pity. He did not know if Owen still had power enough to face Telgrin, but he knew that he deserved the chance to try. Mad though he might be, he deserved the chance to try.

"The staff," Owen said, a plaintive edge to his voice. "Give me the staff. Please."

Alexander stepped slowly forward and stuck the end of the staff through the bars. Owen grasped the glossy ebon shaft with his free hand and drew it to him, cradling it in the crook of his arm. He did not touch it as one might normally touch an object; rather he touched it like a friend, a lover, with a soft and yielding caress. "So," he whispered. "After so long."

Alexander was relieved to have the staff out of his

possession. It had by now numbed almost his entire body, and made him feel as if he was floating in air, set loose from the moorings of his body. He felt changed by his contact with its dreadful power, and not for the better.

Suddenly Owen held the staff crosswise before him. He seemed larger, more powerful, now. His entire attitude spoke of confidence and command. No longer was he a figure to be pitied. He was a creature mighty and terrible.

"Stand back," he said. Alexander hastened to do as he was told, retreating into the chamber's far shadows. Anything could happen now, he knew.

Owen spoke a single whispered word. The crystal on the top of his staff flashed bright, and there arose a piercing high-pitched squeal. The bars of his cell shuddered, were still for an instant, then shuddered again. Alexander could see them vibrating faster and faster, until their outlines became a soft blur.

Suddenly the bars exploded outward, shattering and sending forth a shower of glowing shards. Alexander covered his face with his forearm. He heard the fragments ringing as they struck the stone floor, but none of them touched or came near him.

When he lowered his arm, he saw Owen stepping through the shattered bars. The beheaded man stood in the center of the chamber, a white nimbus flickering about him, as he held aloft his dark staff.

"*At last, I am complete again!*" he cried.

Owen turned suddenly to Alexander. He had let go of his head, and now it was floating above his shoulders. Alexander supposed that this really ought to look less horrific, but somehow it did not. It looked quite awful.

Owen said, "You must take Princess Lydia and leave this place, Alexander. See that she is safe and cared for."

"I will do my best, King Owen."

"Before you do that, however, there is one last thing that you must do here."

Alexander frowned. He was eager to be done with the black castle. Certainly he did not want to be here when Telgrin and Owen finally clashed. "What could there be left to do?" he asked.

"Near the gatehouse there are some steps that lead down into a deep well. At the bottom of that well you will find a large golden pin embedded in the paving stone. You are to remove this pin. It may not be easy, but you must do it."

"What happens when I remove the pin?"

"It will set the castle free from the moorings of

the earth. Be sure to take the pin with you. Without it, the castle will not be able to come to ground again. Whatever happens now, Telgrin must not be allowed to threaten any other innocent kingdoms."

Alexander nodded. He could see the importance of this. "Yes, all right, I'll do as you say."

"Thank you. Thank you for everything. But now, you must go. I would prefer that Lydia not see me. I don't think that she would recognize me, but I would rather not chance it."

"I'll be on my way, then." He hesitated a moment, wishing that he could think of something more to say, something that might have some real meaning to the beheaded man; he could not. "Good luck to you," he said, knowing how inadequate that was.

"And to you."

Alexander left Owen and made his way through the various chambers and corridors, until he came to the chamber where Lydia waited. The princess stood high on the steps, peering through the opening between the door and frame. She gave a little jump when Alexander cleared his throat behind her.

"*Oh!*" she said. Then: "You were gone a very long time."

"I tried to be quick."

"I don't suppose that you'll tell me what you were up to."

"I don't suppose."

"Can we get out of here now, then? It's really rather depressing."

"Yes. But we must be quiet from here on."

''Well, of *course*.''

Alexander led Lydia through the open door and up the stairs. Cautiously they entered the corridor above and moved silently along it. Alexander expected to see one of Telgrin's knights come suddenly from one of the intervening doorways, but none did. After several tense minutes, they at last reached Telgrin's throne room.

Alexander paused at the threshold to that shadowy chamber. It appeared unoccupied, but even so the thought of embarking across its vast expanse was intimidating. Telgrin and his knights could appear at any moment while they were in the throne room, and there would be no way that they could hide from them. Alexander knew that they had to risk it, for it was the only way out of the keep. He did not like it, though.

At last, doing his best to swallow his fears, Alexander began moving through the chamber toward the main entrance, Lydia at his side, their footsteps sounding alarmingly loud on the marble floor. Something inside of the prince flinched with every step they took. He was sure that they would be discovered before they could reach the door.

Alexander was pleasantly surprised when they reached the chamber's entrance without being challenged, but he was not about to congratulate himself yet. They still had the antechamber to brave, and he knew there was a very good chance that one or more of Telgrin's knights was standing guard out there.

Heart beating fast, the prince put his hands on the massive door to the antechamber and hesitated a moment. It took a strong effort of will for him to finally grasp the elaborate brass handle and pull the door open. Peering through the gap between the door and its frame, he expected to find himself facing the black and unfathomable helm of one of Telgrin's knights, but the antechamber was empty. Numbly, Alexander gestured for Lydia to go through. He followed her into the antechamber.

He had not expected it to be this easy. That very ease had begun to arouse his suspicions. He could not shake the feeling that they had been allowed to get this far, for reasons he could not comprehend. The feeling was not strong enough to make him turn back now, when they were so close, but it was enough to make him extremely nervous.

Making it out of the keep was the least of the problems that they faced, of course. The real trick was going to be getting out of the castle itself. At this point, however, he had lost the ability to think that far ahead. He had to take one thing at a time.

Alexander unbarred the heavy outer door, wincing at the loud grinding it made. He swung the ponderous door open and motioned for Lydia to go through. She did, and he followed quickly. He pulled the door shut behind him; it seated in its frame with a muffled *thump*.

They were now on a stone landing outside the keep, from which steep steps descended to the floor of the courtyard. Alexander paused here, while he scanned the dark court for the slightest sign of danger. There was nothing; it appeared deserted.

Above, the sky had acquired the deep purple glow that presaged the dawn. Had he really spent the entire night going from one part of the castle to another, and from one danger to the next? It seemed incredible. Yet, tired as he was, it could as easily have been a week.

Alexander went down the steps, still unable to shake the inexplicable sense of doom that had followed him since he had left the dungeons. When he came to the bottom, he started immediately across the courtyard, in the direction of the gatehouse. Lydia bobbed along at his side, seeming to feel nothing of his misgivings.

When they reached the very center of the courtyard, misgivings abruptly turned to the certain knowledge that they had been walking into a trap. The first evidence of this came from straight ahead, from the tunnel in the center of the gatehouse: the ringing spurs and soft rasp of metal on stone that signified the approach of at least two of Telgrin's dark knights.

Alexander stopped abruptly, then turned toward the great tower. Hearing the same ominous sounds emanating from that direction, he turned back toward the keep. Four knights were at that moment coming from around the structure, two from either side. Moving at the same steady, unhurried pace, the knights started to close on Alexander and Lydia.

Alexander spun all the way around, shooting quick glances about him. Two knights had emerged from the tunnel in the gatehouse, three from the great tower, another three from the vicinity of Lydia's house, and two from the west corner tower. With a sinking heart, Alexander realized that there must be others who had not yet appeared.

Although Alexander knew full well that escape was probably impossible, he grabbed Lydia by the hand and tried to pull her toward a gap between the knights. After they had taken only a few steps, another knight appeared in front of them, seemingly from nowhere. Alexander wheeled about and took a step or two in a new direction, but found his path again blocked.

It was now quite clear that there was nowhere to run to. Black knights were converging from all directions, none of them speaking, their masked faces staring blankly ahead. The knights formed a wide ring around Alexander and Lydia, then stopped and stood perfectly still. All was silent for a moment, and the prince found time to wonder what would happen next.

He did not have to wait long to find out.

"I told you that you would never escape this castle alive. It's a shame that you did not believe me, for you could have saved us both a great deal of effort and pain." The dry, rasping voice came from close behind Alexander. The prince recognized the voice immediately. It belonged to Telgrin.

Slowly, with as much dignity as he could muster, Alexander turned to face him. The magician-king had somehow managed to appear silently within the ring of knights, four or five yards from Alexander and Lydia.

Alexander saw that Telgrin had made a new addition to his dark wardrobe. A patch of black silk now covered one eye, held in place by a thin cord that circled his bald head at a jaunty angle. When Telgrin caught Alexander staring curiously at the patch, he said, "Do you like it? It comes courtesy of our last encounter. Surely you remember? When you threw that spell at the image into which I had invested myself?"

"But that was just an image of light," Alexander said, perplexed. "It wasn't you, really."

"Unfortunately such fine distinctions mean little when it comes to magic. A high degree of sympathy existed between the image and myself at the moment when you threw the spell. You see the results. I may never recover the sight in this eye, thanks to you."

Alexander thought that it would be inappropriate to express regrets for the incident, since those regrets would not be deeply felt. "You *were* trying to kill me at the time."

Trembling slightly, Telgrin's thin lips assumed a ghastly expression that was somewhere between a snarl and a smile. In a confidential tone, he said, "You know, Alexander, I am not normally given to strong emotions. I do not often make declarations of animosity, for these do not agree with my usually thoughtful and scholarly nature. I must, however, tell you that I hate you. Yes, hate you, without reservation or stint. I wish to see you dead, preferably after a program of long, painful, and disfiguring torture.''

Telgrin paused for a moment, glaring at Alexander with his remaining eye, and then continued in the same tone: ''The wonderful thing is, I have the power to make it all come true. All of it—the pain, the disfigurement, the death. I tell you, sometimes it's a truly marvelous thing to be me.''

Telgrin's speech did not seem to require a response, so Alexander said nothing.

Telgrin said, ''Now that I've confided that to you, perhaps you will tell me where you've hidden my staff. If you tell me freely, perhaps I will start to feel more kindly toward you. I might then be willing to kill you quickly and painlessly.''

''No, I don't think I'll tell you. It would spoil the surprise.''

''Surprise? What surprise?''

''You'll see.'' Alexander gave him a mysterious smile.

''Hmph. Do you think that you can play such foolish games with *me*? You will soon learn better, I assure you.''

''I'm not playing any game,'' Alexander said simply.

Telgrin frowned. ''I'll give you one more chance to tell me what you've done with my staff. After that, the torments begin.''

''I will not.''

''Have it your own way, then. I can't say that I'm altogether displeased.'' Telgrin raised his right hand,

and a cruel light showed from it, an unwholesome amber in color.

"You may not enjoy this," the magician-king said, "but I certainly will."

At that moment Lydia dropped Alexander's hand and stepped in front of him. "Telgrin, *no!*"

Narrowing his eye, Telgrin lowered his hand a little. "Move out of the way, Lydia. I'll deal with you later."

"No. I won't let you hurt him."

"You don't have any say in the matter, Lydia. I intend to marry you, but that doesn't mean that I have to listen to what you have to say."

"You *do* have to listen."

Telgrin gave an exasperated sigh. "Princess Lydia, you are proving to be a great disappointment to me. First you take up with this adventurer, and now you dare to take his side against your own betrothed. Have you no loyalty? Ever since the death of your father, I've seen to it that you have been sheltered, fed, and protected. I've kept you safe from the attentions of other men, and from the disturbing influence of excessive freedom. All I've ever asked in return is that you marry me, and that you not burden me with your opinions. And now this. I must tell you, it is most disillusioning."

"You must not hurt him. I won't allow it."

"Lydia, Lydia, don't you understand? A man wants to idealize the woman he is to wed. This becomes extremely difficult *when she keeps bloody carping at him.*"

"There must be some way that I can persuade you. Please."

Suddenly Telgrin got a crafty look on his face. "That depends. Can *you* tell me what he did with my staff? If you can tell me that, then the torments I have planned for him may not be necessary."

"No," she said. "He went away for a while with the staff. When he came back, he no longer had it. He wouldn't tell me what he'd done with it."

"Well, then, perhaps now you can coax him to tell you what he did with it."

Lydia gave Alexander an uncertain look from over her shoulder. "No, I don't think he will tell me that," she said reluctantly.

"Then there's really nothing to discuss, is there? Move aside and let me do what I must."

"Wait! There is *one* thing that we can discuss still. You say that you want to marry me. Very well. If you let Alexander go, I promise that I will stay here and marry you willingly. I will do my best to make you a good wife."

"You would do this?"

She drew a deep breath. "Yes."

"And all I have to do is let this man go?"

"Yes."

Telgrin raised his face skyward and made a short, barking sound of frustration. After a moment he turned his attention on Alexander. "Do you see what you've done? You have stolen the affections of Princess Lydia. She's now willing to marry me, merely to save your worthless life. Willingly! Well, I won't have it, I tell you. She shall marry me unwillingly, or not at all!''

Listening to this exchange, Alexander became convinced that Telgrin was even madder than Owen, and with less cause. He was astonished.

The magician-king angrily gestured to two of his knights. "You—and *you*. Take the princess back to her quarters. Drag her there, if you have to."

The two knights began to converge on Lydia, when suddenly a dazzling ball of green flame arced down from the keep and landed before them. The ball of flame burst upon the pavement, and its energy rose up in a rush, to form a flickering barrier. The two knights put up their hands before them and began staggering back, step by hesitant step.

Alexander could feel the unworldly energies of the green fire upon his face. It possessed no real heat, and did not even seem particularly unpleasant. He could only assume that its effect upon the knights was somehow different.

"*No!*" came a commanding voice, which echoed throughout the courtyard. "You will leave the princess alone!"

Alexander looked toward the place where the voice had originated, which proved to be the top of the stairs that led to the keep's entrance. He saw him there, standing quite still, staff in hand, ruined garments fluttering in the breeze, his head floating slightly above his shoulders: Owen.

Telgrin turned a perplexed look toward the newcomer. "Who are you, that you interfere in my affairs? What are you doing with my staff? Don't I . . . know you?''

"I know *you*, Telgrin. I remember you from long ago. Perhaps I have changed since then, but that is to be expected.''

Alexander had the pleasure of seeing recognition finally dawn on Telgrin's face. The magician-king's pale cheeks somehow managed to turn even paler; they would have made a marble statue appear dark by comparison.

"*You!*''

·23·

"Yes, Telgrin. It is I," Owen said, as he started slowly down the steps. "I'm pleased that you remember."

"It can't be! I sealed you away myself. There's no way that you could have escaped."

"Yes, you were exceedingly thorough—but not quite thorough enough, it seems."

Owen reached the bottom of the steps, then strode across the courtyard, until he reached the circle of knights. "Let me through," he commanded. The knights hesitated, their armor rustling faintly, as they shifted from foot to foot.

"Let me through," Owen said again, a sharpness to his voice. Slowly, with the appearance of deep reluctance, the knights parted and let him by.

Owen took his place within the circle, at the opposite pole from Telgrin, with Alexander and Lydia standing between. Fixing Telgrin with a scornful gaze, he said, "It has been a long time."

"Not nearly long enough."

"No, I'm sure *you* wouldn't think so."

Lydia was staring at Owen with horrified fascination, eyes wide with awe. "Who *are* you, sir?" she said.

For an instant Owen's manner seemed to soften, and his eyes filled with a gentle sadness. "A friend, here to avenge your father's death."

"My father? He died of a fever."

"No, he didn't. That's just what Telgrin told you, to conceal his guilt."

"Telgrin?"

"It was Telgrin who killed your father."

Lydia turned on Telgrin. She studied him for a moment, and gradually her gaze came to project a bitter reproach. *"You.* It's true, isn't it?"

The magician-king threw up his hands, and said, "Oh, I see the way of it. It's blame-everything-on-Telgrin time, is it? Well, if we're going start resorting to the truth, perhaps we'd better have all of it. Do you see that creature behind you, my dear, that hideous walking corpse? He—"

"Alexander!" Owen said sharply. "Catch Lydia!"

Perplexed, Alexander gave the beheaded man a questioning glance. There was no apparent reason to catch the princess; she was just standing there beside him. In that same instant, however, Owen raised his left hand and twitched two fingers. Suddenly Lydia's eyes rolled up in her head, her knees buckled, and she started to sag to the pavement.

Alexander managed to catch the princess under the arms and keep her from falling. She seemed remarkably heavy, for a person of her size.

Telgrin took this in with an expression of surprise,

then he fixed Owen with a baleful glare. "Not fair, not fair! You should have let her hear the truth about just who and what her father is."

"No," Owen said. "I will not allow you to hurt her in that manner. You have already done enough damage."

"Not allow! You have a high opinion of yourself, sir. I care not for what you will or will not allow. I am master of this castle now. Your day is done."

"My day has come again."

"Do you think so? Much has changed since I was your humble apprentice, Owen. I have studied deep the obscure lore of our trade, and practiced my art for every day of the past ten years. I am now more than your equal, even without the staff."

"As to that, we shall see. It's just the two of us now, your power against mine."

"Not entirely." A slight, secretive smile came to Telgrin's lips. He let his gaze play over the circle of knights for a moment, then said, "My knights, my devoted defenders, take them! Take them all!"

The knights shifted slightly in their circle, but otherwise they did not move. It appeared to Alexander that each of them was waiting for some other member of their company to be the first to obey their king. He suspected that they somehow sensed Owen's power, and were afraid to face it.

"Take them, I say!"

This finally goaded the knights into motion. Their circle began to contract, in a slow, step-by-step fashion.

"Call them off, Telgrin," Owen said quietly.

"*Ha!*"

"As you wish it, then." Owen raised his staff, and its crystal flashed silver-white. Alexander could feel a rising vibration in the air; the pavement trembled under his feet.

The knights stopped their progress for a moment, then pushed ahead again, each step more ponderous than the last. The vibration had grown painfully strong now. The prince could feel it beating against his flesh, with a bruising force. His ears began to ache.

The knights were forced to stop again. Their armor rattled and shivered, and their outlines blurred momentarily. Then, suddenly, the helm of one of the knights flew off, seeming to explode upward. Where the helm had been, a fiery face was revealed, showing an expression of dismay in that instant before it flared into the early morning sky, and was gone. The knight's empty armor wavered and crashed to the pavement, just as a second knight lost his helm.

One after another, Telgrin's knights were in this manner dispatched, their flickering green faces shooting into the heavens, their black armor crashing to earth. In a few moments, it was all over. Not a single knight still stood. Their vacant armor littered the courtyard like the dead husks of enormous black beetles.

Owen lowered his staff. The vibration ceased instantly, though Alexander continued to imagine that he could feel it thrumming against his flesh for a long time after it was gone.

Telgrin gazed upon the scene with a dumbfounded expression. "What have you done!" he cried. "My collection, my beautiful collection! Priceless! Irreplaceable!"

"I've set them free," Owen said.

"So help me, I'll destroy you for this!"

"Try."

Alexander quickly realized that he did not want to be caught in the midst of a battle between two such powerful magicians. Awkwardly, he scooped Lydia into his arms and hastened out of the way, stepping over the remains of one of Telgrin's knights. When he was a few yards away, he turned and looked back.

Just as he did, he saw Telgrin mouth a short phrase and make an abrupt gesture with one hand. Suddenly a fleeting vee of distortion, an obscure curdling of the air itself, took form and raced across the courtyard at Owen.

The beheaded man interposed his staff between himself and the oncoming distortion, then swept it to one side. The vee of distortion veered away and struck the keep with a resounding crash. Alexander saw an overhanging stone cornice shatter and crumble into dust.

Telgrin threw another vee of distortion, but Owen swept it off to the other side, where it crashed harmlessly into the outer wall. The magician-king threw a third and more powerful vee, and this time Owen caught it with the extended head of his staff. The distortion swirled and turned back upon Telgrin, who cried out in alarm and crossed his arms before his face. A dim screen of light appeared before him and seemed to absorb the brunt of the impact. Even so, Telgrin staggered back a pace, and looked momentarily dazed.

Owen held his staff out before him and made a churning gesture with it. A thick white mist began to boil up from the courtyard's pavement, rising quickly. It was already up to Owen's knees, when the beheaded man turned to Alexander, and said, "This mist should give you some cover. Take Lydia to safety. She is merely sleeping, and will awaken soon."

Alexander swallowed hard. "I will."

Owen pointed to the left of the gatehouse. "Remember the pin. You must take the gold pin with you. Now hurry."

Alexander felt that he wanted to say something, but he was not sure what, and there was not any time. Holding Lydia in his arms, he started away across the courtyard, the billowing fog now up to his shoulders.

Behind him, he heard Owen's voice, echoing like thunder: "Now, Telgrin, you shall be made to pay for your crimes."

Alexander saw a flash of light, which showed briefly upon the battlements of the outer wall, and then a dull, rolling boom. A moment later, Telgrin said, "You'll have to do better than *that*, if you wish to make me pay for anything."

"Try this, then."

There was another flash, much more intense than

the last, and the resulting *boom* was almost enough to knock the prince from his feet. "Better," Telgrin said, sounding perhaps a little breathless. "But still not good enough. Maybe if you had tried something like *this*."

There was a rushing sound, like the sound a fire makes when it first takes hold, only much louder. The rising mist was for a moment tinged with red. The castle's foundations trembled perceptibly.

"Very good, Telgrin," Owen said. "You have learned a little something in the last ten years. But have you learned enough to ward against *this*?"

And so it went. There were clashing sounds and shrieking sounds, hissing sounds and rushing sounds, booming sounds and roaring sounds. There were brilliant flashes. There were sullen glows. There were explosions that shook the castle.

Alexander had no desire to turn to see what was occurring. He wanted merely to escape with his life, and that of the princess Lydia. He was afraid that the mist would close so thick about him that he would lose his way, but it never seemed to get as dense out toward the outer walls as it was at the center of the courtyard.

At last he reached the gatehouse. As he moved to the left of it, he saw an open arch before him, darkness behind it. This was, he assumed, where the well that Owen had spoken of was located. When he reached it, he finally risked a look back over his shoulder. He caught one glimpse of what appeared to be a colossal dragon made entirely of a vivid blue light rear from the mist and then disappear again into the soft whiteness. After that, Alexander hurried to take shelter under the arch.

He found a small, bare space within. To one side was the foot of a stair that ascended into the gate-house; to the other was a round opening. By now, his arms were starting to ache. He carefully put Lydia down on the stairs, and saw that she was starting to awake.

Lydia's eyes opened dreamily. "Alexander," she said softly. "What happened?"

"You fainted." This was a true, if incomplete, explanation.

"Really? That doesn't sound like me."

"It has been a long night."

"I . . . suppose."

Just then, a thunderous crash sounded from the courtyard. Lydia opened her eyes wide. "What was *that*?"

"Telgrin and . . . the newcomer are engaged in a magical battle."

"I hope Telgrin has his head handed to him."

All in all, it was Alexander's judgment that this would be appropriate.

"Listen, Lydia," he said. "There's something that I have to do before we can leave the castle. It shouldn't take long. Will you be all right if I leave you here alone?"

She looked at him for a moment, her eyes fearful, her lips pressed firmly together. "I— Yes, I'll be all right."

"Stay put, then. I'll be back in a moment."

"I'll be here."

Alexander acknowledged Lydia's warning with a quick nod. He left her on the stair, while he went to examine the round opening in the paving stones. Beneath the opening was what appeared to be a dark well, with narrow steps cut into its walls, spiraling as they descended. The well seemed to go very deep.

It was with some reluctance that the prince started down the steps and let the deep gloom of the well enfold him. He wished that he had a torch, at least.

·24·

At first it seemed that there was no light at all within the well. Alexander was forced to descend the steps with cautious deliberation, lest he miss a step and go hurtling down into the darkness. When he found himself becoming dizzy, he realized that he had been holding his breath, and he made a conscious effort to breathe normally. He wondered how far down would he have to go before he finally found the golden pin that Owen had told him about.

After he had been descending for a minute or two, he realized that the darkness was not total, after all. A faint yellow glow was filtering up from somewhere below, becoming stronger the farther down he went. He quickly realized that this vague illumination did not help his progress at all, and may actually have hindered it, for it made the steps look shorter and steeper than they were.

The sounds of the magical duel echoed within the well, distorted and unnaturally lengthened. Some sounds boomed loud and echoing, others seemed strangely muted.

Alexander became frustrated by the laggardly pace

he was forced to keep. He was afraid that Telgrin would win the duel, and then their best chance for escape would be gone. He was not at all certain that Owen, after ten years locked away in the castle's deepest dungeon, would be able to stand long against Telgrin. The prince desperately wanted to be outside the gate before the battle ended. Once he had taken the golden pin, they might end up trapped in a ceaselessly floating castle with a victorious Telgrin.

The yellow glow soon became very bright. When Alexander glanced over the side of the steps, he saw that he had almost reached the bottom. The floor of the well was of fine grey stone, he saw. At the center of it was an object that he could not quite make out, but it appeared that it was from this object that the glow originated. From this angle and distance, it looked a little like a candlestick set into a slight depression.

Emboldened by his nearness to the bottom of the well, Alexander increased his pace. Eventually he came down from the last step and glanced up. He saw only a tiny circle of grey light, which he realized was the morning light showing through the top of the well.

He looked down. The floor of the well had been set down in a spiral pattern, turning from a small, round hole. Projecting from this aperture, at a shallow angle, was an oval rod.

The rod was widest at the top, which was round and smooth, and narrowed all along its apparent length. The prince would have thought that it was forged of gold, if it were not for that uncanny yellow light that it emitted. When Alexander knelt beside it for a closer look, he saw that there was a band of faintly inscribed symbols near the top, none of which he recognized.

This had to be the pin that Owen had spoken of, Alexander knew. When he pulled it from the hole, the castle would be set free of the bounds of the earth.

The prince hesitated for a moment, unwilling to touch that luminous metal, but at last he gathered his courage and grasped the pin just below the top. He began to pull on it, but it did not want to move. It almost seemed to have been set into the stonework with thick mortar.

Alexander changed his grip and tried again. It did not move at all. He pulled with all his might, until he could feel the blood come hot to his cheeks and his shoulder start to feel as if it was going to disjoint— but to no avail.

With a gasp, Alexander let go of the pin and went to lean against the side of the well, while he tried to catch his breath. He thought about the problem for a moment, and eventually came to a possible solution. When he was well enough rested, he returned to the pin.

This time he positioned himself directly over it. Squatting down and grasping it with both hands below his knees, he exerted the full strength of his legs against it. At first this approach seemed equally futile. Then, at last, the pin began to shift slightly, making a loud grinding sound as it did so.

Little by little, the pin slipped from the hole in the

floor, until it abruptly gave up all resistance. The suddenness with which this happened was such that Alexander was almost thrown back against the wall before he could compensate. After managing to catch himself, he pulled the rod the rest of the way from the hole.

In all, the rod was more than five feet in length, narrowing to a sharp point at the far end. The last two feet were coated with a residue of moist earth. It looked rather like a giant, glowing brooch pin, dirty at one end.

Alexander had only the barest instant to enjoy his triumph, for suddenly there came a ponderous rumbling from deep below him, and then an abrupt, violent lurch. He was thrown hard against the side of the well, which he clung to as best he could, momentarily overcome by an intense sense of disorientation.

He knew what was happening, but only because he had been told what would happen. The castle was rising.

Realizing that he had to hurry lest the castle rise too high to escape, Alexander grasped the pin tightly in his right hand and started up the steps. In one respect, his ascent was easier than the descent had been, for now he had the light of the pin to guide his feet. In another respect, however, it was much more difficult and dangerous. The castle was not rising entirely evenly, and several times it pitched abruptly to one side or another, threatening to cast him into the dark heart of the well.

Somehow he managed to make it safely to the top

of the well, though his head was by then reeling from the exertion. He leaned up against a nearby wall, gasping, until he recovered enough to move away.

Lydia was where he had left her, there on the bottom of the stairway. She rose and dusted herself off as he approached her.

"Come," he said, heart still pounding. "The castle's starting to rise. If we delay too long, we won't be able to leave without killing ourselves in the fall."

"I'm ready."

They went through the arch into the courtyard. The mist had begun to thin by now. Except for a few pockets, it existed only as a soft milky haze, allowing Alexander to clearly see that Telgrin and Owen were still engaged in their terrible battle—which meant that Owen had lasted longer than the prince had suspected he would.

It had apparently been an awesome struggle. The courtyard was deeply pocked by the destructive forces the two had wielded, the steps to the keep had been reduced to a pile of rubble, and the great tower seemed to be listing to one side.

It appeared that Owen's valiant fight was nearly at an end, however. Telgrin had somehow produced a great sword fashioned entirely of searing blue light, which he was wielding with considerable vigor against the beheaded man. Owen had only his staff to defend himself, and although he seemed able to parry the magician-king's mighty strokes with that staff, at least so far, he was being driven steadily back. Each blow flashed like lightning. Each blow sounded like thunder. Each blow forced Owen to give ground.

Alexander made himself look away. "Come," he said. "We don't want to be here if and when Telgrin wins this battle."

Lydia resisted his attempt to hurry her along, however. "Shouldn't we try to help the stranger?"

"I wish I knew how, but I don't." Alexander knew that Owen would not thank him if he were to endanger Lydia in what would likely be a vain effort to save him from Telgrin. "We must go now, or it may be too late."

The princess yielded reluctantly to Alexander's urging, and the two turned and entered the long passage piercing the gatehouse. Before him, the prince saw that the delicate light of dawn was starting to steal across the sky. The gate showed an expanse of pale blue sky, crisscrossed by black bars.

Alexander almost stopped dead in his tracks. The portcullis. He had forgotten about the portcullis.

"Keep going," the prince told Lydia, as he raced ahead. "I must raise the portcullis!"

There was a door on the right, just before the portcullis. Already out of breath, Alexander pushed the door open with his shoulder and embarked immediately up the stone stairway that lay just within. He took the steps two at a time, until he reached the top and entered an austere and utilitarian room.

There was a big fireplace centered on one wall of the room, with a great iron cauldron hanging within, which Alexander knew was intended for the production of boiling oil, to be poured down on an invading enemy. In the center of the floor was a constellation of large holes that looked down on the passage below. These were known as "murder holes," and they were one of the places through which boiling oil might be poured. Beyond them was the large winch that could raise and lower the portcullis.

Taking care not to step into any of the murder holes, Alexander made his way swiftly to the winch. He grabbed hold of the iron lever and began frantically winching up the portcullis. This took considerable effort and, more importantly, time. Alexander had the sinking fear that it was already too late to exit the castle safely.

As soon as the prince knew that he had raised the portcullis sufficiently, he raced back across the room, down the stairs, and out into the passage. He saw Lydia standing a few yards away, staring back toward the castle's courtyard.

"Lydia," he said urgently. "We've got to go. *Lydia.*"

When she did not respond, Alexander wearily made his way up the passage to her. He saw then what it was that so fascinated her, and he could not blame her. The duel between Owen and Telgrin appeared to be nearing its conclusion. Owen had been backed up to the ruins of the keep's steps, and now there was no place left to which he could retreat. Telgrin was swinging his blazing sapphire blade with increasing confidence, while Owen's parries were becoming more and more feeble.

At last, as it had always seemed it must, Telgrin's

flashing blade got through Owen's defenses, in a tremendous sidewise cut. It would have severed Owen's head from his body, had his head not already been severed and merely floating in the approximate position that it would normally occupy. The head bobbed up suddenly higher, and Telgrin's blade swished harmlessly through the enlarged gap.

The force of the unimpeded stroke drew Telgrin off-balance. He recovered quickly, but by then the end of Owen's staff was streaking toward his own head. He did not see the blow coming. He could not, since he no longer had a functioning eye on that side of his head. Alexander had taken care of that.

Owen's staff struck home. It was not an especially powerful blow, but it was a deft blow. Telgrin fell over backward. The sword of blue light flew from his hand, landed a few yards away, and promptly dissolved into a shimmering sapphire pool.

After planting his foot on the chest of the unconscious Telgrin, Owen lightly placed the glowing end of his staff on Telgrin's forehead. He said, ''What I once gave you, I now take back. What you once were, you are again.''

Telgrin's form became oddly indistinct. It seemed to be shifting, changing, right there before Alexander's eyes, in a bizarre and disorienting process. When the form became solid again, it was not Telgrin who lay there, or at least not the Telgrin that Alexander knew. It was instead a thin and unappealing youth of eleven or twelve. There did, however, seem to be something about the youth's features that vaguely suggested Telgrin.

Alexander knew what Owen had done, or he thought that he knew. Somehow Owen had returned Telgrin to what he was before the betrayal, even before he had taught him his magic, returned him to the powerless scullery lad he had been at the beginning. Thinking about it made Alexander suppress a shiver. He guessed that the scullery lad who had been the magician-king Telgrin would not have an easy time of it from this day forward.

Suddenly Alexander remembered where he was, and that was in a castle slowly rising off the ground. He touched Lydia's arm. "Come," he said. "If you want to leave here, it's got to be now."

"I'm coming now." As she turned, Alexander could not help but notice the serene and untroubled look on her face.

·25·

Alexander stood for a moment on the edge of the rising castle, wondering how many bones he would break if he jumped. Already the castle had risen a substantial distance from the ground, and it was still going up, as it continued to hover above the spot it had once occupied. The ground below was sandy and marshy, but jumping from this height would still be a chancy proposition.

Lydia stood slightly behind the prince, using him as a barrier between herself and the precipitous drop. This was only prudent, Alexander thought. The castle was still listing slightly from side to side as it went up. A larger-than-expected lurch could well send them toppling from the edge.

"I don't think I want to jump," Lydia said. "It looks awfully high."

Alexander scowled and said nothing. She was right, of course. But if they did not jump, how could they get down? A rope, perhaps. Where could he find a rope? If they delayed too long, even a rope would not help.

Suddenly he heard someone calling his name. "*Al-*

exander! Ho, there! Alexander! Here! Down here!"

Frowning, Alexander carefully scanned the land below, until he at last spotted him: Cyril. The young wizard was just coming out from behind the cover of the trees, waving his hand over his head as he went.

"Cyril!" Alexander called out. "Am I glad to see you! Can you think of any way for us to get down from here?"

The young man stopped and appeared to consider the question. "I could attempt to fly you down."

All in all, Alexander thought he would rather just jump. "I . . . don't think that's such a good idea. Can you think of anything else?"

"A rope! A magical rope! That isn't one of the major spells, so I don't think anything can go wrong, much."

"Do you have such a thing?"

"I could make one. Just a moment. Let me think."

Pensive, the young magician patted over his clothes, apparently trying to think of what he had on his person that he could use. After a moment, he seemed to get an idea.

With hasty, fumbling fingers, Cyril unfastened his cloak, grasped the top of it firmly, and tore from it the slender cord that one normally used to tie the cloak about one's neck. After discarding the torn cloak, he held the cord out before him in both hands. Closing his eyes, he said a few soft words.

One end of the cord twitched and abruptly rose up, so that for moment the cord looked like a small, dark snake poking its head up from its coiled body. Cyril said a final word, and opened his eyes.

Undulating like a small fish making its way along the bottom of a still pool, the end of the cord climbed gradually higher. The cord seemed to be getting thicker and longer as it rose, becoming six feet long, eight feet long, ten feet long. And still it rose. By the time it poked up over the edge of the castle's pavement, it was already as thick as a rope.

The end of the cord rose over Alexander's head, and slowly went behind him. Turning a curious glance on it, the prince saw it reach past the bottom of the suspended portcullis, turn back, and coil itself several times around the bottom bar. The cord drew itself suddenly taut. When Alexander looked back toward Cyril, he saw that the other end of the cord had wrapped itself around the trunk of a nearby tree. The cord was now a taut line, extending out from the castle at a gentle angle.

Cyril said, "Grab hold of the cord and lower yourselves down. It should be safe enough."

Alexander considered the cord suspiciously for a moment, then gave it an experimental tug. It *seemed* strong enough.

"*Hurry*," Cyril said. "The castle is still going up."

Alexander exchanged a quick glance with Lydia. "Do you want to go first, or shall I?"

After a brief hesitation and a glance at the ground, she said, "I'll go."

"Just be careful, then."

Lydia faced the line and took hold of it with both hands. She swung a leg over, kicking her skirt out behind her as she did so. Straddling the line, she commenced to lower herself over the side of the floating castle.

The princess descended smoothly, sliding along the line on her belly and controlling her speed with both her hands and her knees. When she had nearly reached the ground, Cyril came hurrying over to her and helped her climb down from off the line.

Now it was Alexander's turn. Lydia's chosen method of descent struck the prince as awkward and possibly painful, so he simply threw the golden pin he had been holding over the side, gripped the line with both hands, pulled his legs from the edge of the castle, and began walking his way down it hand over hand.

The line felt soft and oddly spongy in his grasp. He was halfway down before he could overcome the suspicion that it would come apart in his hands, and by then he knew that he was likely to survive any fall intact.

When Alexander hung just a few feet above the ground, he let go of the line and dropped. He took the slight impact with flexed knees, stumbled a bit, and then recovered. He went to stand with Lydia and Cyril, limping slightly.

Cyril clapped his hands together sharply. Abruptly the line let go of both the tree trunk and the castle's portcullis, and the latter end dropped from the sky and fell heavily to earth. The line then began to contract rapidly. In a matter of moments, it had been transformed into a humble cord again.

Alexander gave Cyril a nod. "I'm surprised to see you here."

"I said I would be back after I found supplies. I was fortunate to discover a farm that Telgrin's knights had somehow missed a short distance from here."

"Well, I'm glad you're here."

Alexander gazed pensively at the floating castle. He found it disquieting to see the immense structure hovering there at the edge of the river, rising slowly, the morning sun glittering on its jet-black walls. He would not be happy until it was gone forever from Daventry.

Following the prince's gaze, and his thoughts, Cyril said, "It doesn't seem to be going anywhere, really."

"No."

"Too bad there isn't any wind."

Alexander started to nod, then an idea suddenly occurred to him. He gave the apprentice magician a speculative glance. "Uh, Cyril, since you've already raised your magic within you, why don't you help the castle on its way?"

Cyril frowned. "I don't know if I should."

"Just give it a little nudge."

"A nudge?"

"Just a nudge."

"Well . . . if you think it would be all right."

"I do."

"I will see what I can do, then. Stand back."

Alexander drew Lydia to one side, while Cyril contemplated the castle with an attitude of intense concentration. After a time, he closed his eyes and raised his arms high. He muttered a phrase under his breath.

The morning's light dimmed, becoming dusky and enervated. A strong wind gusted up from nowhere. Cyril opened his eyes and spoke a final word, hurling it vehemently at the castle floating overhead. At first this seemed to have no effect, but then a dull boom sounded, echoing like thunder from a distant valley. Shuddering, the castle began to rise at an increased rate. As it rose, it slowly, sluggishly, started to drift across the river. It appeared to be picking up speed as it went.

As the morning's full splendor was restored, Cyril let his arms drop. His shoulders sagged a little. He looked spent. "There," he said. "That's done it. I think I'm beginning to get the hand of this."

"That was just about right, I think," Alexander agreed. "Well done."

"And now, I'm going to go sit under that tree over there for a while, I think. I've come over a bit dizzy."

Cyril went to the tree and dropped wearily beneath it. Putting his back to the rough, grey trunk, he stretched out his legs with a sigh.

"You didn't introduce me to your friend," Lydia said, a hint of reproach in her voice.

"Didn't I?" Alexander said. "Sorry, my mind must be elsewhere. His name is Cyril, and he is apprentice to the wizard Morowyn."

"His magic is very strong."

"Yes, but I'm afraid that he is now paying the price for the spell he invoked."

"Great deeds often exact a great cost."

"Hmm? Yes, I suppose that's true." Alexander started to give the princess an inquiring glance, but she had already turned her back on him and gone to sit under the tree with Cyril. By and by, the two began to chat, their voices soft and very young.

Alexander returned his attention to the black castle. He watched it closely, as it lofted up higher and higher. Already it had drifted across the river and the surrounding marsh; now it was crossing over a thickly wooded ridge. It was revolving slowly as it went, so that by now he could no longer see its sinister gates.

As the prince watched, the castle grew progressively smaller and less distinct, until it appeared only as a dark speck on the horizon. Eventually even that was gone.

When Alexander was finally satisfied that the castle was gone and would trouble Daventry no more, he went to retrieve the golden pin he had discarded as he quit the castle. The pin was sticking up from the sandy soil at the margin of the river, its pointed end buried a full foot and a half deep. He did not suppose that it would be of any use to him now, but he decided that he might as well take it.

The prince pulled up the pin, then turned and went up the slope, to rejoin Lydia and Cyril. The two were still beneath the tree, he saw. Cyril had his head on Lydia's shoulder, and Lydia's cheek was resting lightly on the top of Cyril's head. They were both asleep.

*   *   *

While he waited for his two companions to awake, Alexander went to sit on a flat rock at the river's edge. He opened his jerkin, reached inside, and took out the sphere that contained his father's soul.

As he held this sphere before him in one hand, he peered into it, trying to pierce the vague and shifting haze that troubled its surface. "Father," he said. "Are you there? Can you hear me?"

After a moment, a face began to take form within the sphere. It seemed to take a long while for it to resolve itself into a specific face, into Graham's face. "Is that you, Alexander?" he said, his voice sounding even fainter than it had before.

"Yes, Father. I am here."

"What news do you have?"

"I've escaped the black castle, the castle itself is gone, and I don't think that Telgrin will be bothering anyone ever again."

Graham showed surprise. "How did all this come about?"

"It's a long story."

"I imagine it must be. I look forward to hearing it, sometime, in better circumstances."

"It shouldn't be long before you are whole again."

"Good, good. That will come as a great relief."

"Are you well, Father? You sound . . . weary."

There was a brief pause, and then Graham said, "I am, a little. It is a disorienting experience, to be taken from one's body and sealed inside a crystal sphere. I can't say that I recommend it."

"I'll try to get you back to Castle Daventry as

quickly as possible. In the meantime, try to save your energy."

"I'll try."

"Is there anything that I can do for you now?"

"I can't think of anything. At the moment, I have few needs."

Alexander hesitated for a moment, not willing to close off communications, yet knowing very well that he should. At last he compelled himself to say, "In that case, I'll let you rest now."

"Yes, very well. Take care, Alexander."

"I'll do my best, Father."

The face in the sphere gradually dissolved, leaving only a vague amber haze behind. Alexander carefully returned the sphere to its place inside his jerkin, near his belt. After sealing up the jerkin, he sat there for a short time, troubled, teeth clenched tightly together, staring into the fast-flowing waters of the river, watching a small patch of white foam swirl in the eddying flood below a large, smooth rock.

His father was growing rapidly weaker. The prince was certain that the king could not last very much longer in his current state. It was essential that his spirit be returned to his body without delay. But it would take nearly two days to reach Castle Daventry on foot, even without the encumbrance of Lydia and Cyril. Two days, two long days!

Deep in his heart, Alexander felt the despairing certainty that his father did not have two days. He would be dead long before then.

·26·

Alexander was half afraid that he would not be able to wake Cyril. On the two earlier occasions when the apprentice wizard had resorted to magic, he had afterward fallen into a long sleep from which he could not be roused. The prince had some hope that this would not be the case this time, for the simple reason that Cyril had not appeared to overreach himself as greatly this time.

Touching Cyril firmly on the upper arm, Alexander said, "Cyril, Cyril, can you hear me? Wake up."

The young wizard woke with a start. His eyes snapped open, and he looked about glassily. "Huh? What? What is it?"

"I need to speak to you."

Cyril lifted his head, which caused Lydia to wake, shift, and sit up straight. "Yes," he said in the reasonable manner of a man trying to pretend that he had been awake all along. "I'm listening."

"I want to ask a favor of you. It is vitally important that I return my father's soul to him as soon as I can. Would you consent to stay and look after Princess

Lydia while I go on ahead? I think that I can move faster alone.''

Cyril considered the request for a moment. At length he said, ''Well, yes, I *could* do that, but . . .''

''What is it?''

''If you go ahead without me, who will undertake the procedure to restore Graham to his body? It's something that will require the skills of a magician.''

Crestfallen, Alexander fell silent for a moment. ''I hadn't thought of that.''

Cyril stared out into space with narrowed eyes. ''You are right, of course. The sooner we can reunite Graham's spirit with his body the better. They've been apart for too long as it is. Hmm. Let me think about this.''

The apprentice wizard rubbed his eyes and ran his hand down his face suddenly. ''Horses,'' he murmured. ''We need horses.''

''Where are we going to get horses around here?''

''That farm I visited yesterday, where I got my supplies— They had horses, I think. I expect the farmer and his wife might be persuaded to loan a couple of them to us. They seemed like good people.''

''It seems to be worth a try. Where is this farm?''

''Not far from here. Not far at all.''

Alexander could see how Telgrin's scavenging knights had missed the farm. Although it was little more than an hour's walk from where the black castle had been located, it was concealed within a small canyon, the entrance of which was densely screened by trees and brush. Only a faint dirt road hinted at its existence.

"How did you find this place?" Alexander asked Cyril, as they ducked under a low-hanging branch and caught their first glimpse of the farm buildings, which were gathered together at the base of a granite ridge.

"I got lost."

As Cyril had predicted, the farmer and his wife— a sober sun-browned couple in their early middle years—proved to be friendly and cooperative. After a short discussion, they agreed to loan the travelers their two horses, and even offered food and lodging for the night. Pleading the need for haste, Alexander had to decline the latter offer.

The horses—one a chestnut gelding, the other a dappled mare—looked very much like the stolid farm animals they were, though the farmer insisted that both horses were well accustomed to the saddle. Alexander had his doubts about this, but he politely refrained from voicing them.

With the farmer's assistance, Alexander soon had the horses saddled and ready. Cyril awkwardly climbed into the mare's saddle and took up the reins. After Alexander swung onto the gelding's back, the farmer helped Lydia climb up behind him.

The farmer and his wife wished them a good journey. With Lydia clinging to him, Alexander maneuvered the gelding around in the direction of the road leading from the canyon. He could hear Cyril and the mare come around behind him.

The horses proved to be solid if unremarkable mounts; Alexander found that he was able to set a good pace and keep to it. Upon leaving the canyon, they paralleled the river at a slight remove for a short time. Then, after turning onto the main road, they crossed over the narrow bridge where the prince had fought the kelpie and, finally, veered away from the river.

Soon they reached the near edge of the Old Wood. They rode along its dense and tangled margin for a little more than an hour, before leaving it behind and turning to enter the low hills that stood between them and Castle Daventry.

The hills stretched on for a long time. The road wove between them, rising and falling gently, until eventually it went between two wooded ridges, and then began to descend rapidly. As the road descended, it hooked around sharply to the right, around the base of a blunt prominence. Here the trees crowded close to the road. There was the trickling sound of a fast-flowing stream off to the left.

As they rode, Lydia would from time to time utter small but delighted exclamations, about the beauty of a stream, of a field of flowers, or of a tree. It was as if she had never seen any of these things before. Alexander began to realize that in truth she probably had not, having spent nearly all of her life locked away behind grey walls.

After they had been riding for a long time, Lydia became subdued and thoughtful. At length, she said,

"So this is the world. It seems so . . ." Her voice trailed off.

"So what?" Alexander asked.

"So . . . big."

"It is that." It was ironic, Alexander thought. Owen had built his castle so that he and his daughter could see all the world. He had spent ten years sealed away inside a tiny cell, and his daughter had grown up friendless, her world limited by a garden wall. It made the prince feel sad to think about this.

As they drew nearer to Castle Daventry, Alexander found himself becoming filled with a terrible impatience. He had to restrain himself from urging his horse to a full gallop, knowing that neither the gelding nor the mare could long sustain that pace.

As the sun slanted low in the western sky and shadows lengthened, the trees gradually thinned, until they merely dotted the rolling green meadows that stretched away from the road on both sides. The road widened and became more firmly packed. A low stone wall crossed the meadow on the right, following the gentle contours of the land, at last to vanish beyond a round hillock.

Finally, coming to the top of a slight rise and clearing a dense clump of trees, Alexander saw it, as he knew he would: Castle Daventry. Its high towers were streaked with the red-gold light of late afternoon, and its circular moat glistened with a mirrored sheen on the side nearest the sun. Alexander thought that he had never seen a more welcome sight in his life.

"See," he said. "We're almost there."

It took them another half an hour to reach the bridge that spanned the moat. By then, the sun had all but disappeared behind the western hills, and the first stars of the evening were appearing in the east. The waters flowing under the bridge were dark and glassy.

Hooves beating a loud rhythm, they crossed over the bridge. Alexander saw that the portcullis was down, so he pulled to a halt before the gate. "Open the gate," he said to the shadowy figures standing behind the portcullis.

"Who's there?" said one of the figures suspiciously.

Before Alexander could answer, the second figure said, "Draw up the portcullis, Bill. Can't you see? It's Prince Alexander." The prince recognized the voice that said this. It belonged to the guard Henry.

"Oh. I beg your pardon, Highness. I didn't recognize you in the dark."

"He's new, Alexander."

"I understand," Alexander said mildly. "Just open the gate, please. We're in a hurry."

"Right away."

The two men called for the portcullis to be raised, and slowly it went up, rattling and clanking as it ascended. When it was all the way up, Alexander nudged the gelding with his heels, urging it through the gate and into the gloomy passage. "Thanks, Henry!" he called over his shoulder.

The guard shouted after him, "*Did you do it? Did you get your father's soul back?*"

"Yes!"

Once through the passage and into the courtyard beyond, Alexander rode directly for the stables. He drew up before the big double doors and called out for assistance. A groom in grey shirt and leather jerkin came out from the stables and helped Lydia down from the gelding, then held the reins of both mare and gelding while Alexander and Cyril dismounted.

"See that the horses are well cared for," Alexander said. "They've served us well."

"Aye, Highness."

Leaving the groom holding the horses, Alexander quickly led Cyril and Lydia across the courtyard. There were few folk about at this time of the evening. Those few there were stopped whatever they were doing when Alexander passed by, probably surprised by the prince's disheveled appearance and the grim look on his face. No one attempted to speak to him.

Alexander climbed the long stair leading up to the keep. He paused on the landing, waiting for Cyril and Lydia to catch up, then pushed open the massive oaken door. The guards standing within the antechamber—there were four of them this time—all moved toward the door, hands going to their weapons. When they saw that it was Alexander who stood within the doorway, they relaxed perceptibly.

"Where's my mother?" Alexander asked, as he entered the antechamber.

"Within, I believe," said one of the guards.

When Lydia and Cyril came into the antechamber, the guards regarded them with immediate suspicion.

"They're with me," Alexander said. Then, gesturing to the princess and the young wizard: "Come on, this way."

One of the guards hastened to open the door leading to the throne room, and Alexander and his two companions went through into the room beyond. The throne room was lit only with the moody glow of the dying day that came through the narrow windows, and it was a moment before the prince saw the shadowy figure who stood alone before the throne of Daventry and recognized it as his mother.

"Mother," Alexander said, as he made his way down the center of the great chamber, footsteps echoing loudly. "I've returned."

Queen Valanice acknowledged him with a smile. "Alexander, welcome home. I've been expecting you."

The prince halted a few feet before his mother. "You have? Why?"

She pointed her chin at the mirror that hung upon the wall across from the throne. "The mirror," she said. "It works again. I saw that you were on your way."

"Of course. I should have guessed."

Valanice extended her arms and stepped to Alexander, wrapping him in a brief but heartfelt embrace. "I'm glad that you're home, Alexander. I was worried about you."

"There was no reason for worry, Mother. I was perfectly fine." As Valanice dropped her arms and moved away from him, Alexander saw the fine lines that had appeared about her mouth and eyes in his absence. He could only guess at the extent of the strain she had been living with in that time.

"How has Father been?" he asked.

Valanice's expression became bleak. "Not well. He appears weaker with every passing hour. The physician does not think that he can last much longer, as matters stand."

Alexander opened the front of his jerkin, reached inside, and brought out the sphere containing his father's soul. "Then we should not delay. It's time that we make him whole again."

Alexander was shocked to see how much his father's physical self had deteriorated in the few days that he had been gone. The king's face was nearly as white as the pillow on which his head lay. A faint, feverish sheen of perspiration showed on his forehead and upper lip. His breathing was shallow and labored, and a tiny whistling sound came from deep inside his breast with each inhalation.

Graham had the appearance of a man in his last hours of life. Looking at him, Alexander could not help wondering if they had come too late.

Alexander stood beside Cyril on one side of the bed. Queen Valanice was on the other side, gazing down on her husband's face with a look of anxiety tinged with sorrow. Lydia was standing far back in the shadows, by the door.

The room's only light came from the single wavering candle on the table beside the bed. It was sufficient to illuminate Graham's face, but after that it shaded away rapidly into grey obscurity.

Cyril regarded the fallen king with a solemn and dispassionate gaze. After a long moment's consideration, he said, "Give me the sphere, Alexander."

For the smallest instant, Alexander hesitated. It was obvious to him that his father's life hung by a fine thread, and now he was about to entrust the delicate procedure that could restore his health to an apprentice wizard whose magical touch had never been fine. Still, he had learned to trust Cyril over the last few days—and, besides, what other choice did he have?

Alexander gave Cyril the sphere.

The young wizard took the glistening object in both hands, holding it propped up on his fingertips. He peered into it with squinted eyes, and said, "Prepare yourself, King Graham. I am about to return you to your body. There may be some momentary sense of dislocation. It will pass."

Keeping it balanced on his fingertips, Cyril slowly lowered the sphere to a level just below his chin. He closed his eyes and whispered a brief phrase in an unfamiliar tongue. A moment passed, in which nothing seemed to happen. Finally, opening his eyes again, he bent to place the sphere down on the blanket covering Graham's chest.

Muttering another phrase, he touched the sphere with one finger, then moved that finger over Graham's forehead. He held it poised there, while he spoke a single word, with an inflection of vehement finality. He touched the finger down lightly on a point just above Graham's eyes, lifted it, and stepped back a pace.

At first Alexander thought that the spell had failed; there seemed to be no change at all. As he was trying to decide whether to speak or not, however, he noticed that the sphere had begun to shine brighter. The increase in brightness was subtle, coming in a series of slow pulses, but gradually it became unmistakable.

When Alexander looked more closely at the sphere, he could see the glowing image of his father's face, growing more vivid and intense with every pulse. The image seemed to leap slightly outside the bounds of the imprisoning sphere whenever the light flashed, and this effect became more pronounced with each repetition.

The pulsing of the sphere became increasingly rapid, until it was only a vague flickering of an otherwise blazing aura, a blackness that came and went almost too quickly for the eye to see. For an instant there appeared to be two Grahams, one a transparent duplicate hanging above his physical form; then the duplicate appeared to settle into the king's body, quickly merging with it. Graham's features were momentarily blurred, but then became sharp once more. He was one again.

The light coming from the sphere vanished abruptly, making the crystal appear dark and lusterless. Graham took in a great gasping breath, his middle rising up in a sudden violent spasm, while his shoulders and hips pressed harder against the bed. He held the breath for a moment, then let it go, making a hissing sound behind his teeth. His tortured body relaxed and settled back again.

His eyes opened. They stared straight up at the ceiling, unblinking, bewildered.

Cyril said, "King Graham, are you there? Can you hear me?"

Graham's eyes slowly tracked in Cyril's direction. "I . . . hear you. I am here."

"How do you feel?"

"I'm not sure. It feels odd to be in a body again. It feels . . . heavy."

"That's understandable. You are tired. You have been through a terrible ordeal. Rest, and soon you will be your normal self again."

"Yes, I will rest—soon." Graham's gaze moved from Cyril to Alexander. The prince could see that his father's confusion was starting to diminish. The look in his eyes was almost normal.

"Alexander," the king said. "You brought me back. There's no way that I can fully express my gratitude."

Alexander smiled, feeling the burden of many days loosen and fall away. He had not realized how heavy that burden had been, until now, when it was no longer there. His relief had cut through the thick haze of his fatigue, bringing a quickness to his thoughts. "There's no need, Father. I am just glad to see you your old self again."

"It will be a little while yet before I am my old self, I'm afraid. I feel very weak yet."

"Cyril's right. You need to rest."

"Yes, in a moment." Graham turned his head, to look upon Valanice. Slowly he freed his right hand from the confinement of his covers and held it up to her.

Valanice grasped his hand tightly with her own. Suddenly she appeared a full ten years younger. "Husband," she said, stroking his brow with her free hand.

"My wife," Graham said softly. "I have much to be thankful for. I have escaped the torments that Telgrin thought to inflict on my spirit. I am in my own body again, in my own home, safe and surrounded by family and friends. But what makes me most grateful is that I am able to look upon your face once again, my dear one. For that is everything."

Valanice laughed softly, and said, "Rest. You are delirious, I think."

Graham settled back with a sigh. "Truly, I consider myself a fortunate man."

·27·

On a fine afternoon in early summer, Alexander stood before the flowering hedge that circled the small house and its surrounding grove. "Open, for a friend," he said, addressing the hedge.

Rustling softly, the hedge split down the middle, and the two sides moved apart, revealing a narrow path between them. Alexander stepped through the hedge, set foot upon that path, and started toward the house. He heard the hedge close behind him.

Alexander had gone only a yard or two, when a barefooted young woman in a white blouse and plain blue skirt came running out of the grove, shouting, "Alexander! Alexander! You've come!" She threw herself into his arms with such force that she almost succeeded in bowling him over.

"Lydia," Alexander said, nearly overwhelmed. "How have you been? You certainly seem well."

"I'm fine, fine! And you?"

"Perhaps not as fine as you, but well enough."

The princess slipped from Alexander's arms and seized hold of his hand. She pulled him toward the house. "Come, Cyril will be so pleased to see you. And Morowyn, too!"

At that moment Alexander saw Cyril come from the grove, carefully balancing an amorphous ball of blue light on the tip of his right index finger. "Who are you talking to, Lydia?" he was saying, the greater part of his concentration focused on the ball. Then he spotted Alexander, and he broke into a smile. "Alexander! It's good to see you again. Look here. See what I've done? I think I'm finally getting full control of my magic."

Alexander thought that the apprentice magician looked thinner than he had been, and perhaps a little taller. "And it's good to see you again, Cyril. You're looking well."

"Never better. Come on, I'll make tea. Morowyn will be pleased that you have come, though I expect he knew all along that you were coming, and he just neglected to tell us. He loves a good surprise, does Morowyn."

Alexander sat in the shade of the tree that had been a man, a full mug of tea balanced on his thigh, watching Cyril and Lydia entertain themselves with Cyril's ball of light. The pair were a few yards away, in an open area, the colorful spikes of foxglove and blue lupine rising behind them. They were playing catch with the ball, but they did not use their hands, relying instead on the power of their minds to catch the ball and loft it back and forth. All the while, they kept laughing and mocking each other's attempts to return the ball. They seemed happy.

"How is your father now, Alexander? Has he quite recovered from his treatment at the hands of Telgrin?" Morowyn asked in his deep, hollow voice.

"Yes, he's fully regained his strength. He is the same as he always was, now."

"That's good. It could easily have been otherwise."

After a moment's pause, Alexander said, "I hope that Lydia isn't proving too much for you to handle."

"Too much for me to handle? No, not at all. She is a very active young woman, it's true, but I've come to appreciate activity, if only in others. I've enjoyed having her here."

"How are her studies progressing?"

"Very well. She has a real talent for magic. Soon she may even surpass Cyril, which would be no small feat. She says that one day she will find a way to reverse the spell that afflicts me, without killing me. I almost believe her."

"Well, if determination were enough to do the job, I'd say that you could count on it. And, of course, powerful magic does run in her family."

"Yes, the unfortunate King Owen. Do you think that he would approve of her life here? She is a princess, but this is no palace. The amenities are rather basic, I'm afraid."

Alexander paused to watch Lydia, as she pursued the ball of light into the patch of foxglove. She was smiling, and the sun was bright on her face. Holding one hand before her, she made the ball stop in midair and then reverse its path. She gave a triumphant shout.

"I expect that he would be pleased," Alexander said.

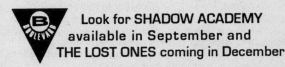